What Others Are Saying...

Read *A Harvest of Hearts* and fall in love with these characters as they work to meld two strong desires into one.

—Diana Lesire Brandmeyer
Author, *Wyoming Weddings*, *Hearts on the Road*, *We're Not Blended*, *We're Pureed*, and *A Bride's Dilemma in Friendship, Tennessee*

A Harvest of Hearts is an edgy Amish story without compromising the traditions of the Amish. You will not want to miss this book!

—Cindy Loven
Book reviewer, cindylovenreviews.blogspot.com

Laura V. Hilton has a winner in her second installment of The Amish of Seymour series. *A Harvest of Hearts* is a tender story with all of the elements necessary to keep you turning the pages: a pretty, plucky heroine in Shanna and a handsome, patient, true-to-the-faith suitor in Matthew. Together, they learn lessons in love, life, sacrifice, faith, and family. This book will involve you from the start with well-written prose, humor, and sweet, romantic moments.

—JoAnn Durgin
Author, *Awakening*

Laura Hilton weaves a delightful tale that encourages readers not to give up on their hearts' desires.

—Susette Williams
Author, *New Garden's Conversion* (appears in the anthology *The Quakers of New Garden*)

A *Harvest*

a novel of *Hearts*

The Amish of Seymour

A Harvest of Hearts

a novel

LAURA V. HILTON

WHITAKER
HOUSE

A HARVEST OF HEARTS
The Amish of Seymour ~ Book Two

Laura V. Hilton

ISBN: 978-1-60374-256-6
Printed in the United States of America
© 2011 by Laura V. Hilton

Whitaker House
1030 Hunt Valley Circle
New Kensington, PA 15068
www.whitakerhouse.com

Library of Congress Cataloging-in-Publication Data

Hilton, Laura V., 1963–
A harvest of hearts / by Laura V. Hilton.
    p. cm. — (The Amish of Seymour series ; bk. 2)
  Summary: "Shanna Stoltzfus thought she'd turned her back on the Amish for good, but handsome newcomer Matthew Yoder forces her to reconsider where her home and heart lie"—Provided by publisher.
  ISBN 978-1-60374-256-6 (trade pbk.)
  1. Homecoming—Fiction. 2. Self-actualization (Psychology)—Fiction. 3. Man woman relationships—Fiction. 4. Amish—Fiction 5. Seymour (Mo.)—Fiction. I. Title.
  PS3608.I4665H37 2011
  813'.6—dc22

2011025928

2 3 4 5 6 7 8 9 10 ᴜ 18 17 16 15 14 13 12

Dedicated to:

Steve, *my best friend,*

Loundy, *my favorite song,*

Michael, *my adventurous one,*

Kristin, *my precious daughter,*

Jenna, *my sunshine,*

Kaeli, *my shower of blessing,*

And God, who has blessed me with these.

In loving memory of Allan and Janice Price, my parents; my grandmother, Mertie; and my uncle Loundy, each of whom has blessed me with some knowledge of our Pennsylvania Dutch ancestors.

Also, to Tamela, my agent, for not letting me give up and for giving sage advice.

Acknowledgments

I 'd like to offer my heartfelt thanks to the following:

The Swartz family, for allowing me a look at the inside of an Amish home and the outside layout of their farm. And for giving me a taste of their homemade jams and jellies.

Susanne Woods Fisher, for contacting her sources to settle a few questions to which I couldn't find the answers.

The residents of Seymour, for answering my questions and pointing me in the right directions.

The Ozark Folk Center in Mountain View, Arkansas—specifically, Scott Reidy—for giving me a crash course in blacksmithing.

The amazing team at Whitaker House—Christine, Courtney, and Cathy. You are wonderful.

My agent, for believing in me all these years.

To my critique group—you know who you are. You are amazing and knew how to ask the right questions when more detail was needed. Also, thanks for the encouragement.

To my husband, Steve, for being a tireless proofreader and cheering section, and my sons, Michael and Loundy, for taking over the kitchen duties when I was deep in the story.

Glossary of Amish Terms and Phrases

ach	oh
aent	aunt
"Ain't so?"	a phrase commonly used at the end of a sentence to invite agreement
Ausbund	Amish hymnal used in worship services. Includes lyrics only.
bitte	you're welcome
boppli	baby or babies
bu	boy
buwe	boys
daed	dad
danki	thank you
dawdi-haus	a home built for grandparents to live in once they retire
Englischer	a non-Amish person
frau	wife
grossdaedi	grandfather
grossmammi	grandmother
gut	good
gut nacht	good night
haus	house
hinnersich	backward
"Ich liebe dich"	"I love you"
jah	yes
kapp	prayer covering or cap
kinner	children
kum	come
maidal	an unmarried woman
mamm	mom
naerfich	nervous
nein	no
onkel	uncle

Ordnung	the rules by which an Amish community lives
rumschpringe	"running around time," a period of adolescence after which Amish teens choose either to be baptized in the Amish church or to leave the community
ser gut	very good
verboden	forbidden
"Was ist letz?"	"What's the matter?"
welkum	welcome
wunderbaar	wonderful

Chapter 1

S hanna Stoltzfus felt something brush against her hair, just above her left ear. She swatted at it. When she touched flesh, she jumped, her attempts to pray forgotten, and raised her head from the steering wheel to see maple-stained fingers, complete with calluses and a small cut.

The hand pulled back. "Is something wrong? Are you hurt?" a deep voice asked.

She looked up into incredible gray eyes belonging to a drop-dead-gorgeous Amish man. He grasped his straw hat in the long fingers of his right hand. His light brown hair shone with natural blond highlights. She'd paid big bucks for streaks like those. He also had a strong, clean-shaven jaw. Nice. Too bad he hadn't been around when she'd been Amish. She definitely would have noticed a hunk like this. Might even have considered staying.

"Lost, maybe? I can direct you back to the main road. Where did you want to go?"

"Anyplace but here. Mexico sounds good." She swallowed her trepidation and aimed what she hoped was a wry smile at him. When she reached for the door handle, he stepped out of the way. "You must be the houseguest Mamm mentioned in her letters. Matthew Yoder from Pennsylvania?" She swung her legs out of the car and extended a hand. "I'm Shanna."

"Shanna." He seemed to freeze. A little smile played on his lips. "Shanna," he repeated.

She didn't know quite what to think. He said her name as if it meant something special. Then, he blinked. "I'm Matthew, jah."

He held out his hand, but before his hand could touch hers, she fixed her gaze on his brown fingers. He hesitated and then rubbed his hands together, as if to check to see if the stain was still damp. Then, he pulled back. "Shanna."

His tongue seemed to trip over her name this time. Or maybe he'd heard some negative things about her. Her stomach churned. She shouldn't be here. But where else could she go?

"I guess they are expecting you?"

"Nein. Not really." Shanna stood and looked up at him. The top of her head barely reached his jaw.

His gaze skimmed over her. She wondered what he thought as he studied her faded jeans, T-shirt, and flip-flops. She looked down at her toenails. Good, they were painted with pink polish. Except that the paint on one of her big toes had a huge chip in it. She wished she could reach for the bottle and repair the damage. As his gaze traveled back up, she repressed the urge to smooth her hair. It wouldn't have done much good, anyway. She'd driven the whole way with the windows down, so it would be hopelessly tangled.

His forehead wrinkled, and there was no hint of recognition in his eyes when they returned to her face.

"You have no idea who I am, do you?"

Matthew raised his eyebrows and his gaze met hers. "Nein. Should I?"

Unexpected pain shot through her. Daed had made good on his threat to reject her. "Figures. He probably forbade everybody to say my name. I'm surprised he allowed Mamm to write. Or maybe he doesn't know."

Confusion flashed across Matthew's face. "So, you think your mamm lives here, and she isn't expecting you?" He shook his head, his lips curling into a sympathetic half smile. "This is the home of Levi and Deborah—"

"Stoltzfus. Jah, I know. I'm their oldest daughter."

Matthew's smile slipped, and he blinked, cutting off her view of those gray eyes for a brief moment.

"You know, you have beautiful eyes." She stepped closer, then turned to shut the car door. "My things are in the back. But I guess maybe we should leave them there until we find out if I'm allowed to stay. Mamm said I would be welkum, but Daed has the final say, you know." She bit her lip and tried to force her fear of the imminent confrontation out of her mind. It didn't work. And since her little brothers and sisters hadn't gathered around to welcome her, she wondered if her family was even home. She looked around for the buggy, or some sign of life other than the handsome Matthew. She didn't notice any.

"Jah. Probably should wait." He blinked again when she turned to face him.

"Well, shall we?" She walked past him, around the front of the car, and toward the porch. At the top step, she hesitated and glanced back. Matthew stood where she'd left him, watching her. He didn't even try to hide it by looking away. A shiver worked through her, but she ignored it. He'd probably never met anyone like her before. Daed always said she was too outspoken. She sighed. "I guess I should ask. Where is Daed?"

He motioned behind him. "In the shop."

"Great." Postponing her reunion with him would at least give her time to see Mamm and her little sisters before she was kicked off the property.

If that happened, Shanna hoped this gorgeous Amish man wouldn't witness her humiliation. She felt ashamed enough of her modern clothes, now subject to his intense gaze. She was so underdressed, she might as well have shown up at a formal event wearing boxer shorts and a paint-spattered T-shirt.

Did Mamm still keep her Amish clothes hanging in her bedroom closet?

She scowled and turned toward the house. It would take more than a good-looking man to get her to change into Amish clothes. She hadn't been able to wait to leave the Amish life behind, and she wasn't about to return to it.

Well, she would stay for the summer, if permitted. But no longer than that.

And if Daed wouldn't let her? She'd deal with that when the time came.

Matthew stared at the front door, through which the green-eyed beauty had disappeared after only the briefest look back, as if checking to see if he followed her. And he probably would have, if his feet hadn't felt rooted to the ground.

He mused over their brief conversation and allowed a smile to play on his lips as he grappled with the sense that he'd glimpsed into his future.

"Shanna," he whispered her name again.

He hadn't meant to touch her hair. He'd noticed the open window, and he'd simply reached in to touch her shoulder. But she'd moved, and instead of the gentle tap he'd intended, his knuckles had buried themselves in her soft, golden tresses.

Inappropriate.

Even worse, he hadn't wanted to pull back.

Matthew swallowed, lifted his legs to see if they would still move, and turned toward the shop. He couldn't remember what he'd needed to go to the house for, anyway. No point in looking like a bigger fool in front of her.

When he pushed the shop door open, Levi looked up from where he stood, hunched over and sanding a wooden chair. "Did you get the key?"

Matthew shook his head. "I forgot what you sent me for." Ach, this was worse, having to admit to his mindlessness. Heat rose up his neck. "Um, there's a girl...your daughter. She was in her car. Said something about staying."

A look of hope flashed across Levi's face. His shoulders straightened, and a bright smile lit his face and eyes. He put down the sandpaper and moved toward the door, then stopped, his shoulders slumping. "Probably not for long."

Matthew couldn't quite read any of the other emotions that flashed across the older man's face.

"Is she shunned?" Matthew asked hesitantly.

Levi shook his head. "Nein, not formally. But I'd hoped denying her a place in the family would bring her back home." His expression hardened. "And maybe it would have. But my frau...."

He didn't need to say more. Matthew nodded in agreement. Shanna had mentioned letters in which her mamm had said she'd be welcome. Deborah must have gone behind Levi's back and kept in contact with her daughter.

It was none of his business, but he decided to ask, anyway. "Will you allow her to stay?"

He hoped Levi would say "Jah," the fascinating creature could stay. But another part of him wanted a decidedly firm "Nein." He hadn't been around her more than five minutes, and already she'd messed with his insides.

"I don't know." Levi scratched his head. "I'll have to think on it."

Matthew chuckled. "Maybe in the barn loft."

Levi's mouth curved up in a grin. "Might be best."

"I'm teasing." Matthew moved toward the door. "I'll go get the key you wanted. Sorry I forgot it earlier."

"Jah." Levi picked up the sandpaper and went back to work. "And I'll think on it. Gives her a few more minutes with her mamm, anyway, in case I decide not to let her stay."

After hugging Shanna, Mamm resumed peeling apples at the counter, where a recipe for apple turnovers was propped against the flour canister. Shanna picked up a knife to help with the paring, as she had countless times before. Mamm chatted nonstop, talking about Shanna's sisters, who were at friends' houses today, and about the garden. Not one mention had been made about whether she was permitted to stay. A piece of apple skin dangled from the peeler, ever lengthening as Mamm worked the apple around and around. It had always been a challenge for Shanna to try to pare the entire apple without breaking the strip, like Mamm did.

She'd never succeeded.

Yet another sign of failure. Another reason why she'd never be an Amish frau.

That, combined with the old-fashioned clothes and her intense dislike of the wringer washer. She'd hated that thing ever since getting her hair stuck in it as a young girl. She had always been afraid that the contraption would pull her whole head through the rollers, try to press it flat, as it did the garments, and leave it abnormally shaped.

That was almost reality. Spiritually, she was abnormally shaped. God had never intended her to be Amish. It must have been a fluke for her to have been born into an Amish family.

Shanna pushed the thought away. Why was she even thinking about this stuff? She'd settled it long ago, for pity's sake, so that she could enroll in college to earn her nursing degree. So that she could live and work in the real world. And wear real clothes. And...well, there were many other benefits of being Englisch.

Yet those scrubs she had to wear to her clinical rotations could hardly be considered real clothes.

Her stomach felt as if a whole flock of Canada geese had landed in it, honking, with wings flapping, as they did when they passed through during migration. It had to be the fault of that young man—the one who'd come out to her car and caused her heart to flip-flop like the bottoms of her sandals.

Matthew Yoder.

A good Amish name, for someone who appeared to be a good Amish man.

As if she'd summoned him by thinking his name, the door opened, and Matthew strode into the room, heading straight for the key rack that hung on the wall. Not that there were many keys hanging there. Why would they need them, when they had absolutely nothing worth stealing? Well, Daed's tools were valuable. But he was out there with them now, so Matthew would have no need to unlock the shop.

She watched as Matthew took a long skeleton key from the key rack. The barn key. One of the doors there led up to a loft she'd never been allowed to enter. She didn't know what Daed kept in there, just that he'd built stairs to replace the ladder leading up to it.

Matthew palmed the key, then turned toward the door, moving with an even stride. Not once did he look in her direction.

Had Daed said something to dispel the friendliness he'd shown her earlier?

Mamm turned around. "Ach, Matthew. I didn't realize that was you. Kum meet Shanna. She's our oldest. Attends college up in Springfield."

Matthew hesitated by the door, then turned, his gaze skimming over her. "Welkum, Shanna." His tongue didn't trip over her name so much this time. And he didn't indicate they had met in the driveway.

"This is Matthew Yoder from Pennsylvania," Mamm continued. "He came down in the swap I mentioned in my letter, where we traded buwe with a community in Lancaster. Matthew is looking for farmland hereabouts."

"I hope you can find some," Shanna said. Farmland wasn't readily available in this part of Missouri, as far as she knew. But then, she didn't keep track of such things. She wasn't in the market for land.

Matthew grinned. "I have my eye on a piece not too far from here. Belongs to an Englischer, so the haus would need some work to be made suitable."

She knew that would mean taking out the electrical lines, removing the screens from the windows, and installing a woodstove, among other things. All silly rules. Why no screens? Okay, she knew the answer: to keep God's view unobstructed. But, really. He could see through screens! And keeping the bugs out would hardly prevent people from going to heaven. Shanna shifted her feet to hide her shrug.

"The barn isn't adequate, so we'd need to have a barn raising to replace that, too," Matthew went on, as if he hadn't noticed her reaction. "But that's if I get the property. I'm praying on it."

"Might not want to pray too long. Someone might buy it right out from under you," Shanna quipped.

"Then, that would be God's will, ain't so?" Matthew looked into her eyes and held up the key. "I'd best get this out to Levi."

Mamm put the apple she'd just peeled in the bowl beside her. "Tell him that Sha—his daughter is home."

So, Daed had forbidden them to mention her name. Nausea roiled within her, and bile rose in her throat. Why was she subjecting herself to this? She shouldn't have come. Maybe one of those pay-by-the-week establishments in Springfield would have room. If she could afford it.

Matthew's gaze stayed locked on her. "Ach, he knows. I'm sure he'll be up in a bit."

His expression told her nothing about Daed's intentions. The Canada geese resumed their wild flapping in her stomach. She wasn't sure if it was due more to the compassion in those beautiful gray eyes or the news that she'd be facing Daed long before she was ready.

Mamm picked up another apple. "Don't worry yourself. He'll let you stay."

Shanna wasn't too sure.

A thump sounded on the front porch. Then another.

Shanna clutched her stomach, afraid she'd be ill. The next second, Daed stood in the doorway.

Chapter 2

When Matthew heard a sound, he turned and found Levi standing in the doorway. For a second, he thought Levi had grown impatient and come up to the house to get the key himself. But then, he saw Levi's eyes, watched him seek out Shanna like a man who'd been too long denied a glass of cold water.

The look disappeared as fast as it had come. Levi straightened his back, pulled the door shut, and stood there, legs spread, surveying his daughter like he'd stared at Matthew when the bishop had first brought him by the Stoltzfuses' farm, asking if they could make room for one of the Pennsylvania buwe. Matthew had been certain Levi could see clean to his soul with that gaze.

And now, that hard look was directed at the beautiful girl not three feet away from Matthew. He frowned, pocketed the key, and slipped past Levi. He reached the door as Levi said, "You think you'll find a welkum here?"

Matthew stepped outside, shutting the door firmly behind him. He should go finish staining the table he'd been working on instead of eavesdropping on a conversation that didn't involve him, didn't concern him, and didn't affect him.

Well, maybe it concerned and affected him—a little. That depended on Levi's decision.

Shanna. He let the name play over in his mind as he walked the length of the porch to the steps. He'd never heard that name before. It certainly wasn't common in his Amish district. But it was pretty. And it seemed to fit the woman, somehow.

Nein, he wouldn't stand there on the porch, listening as if he had a vested interest in the conversation going on inside that door. He went down the three wooden steps to the right side of the unfinished porch and headed across the circular gravel drive that separated the haus from the barn and the shed, where the carpentry shop was located.

That was another thing wrong with the Englisch farm he'd looked at. The barn was too far away from the haus. Yes, the problem could be fixed with a barn raising. But Shanna was right. If he dawdled too long with the decision, someone else would snatch up the property. And it was the only piece of land for sale in the same district where his best friend, Jacob, resided. He'd like to stay in the area. Maybe he'd contact the realtor and take another look at the farm.

Inside the shop, Matthew breathed in the combined scents of sawdust, lumber, and stain. He loved those smells. Good thing he'd landed in an Amish family that made their living by crafting quality furniture. He'd always enjoyed working with wood, but it'd been more of a hobby. His life had been centered around the land. And he had dreams for his own property. Dreams that included—

A car door slammed, followed by an engine revving.

Levi must have said nein.

A mix of emotions flooded through Matthew. He moved to the doorway of the shop to watch Shanna drive out of his life.

To his surprise, she stopped the car outside the door and rolled down the window. "Get in."

Shanna let the car idle as the Amish man stood there staring at her like she'd spoken in some foreign language. Okay, so she'd used Pennsylvania Deutsch, but she hadn't been away from home long enough to forget her native tongue. Matthew Yoder should have understood her just fine.

"Why would I want to get in?" Matthew moved out of the doorway and approached the car.

Shanna smiled. "I have need of your brute strength."

"Is that so." Matthew's lips curved in a crooked grin.

"Jah. Daed said I could stay in the apartment."

He raised his eyebrows. "The apartment?"

"It's my onkel's. He's Englisch, and he wanted Daed to remodel an unused loft in the barn into an apartment, with electric and everything. The one above the cows."

Matthew looked at the barn, not twenty feet from where he stood. "You want to drive me to the barn?"

His tone said, "What, are you out of your mind?" Now that she thought about it, maybe she was. Certainly, he had no reason to want to help her. She was capable of unloading her suitcases and boxes. After all, she'd loaded them by herself, carrying them down three flights of stairs from her dorm room, before she'd left campus that morning. She'd waited until the last minute before leaving, hoping for another option. Something other than going home.

"I'll meet you there," he said.

She forced her attention back to the topic at hand. His incredulity must have had nothing to do with her insinuated request for help but with her offer to drive him the short distance.

Well, there was that. But he had no idea how many stairs she'd already climbed that day. Her legs threatened to cramp just thinking about facing more. At least this loft wasn't high. And it was finished, so she'd have privacy. She'd dreaded the thought of sharing a room and a bed with her little sisters.

Shanna backed the car up to the barn by the double doors, which were open, and then pushed the button to unlatch the trunk. When she stepped out of the car, Matthew appeared at her side.

He reached into his pocket and pulled out the skeleton key. "Is this the key to the apartment?"

Shanna shook her head. "Nein. That's to Daed's area. The apartment is right here." She nodded to a door on the near left while pulling a key out of her pocket. She handed it to him and grabbed a box.

"I'll do the lifting." Matthew took the box from her. "You get the door." He handed the key back. "Unless you needed my brute strength to hold that big, heavy door open."

She laughed at his dry wit and unlocked the lightweight door. Matthew walked past her and climbed the short flight of stairs. There were only twelve steps, yet her legs ached at the sight of them.

He stopped at the landing. "Wow, I had no idea this was in here. It's a small haus, ain't so? Bedroom, living room...no kitchen, though." He put the box down on the living room floor and came back for another load. "You'll be eating with the family?"

"I don't know. I didn't give Daed the chance to say much—except that I had to find a job for the summer and pay Onkel Micah for the electric I'll be using. He's the one who pays the bills for this apartment, since it's against the Ordnung to have power. Daed had to get special permission from the bishop before he was allowed to remodel this loft. But Onkel Micah travels a lot; he and his wife drive all over North America in their little travel trailer, and they wanted this apartment for a home base. They won't be back until the fall." She looked around for something heavy with which to prop the door open.

"I'll get the boxes. You stay here." Matthew loaded two more boxes into his arms and walked past her again. "So, this Onkel Micah used to be Amish? He wasn't shunned?"

Shanna nodded. "He left to marry my aenti Billie. She's Englisch. And nein, he wasn't shunned, because he hadn't joined the church when he left." Daed certainly showed more kindness to him than to his own daughter. He'd welcomed Onkel Micah home but then had virtually shunned her. Not fair. She ignored the pain by focusing on the man walking up the loft stairs. He was a heartthrob, for sure. Too bad he was Amish. She watched as Matthew disappeared into the living room, then reappeared a moment later.

"I expected to hear something that would explain your name." He trotted past her again.

"Shanna? I was named after both my grossmammi. One was named Hannah, the other Sara. My parents kind of shoved the names together."

The knowledge made Shanna glad, even though her name was another reason she didn't fit in the family. She was the only *S*. All her brothers' and sisters' names started with *J*.

"Hmm. I never would have guessed." He bumped the car door shut with his hip. "That's everything in the backseat. You got much more in the trunk?"

"A few more boxes."

Matthew grunted as he hefted one of them. "What's in here? Books?" He headed up the stairs.

"Textbooks, jah."

"Am I going to be hauling this all back down when school starts again?"

Shanna grinned. "Are you offering to?"

His long glance told her nothing, but he went out to the car and hoisted another box from the trunk.

"I'll take you to McDonald's for a Caramel Frappé to say danki."

"Hmm. I've heard that term before. Caramel Frappé. Don't tell me that you're hooked on that stuff, too."

Too? Who else was hooked on it? Shanna tilted her head. "Well, it's not a Starbucks Frappuccino, but it's the closest thing to it in Seymour. I wonder if McDonald's will let me have my old job back for the summer. Guess I should ask."

"Sounds like a foreign language." Matthew shook his head but didn't say anything else as he went back to the car for the last box.

"I'll unpack later," Shanna said when he came back down. She shut the door behind him. "Can you go for a koffee now? I need to stop at the store for a few things."

"Do you need my brute strength for the shopping, too?" He adjusted the straw hat on his head.

"Will my response determine your answer?"

Matthew frowned. "I'll need to give Levi the key he asked for and check with him before I go. He is my boss, after all."

Shanna closed the trunk and headed for the front seat. "Hurry back."

Matthew gave her another look she couldn't decipher before he turned away.

When Matthew entered the shop, Levi was putting the finishing touches on a chair. Matthew placed the key on the counter nearby, then hesitated. "I moved Shanna's things into the apartment. She wants me to go into Seymour with her. Said something about going shopping and seeing about getting her old job back."

Levi grunted. "Never should have allowed her to take that job in the Englisch world. Gave her too many ideas."

"It happens." Matthew shrugged. "Maybe she'll come back to the faith."

"I pray so." Levi picked up the key and pocketed it. "Danki for helping her. I guess you can go with her to town, if you'd like. At least I'll know she'll get home safely."

"She'll be the one driving. Maybe you shouldn't be so confident...?"

"Hmm. Maybe so." Levi looked up and grinned at Matthew. "Have fun. You can finish when you get back."

"Okay. If you're sure." Matthew went out, headed toward that little blue car where Shanna waited.

"He said jah?" Surprise was evident in Shanna's voice and her raised eyebrows. However, she didn't elaborate. Instead, she waited as he climbed into the car next to her and then reached for the gray seatbelt. After eyeing it for a moment, he snapped it in place. He hated the tightness of these harnesses across his chest, but Englisch law required them.

"He said go if I wanted to." No need for her to know the part about seeing her safely home. He wanted to ask about the situation between her and Levi but decided it would be way too nosy. Some Amish fathers did cut off their children in rumschpringe if they ventured too far away from home base. And Shanna clearly had.

His gaze skimmed over her lacy pink shirt and low-cut jeans. Her flip-flops looked like they must hurt her feet, the way they wedged a hard-looking plastic thing between each of her big toes and the toe next to it. But what did he know?

Well, he knew that if he'd met her on the street, he never would have guessed her to be Amish.

Most Amish girls didn't stop wearing plain clothes during their rumschpringe.

"Your mamm said you're going to school in Springfield. What for?"

"Nursing. I'm working on my degree. It'll lead to a good job when I finish. At least, I'm hoping so. I still have another semester of school and then a semester of clinical rotations before I graduate."

He looked down and studied his stained fingers. "Why did you come home, then, if you're in school?"

"School lets out for the summer. All my friends were going on a medical mission trip to Mexico, but it cost a lot of money, and, well, I couldn't exactly ask my family for donations. I earned some money toward the trip, but nowhere near enough to cover it, so I gave it to a friend who needed some." There was a pause as she maneuvered her car around a washout in the dirt road, then picked up speed again. "I found a job for the summer in Springfield, but, you know, apartment leases require the first and last month's rent, plus a yearlong agreement, plus a security deposit, and I couldn't come up with all that, either. I have grants and scholarships to fund my education. Not that much extra money, you know? I had no choice."

That explained the comment she'd made earlier about wanting to be anywhere but here, even Mexico. She'd actually wanted to go. Little else in her dialogue made sense. He had only a vague idea what grants, scholarships, or security deposits might be. "What about your job in Springfield?"

She shrugged, then made a right turn on red onto the four-lane highway that had him grabbing for the door handle. A truck whizzed by on the left, so fast that her car shook. "It was at another fast-food restaurant. If I worked there and stayed here, my paycheck wouldn't even cover my gas. So, I quit. Hopefully, I'll get hired on here in town." That fast truck didn't appear to have fazed her.

It seemed his heart had found a permanent home in his throat. He swallowed. Hard. "You didn't stop at that red light," he said quietly.

She glanced at him. "I totally paused. No one was in the right lane." She clicked the turn signal, then began to merge the car into the other lane.

"Maybe I should drive on the way home. Your daed said he wanted you to come back safely."

Laughing, she reached over. He tried to lean away, but she snatched his hat off of his head and waved it triumphantly. "Jah. Sure. Let's see your driver's license, Matthew Yoder."

Chapter 3

Shanna tucked Matthew's hat between her and the door, and drove up to the light. It was green, but she waited for two cars and a semi to go through, then she turned left onto the road leading to McDonald's. She maneuvered the vehicle into the parking lot. Winking at Matthew, she plopped his straw hat on her head, remembering too late the old saying that a woman who wore a man's hat was indicating she wanted him to kiss her.

She licked her lips. Would he? Maybe on the cheek?

His eyes widened, and he shifted his gaze away from her, focusing on something out the front window. His mouth gaped a little. "Shan—"

A thud silenced him, and Shanna slammed on her brakes. Had she hit another car that was backing out? She looked ahead. Even worse. She'd rammed the left side of a buggy that'd been waiting in the drive-through lane. Her stomach roiled. What if the driver recognized her and told Daed?

She jammed the gearshift into park and hopped out of the car, noticing how the buggy listed to the side. Ugh. She'd broken a wheel. At least she hadn't permanently destroyed the buggy or killed the horse.

The driver, a man, got out of the buggy on the far side and came around the back to meet her.

"Are you all right?" She didn't recognize him, but she'd been out of the community for a while. People changed.

"Jah, fine. And the buggy will be, too, ain't so? I'll need to find a ride." He stroked his beard as he surveyed the damage.

"We'll take you where you need to go, Amos." Matthew came up beside Shanna and wordlessly slid something into her hand.

She looked down. Swallowed. It was a Pennsylvania driver's license. Valid, too, according to the date. He must have gotten it during his rumschpringe. She grimaced and handed it back to him, watching as he slid it back into his pocket.

A middle-aged woman approached them. "I called the police. They're on their way."

Shanna sucked in a breath. She couldn't afford a ticket. Why hadn't she kept her eyes on the road instead of teasing Matthew with his hat? Flirting with him, like a silly schoolgirl?

The police arrived before Shanna had mentally prepared herself. Thankfully, they came without lights and sirens. She'd attracted more than enough attention as it was. She may have left the community, but she still disliked being in the spotlight. It made her feel extremely vulnerable. And she hated that.

The police officer looked at her from beneath his wide-brimmed hat. In his left hand, he held the ticket book, along with her license and registration; in his right, a pen he must have lifted from a bank. He glanced again at the license and vehicle registration. "So, Ms. Stoltzfus." He looked up with a smirk. "Were you paying more attention to the handsome young man next to you than to the road?"

"Yes, sir." Shanna felt heat rising to her cheeks. She didn't dare glance at Matthew, who stood silently, supportively, beside her. Hatless. What did he think about her confession now that she'd openly admitted she'd been flirting?

The police officer handed Shanna the ticket and her papers, then turned away, promising to send someone to transport Amos's buggy to a blacksmith shop. "And it's okay to move your vehicles out of the drive-through lane," he added.

Shanna pulled in a deep breath and held it, waiting for the officer to return to his vehicle. Then, she released the air with a sob as despair washed over her in a flood. Slumping, she turned and flung herself against Matthew, tears scalding her eyes. "I can't afford this. Why did God leave me behind when I left the Amish?" Okay, she knew better; God hadn't left her. She was the one who attended church only sometimes, and, since leaving home, her relationship with Him had steadily gone downhill.

"He didn't." Matthew stood there, unmoving, for a moment. But in the next moment, his arms moved to surround her, somewhat awkwardly, as he surrendered his strong shoulder.

With one hand, Matthew tugged his hat free from Shanna's grasp and set it on top of his head. Then, he pulled her tighter against his chest and allowed himself to enjoy holding her. It was likely to be the only chance he'd ever get.

He took half a step back and freed his arm again to smooth her hair away from her face. Then, he took a fortifying breath. He'd make sure this was the only time he held her. Especially in light of her admission to flirting. With him. After all, a relationship between them wouldn't be happening.

He sucked in another breath, hoping she didn't notice his unsteadiness or hear his pulse pounding in his chest.

He didn't know how long he'd stood there, holding her. But all too soon, she pulled away, squared her shoulders, and wiped her eyes. "I'll be okay."

Jah. Of course, she would be. He was more worried about himself.

He watched as she marched over to her car, ducked inside, and backed it away from the buggy, whipping it into a vacant spot. Maybe his concern stemmed more from the thought of riding in a car with her behind the wheel again than how she affected him.

How had she ever managed to drive around Springfield without wrecking her car and taking her life—or someone else's? He cringed, remembering the traffic he'd seen when he'd gone through that city, and glanced at her car, now safely parked in between the yellow lines, with a black pickup truck on one side, a red one on the other.

Well, there were some dings on her car. Several, actually. Small dents. Apparently, she hadn't kept it completely scar free.

She stepped out of the car and came toward him. "I need to use the facilities," she said simply before turning and darting in the side door. Through the window, he watched her make a beeline toward the back of the building, where the restrooms were.

Matthew turned and sauntered over to where Amos Kropf waited with his broken buggy and his horse.

"Never thought you'd take up with an Englisch girl." Amos nodded toward the building.

Matthew shook his head. "Levi Stoltzfus's daughter. I just met her. Today."

Had it been just this morning? So much had happened since then. And it seemed like he'd known her forever. His heart had recognized her.

"You have to watch those Amish girls who veer so far from home during their rumschpringe. Some of them never return."

"I know." Ironic that he was being warned about a girl he barely knew. One he found much too fascinating.

"I was going through the drive-through to get my lunch. Working on a construction site on Garfield Street." Amos frowned. "Guess I'll go in and get it now. I'll catch a ride home later, so I won't need a ride from her." He gave an exaggerated shudder and looped the reins around a fence post. "Danki for offering."

Matthew nodded. For a moment, he wondered if maybe he shouldn't look for another ride home for himself. But then he shook his head. Shanna had gotten him there safely. Well, in a manner of speaking. She'd get him home. And, thinking of her.... He should probably go inside and check on her. It shouldn't take her this long to wash her face. He followed Amos to the building and entered after him. Immediately, he noticed Shanna leaning over the counter, talking with a man. Her shirt, untucked, revealed an inch or so of skin. He looked away, embarrassed.

The man gestured off to the side, and, in the next moment, Shanna pushed through a half door and disappeared into the recesses of the building.

Amos had taken a place in line, so Matthew turned around and looked for a seat. Almost all the tables and booths were occupied, some with only one person, but most with three or four people. He turned to face the counter and leaned against a support post to wait for Shanna.

The crowd thinned, and one of the women behind the counter looked at him. "May I help you?"

He shook his head. "Just waiting." Then, he frowned and stepped forward. "Uh, maybe, yes. Two Frappés."

"Excuse me?" The woman's eyes narrowed.

Matthew looked above her head and skimmed the menu. "Uh, two Frappés. One caramel, and one, uh...actually, both caramel." He didn't know what kind Shanna would want. He didn't even know if he liked them, never having tried one. The cappuccino he'd had once had been good. A bit sweet for his taste, but good. But she had mentioned a Frappé. It was the least he could do.

When the drinks were ready, Matthew took one in each hand—he hadn't expected them to be a type of iced coffee—picked up a couple of straws, turned around, and saw a booth that had emptied. He sat down and picked up an abandoned section of the Springfield daily newspaper. Sports. He scanned the headlines. Seeing nothing of interest, he set the paper down again, stuck one straw into one of the cups, and took a sip. Was this drink made out of pure whipped cream? It was way sweeter than cappuccino.

A few minutes later, Shanna came over to the table, carrying two clear cups identical to the ones he'd purchased. She glanced at the cups on the table and laughed. "Are you ready to go? I have shopping to do, and they want me back to work for the supper shift tonight."

Matthew blinked at her. "You got hired?" Levi wouldn't be pleased. But Matthew doubted he'd say anything to Shanna.

"Why did you think I wanted to come here? For the koffee I promised you? I needed a job. Thought I told you that." She turned away. "I have the uniform already, so we're all set."

Matthew grabbed the two iced coffees from the table and followed her to the door.

Someone had loaded the broken buggy onto the back of a trailer and was securing it. Amos stood off to the side, holding his horse. Looked like the animal had been taken care of.

"Want me to drive?" They'd had enough hits and near misses today for his taste. He put both of the cups on the hood of her car.

After a moment's hesitation, she set down one of the cups, reached into her pocket, and handed him the keys.

He hadn't expected her to let him.

Matthew pocketed the keys, then looked down at the two coffee cups. "I suppose I should offer one of these to Amos. We don't need four of them."

"I can take it over," Shanna said. "I should offer to pay for the transport and repairs of his buggy, anyway. It was my fault."

Matthew shook his head. "Nein, I'll offer. You aren't Amish."

Shanna dipped her head. She'd forgotten the rules about taking things from the hands of Englischers. "I'll pay you back, then, if you'll let me."

Matthew shrugged, then picked up a coffee cup and headed in Amos's direction. Shanna moved the two drinks she'd bought to the cup holders in the console of her car. When she looked up again, she saw Amos take a sip of coffee and the trailer driver pocket his wallet. Matthew started toward her. "All set, then. Sure it's okay if I drive?"

"It's fine." Except she felt like an idiot, knowing Matthew considered her an unsafe driver. But it was her fault for showing off and flirting with him. "How much do I owe you?"

"Not much. Don't worry about it." Matthew slid into the driver's seat. "We'll discuss it later."

She scooted into the passenger seat, closed the door, and watched as he inserted the key in the ignition, then deliberately adjusted the seat, the side and rearview mirrors, and the steering wheel. Kind of like she had the first couple of times she'd driven. "How much have you driven?" Maybe giving him the keys hadn't been a good idea, after all, despite the fact that he had a license. But then, he had to have passed a driving test to get the license. He must be a halfway decent driver.

"Enough. Where to?" He hooked the seatbelt and looked behind him before putting the car in reverse and backing out.

"The square."

He nodded and pulled out. A few minutes later, he eased the car into a parking space.

Shanna climbed out of the car. "I need a few personal items. I'll be right back. Unless you need something, of course; then you can come in."

He arched an eyebrow. "Thought you said you needed me along."

She shook her head. "I don't think I did. I didn't mean to, anyway. But I wanted you to come."

"Why...?" His eyes widened, and he immediately shook his head. "Never mind. Don't answer that."

Good thing he changed his mind. She didn't want to admit that she'd wanted to go on a date with him, and this would be the closest she'd ever come. Even if the attraction she thought she saw in his eyes were real, there was no way he'd ask her out.

But she'd gotten what she'd wanted. A job. And a sort-of date. Yet now she regretted manipulating Matthew, and what that said about her. She wasn't a very nice person sometimes. No wonder she'd never had a real relationship with a man. Plenty of dates, but nothing more. Shanna forced a grin and shut the car door. Then, she hurried across the street toward the store, making a mental list of the things she needed: shampoo, conditioner....

After making her purchases, she exited the store and jogged back to the car. She opened the passenger door, tossed the yellow plastic bag behind her onto the backseat, and closed the door. "Okay, I'm done. Let's go."

Matthew glanced at her. "Home?"

"Unless you can think of someplace else to go." She said it jokingly, but she half meant it. Maybe more than half. "Maybe we could run away and not bother coming back until the fall semester. Do you have any money? We could still go to Mexico."

"Home it is."

Shanna gave an exaggerated sigh. She'd known she was being extreme. Still, disappointment ate at her.

Matthew backed the car out of the lot and pulled onto the highway. Shanna shut her eyes, not wanting to watch him drive. She knew he'd be the most careful one on the road.

"I'm afraid someone will recognize me driving," Matthew said quietly. "I think I saw the bishop back there. I shouldn't have asked to drive. You shouldn't have let me."

"I'm sorry." She opened her eyes. "I'm really sorry." Then, she noticed an upturned cardboard box on the side of the road, and a bunch of kittens scampering nearby. She gasped. "Pull over!"

Matthew did, and Shanna was out of the car in an instant, scooping up the kittens to save them from certain death. With her arms full of three kittens, she turned to take them to her car, but Matthew was already standing there, box in hand. He set it down, right-side up, on the ground. He picked up a fat black kitten and lowered it into the box, where it mewed and pawed at the sides.

Shanna dumped in the three she held and then turned to catch the last one, which had wandered out into the road. An approaching vehicle swerved into the other lane, and she grabbed the kitten by the back of its neck, then hurried back to Matthew and the other kittens. "It makes me so mad when people dump animals."

He nodded. "Jah. They could have at least dumped them in front of an Amish farm. There is no such thing as too many mouse-catchers."

For a moment, Shanna was tempted to slug his arm and argue that an animal shelter would be a better choice, in case the hypothetical Amish farmer was the type to put the kittens in a bag filled with heavy rocks and take them out to the pond to drown. But she stopped herself. She'd flirted with him entirely too much today. And even though she wanted to, she wouldn't suggest making a trip to Springfield to find the kittens a good home. She didn't have time tonight, anyway, since she had to work.

In her defense, he did seem interested in her, and she was used to the Englisch way of going after what she wanted, even toying with men's affections.

That was wrong. She was wrong. She needed to show more respect to Matthew and his standards.

He loaded the box of kittens onto the backseat of her car. "What are you going to do with them?"

"Take them home." Her daed had drowned more than his share of kittens in the past, despite her tears, but maybe he wouldn't notice them for a day or two. At least until she had some time off work. Then, she'd take the animals into the city, where they'd have a chance at survival.

He nodded and dangled her car keys between them as a horse and buggy came to a stop behind them. A gray-haired man climbed out. Shanna recognized him as the bishop. He hadn't changed at all. She cringed as he eyed her, but instead of berating her, he shifted his attention. "Matthew Yoder. I thought that was you. I must have imagined you behind the wheel of that car."

Chapter 4

M atthew wanted to deny driving the car. But even as the temptation to lie washed over him, he straightened his spine. Lying wouldn't do any good. The bishop had seen him. Amos Kropf had seen him. And, of course, there were the keys, still clutched in his fingers.

He was the one who'd asked to drive, even when he knew that it was wrong for him, a member of the Amish church. And he'd been caught. There was nothing to do but own up to his violation of the Ordnung and accept the consequences.

"Jah—"

"I had an accident with a buggy in town," Shanna said, interrupting him.

Matthew looked at her, noticing the stiffness in her stance. Why had she spoken to the bishop? He hadn't addressed her.

"I shouldn't be behind the wheel of a car after the day I've had. I'm a danger to all the other people on the road. And Matthew knew this. You know how when you take cold medicine, the instructions tell you not to operate heavy machinery? Well, stress can do the same thing."

"Then, maybe you shouldn't be driving. Ain't so?" The bishop's sharp gaze landed on her.

Shanna's grin appeared forced. "I knew you'd see it my way."

The bishop's brow furrowed in a frown. After a long hesitation, he shook his head and turned back to his buggy. Matthew watched him climb in, check for oncoming traffic, and drive away.

The issue was far from over, but it would be pursued away from confusing Englischers. Away from Shanna. Matthew sighed and jingled the keys. He'd always been the good Amish kid, the one who mostly obeyed the rules during his rumschpringe. Getting a driver's license had been his one major act of disobedience, and that was because his best friend had talked him into it.

He shoved the memory away and rattled the keys again, drawing her attention.

She didn't make any move to reach for them.

"Take them."

Shanna did so without argument, sliding them into her pocket. She peered into the backseat, then turned to scan the road, maybe looking for more stray kittens.

"I don't need you trying to cover my transgressions," he told her. "I can talk for myself."

Her mouth parted for a moment, and then she shut it with a curt nod. Glancing up the road, she walked around him to the driver's side, opened the door, and slid inside. Without saying a word to him.

The engine roared to life. Did she plan to leave him there? Stranded? Matthew sucked in a breath of air and hustled around to the front passenger's side. It would be the last straw if she left him standing on the highway.

He was only halfway inside when the tires started to roll. He pulled his other leg in, reached for the door handle, and slammed the door shut as she merged onto the highway.

"You're dangerous!" He shifted his weight to sit correctly, pulled the seatbelt across his chest, and then glared at her. As if she could feel his eyes.

Her jaw tightened.

"Is that why you wanted to be a nurse? Job security from fixing up all the people you injure in traffic accidents?"

A lone tear made a trail down her cheek.

He instantly regretted the words. They'd been more than a bit harsh. But instead of apologizing, he turned away and looked out the window. He'd apologize later. If he made it home in one piece.

How could this woman have even one drop of Amish blood in her? He certainly couldn't see it.

She didn't attempt to avoid the washout on the dirt road when they came to it. She hit the gas and flew over it, seeming to ignore the racket when the car bottomed out.

Jah, Shanna was trouble with a capital T.

So, why did he feel so attracted to her?

Shanna dropped Matthew off in front of the shop door, then drove the car behind the barn, where it would be hidden from sight. Daed had always asked Onkel Micah to park his RV back there, as if he was ashamed to have an Englisch vehicle on the grounds. Few, if any, of the neighbors even knew that part of the barn had electricity, and Onkel Micah always kept the windows covered with cardboard at night, probably so the lights wouldn't be seen.

She would do the same.

But that was as far as it would go. She didn't claim to be Amish anymore, and while Daed may be permitting her to stay on his property, he treated her as an outsider. At least, he had so far today. So, she would respond in kind. She didn't belong here, and she wouldn't make any effort to seek out her family—make that her ex-family—or the handsome Matthew Yoder from Pennsylvania.

She'd done enough damage today, to much more than just the buggy. Her reputation, for one—she couldn't imagine what Matthew must think of her. Dangerous, a bad driver, a flirt, too talkative…. The list probably went on and on.

Pretending she was about to drive off without him? She wouldn't have, really. But the joke had belly flopped. She still felt the pain deep inside. College students pulled that trick on each other all the time. Matthew didn't know that.

Frowning, she climbed out of the car, opened the back door, and lifted the box of mewing kittens. After using her hip to bump both doors closed, she carried the box around to the front of the barn. She hoped Daed wouldn't peek out of the shop and see her. And that Matthew wouldn't tell Daed about them.

Surely, Daed wouldn't notice five extra kittens if no one mentioned them. After all, she'd spied kittens tumbling around in the grass when she'd arrived this morning. She didn't see them now.

A rock settled in the pit of her stomach. Had Daed drowned the kittens while they'd been gone? If so, he would notice the new ones.

Entering the barn, Shanna scanned the shadows. There, in a corner, a kitten wrestled with a mouse. It looked like the mouse was winning. With a grin, Shanna set the box down and scooped up one of the kittens.

"What do you have there?" Daed's voice came from behind her.

Shanna felt her heart rate skitter out of control, and she gripped the kitten tightly, squeezing enough that it squeaked and dug its claws into her hand.

She swallowed and turned to face her father, with the kitten still squealing and squirming for freedom. "They were dumped out on the highway. I couldn't leave them. They were going to get run over. I thought I'd take them to the Humane Society in Springfield."

"You think this looks like the Humane Society?" Daed folded his arms across his chest.

"Nein. But I have to work tonight until close, so I didn't have time. I'll take them there as soon as I can."

"Work?" A shadow flickered through Daed's eyes.

"Jah. I got my old job back for the summer."

"For the summer." Daed's chest rose and fell. "So, I take in stray cats and stray Englisch girls for the summer."

Pain shot through Shanna's heart as she watched Daed frown and move past her. A stray Englisch girl? Was that all she was to him?

Probably so. She didn't belong in this world. She didn't have a family. Not really.

She was just a stray.

Matthew couldn't shake the sense of guilt that haunted him. He stared down at the table he'd been staining, the harsh words he'd spoken to Shanna repeating over and over in his head. He needed to apologize.

He didn't know how.

In all honesty, "safe driver" was the last term he'd choose to describe Shanna. But maybe he should let it go.

Or maybe he should apologize for hurting her feelings.

Well, he'd wait until he'd finished working on the table.

He couldn't concentrate. Instead, the flash of pain across her face and the tear trickling down her cheek—both results of his unkind words—replayed in his mind.

With a sigh, Matthew put the brush down and, leaving the can of varnish open, walked out of the shop. He wouldn't be gone long. Just long enough to apologize and beat a hasty retreat.

After that, he'd stay as far away from that beguiling Englischer as he could.

He didn't see her outside anywhere. Levi's wife, Deborah, stood out by the laundry line, folding dry clothes. The two littlest girls were by her side, one taking the clothes down and handing them to her, the other setting them in the basket. Strange that Shanna wasn't out there with them, visiting.

If one of his older sisters had returned home after a long time away, she'd be with the family, talking up a storm.

With another glance around, Matthew turned to the barn and headed in that direction. A few moments later, he approached the apartment door. Loud music pulsed from behind it. She would never hear him knock over all that noise.

What more could he do except make an effort?

He raised his fist and banged with all the force he could muster.

A few seconds later, he heard the sound of feet pounding down the stairs. The door flew open. Shanna wore different clothes, which looked neither plain nor fashionable Englisch. He realized it must be her McDonald's uniform. Her hair was wrapped in a blue towel, and she held a tiny brush in her right hand. "Hey. You don't need to beat the door down. Kum on in." She turned and dashed back up the stairs, disappearing around the corner.

He couldn't. Shouldn't.

The music radio clicked off, and she stuck her head into the stairwell. "Aren't you coming?"

"Uh, nein. I came to apologize. I didn't mean to hurt you."

She blinked at him. "Ach. I'm so over that. Right now, I'm trying to kum to terms with being called a stray."

A stray? He didn't remember calling her that. Matthew scratched his neck.

"Tell you what. If I had anyplace else to go...." She shook her head. "Daed doesn't love me. He doesn't want me here. I guess that's why I'm out in the barn. Out of sight, out of mind, ain't so? I don't know why he agreed to let me stay. Maybe because Mamm wanted it."

Matthew frowned, remembering the expressions that had crossed Levi's face when he'd found out Shanna had come home. Expressions of joy and hope. And love. "Your daed loves you."

She glanced down at her feet. "Right. And that's why he called me a stray." She heaved a breath, then waved the little brush in his direction. "I need to finish putting my makeup on so I can go to work. Are you coming up?"

He thought she'd been wearing makeup when she'd come home. Why would she wash it off, only to reapply it? Matthew shrugged. "Nein. I need to get back to work."

"Okay. Don't worry about it, Matthew. I'm tough. I can handle criticism."

His brow furrowed. Why did he have trouble believing that? It didn't matter. He'd done what he'd come to do.

"So, what are you called? Matt? Or just Matthew?"

He backed up a step. "My friends call me Matthew." Instantly, he regretted his words. But then again, everyone called him Matthew, except for some of the Englisch. Shanna would probably go with Matt.

Her gaze settled on him. "Gut. I prefer Matthew. It's sexier."

Matthew's face heated, and he reached out to grip the doorknob. He needed the support to deal with this forward Englisch girl. She seemed to thrive on shock.

She grinned. "Shut the door on your way out."

Chapter 5

S hanna closed the door of her car and headed for her apartment, swinging the yellow Dollar General bag beside her as she trudged through the weeds behind the barn. Before she rounded the corner, she paused to stretch her aching leg muscles. Still, she was glad for the work. She'd been back in Seymour three days and had worked every one of them. She hadn't been on the schedule to work today, but she'd had to fill in for somebody who hadn't shown up this morning. And she was scheduled to work every day next week. Good, because she needed the money.

Except she had yet to take the five kittens to the Humane Society. She needed a day off to take care of that before Daed decided to eliminate them. So far, he had ignored their presence, much as he'd appeared to ignore Shanna's. She hadn't seen any members of her family since the day she'd arrived.

Of course, that was partly her fault. When she wasn't working or spending time in town, she was hiding out in the apartment.

As she came around the corner of the barn, the house came into view, and the aroma of roast beef met her nostrils. Her stomach rumbled in response. Shanna pictured the meal—the gravy Mamm always made to go with it, the warm, flaky crescent rolls— and she made a decision. She was tired of living off of burgers and fries consumed during her breaks or granola bars eaten at home. The apartment didn't have a kitchen. There wasn't even a microwave or a mini fridge. But then, Onkel Micah and Aenti Billie usually ate meals with the family when they were in town. She longed for a home-cooked meal. Especially now, with the scent of roast beef along with something sweet, maybe shoofly pie, tantalizing her senses.

How unwelcome would she be made to feel if she ventured up the porch steps and entered through the front door, interrupting the family as they sat down for their evening meal?

Thunder rumbled overhead, drowning out the sound of her growling stomach, though it did nothing to mitigate the ache. She hadn't eaten fruits or vegetables in ages, filling up instead on hamburgers, fries, and cappuccinos at work. Hardly what one would call a balanced diet. She cringed at her outright disregard of everything she'd learned about nutrition in her nursing classes.

Another rumble of thunder. She looked up at the sky, where ominous-looking storm clouds loomed. A raindrop plopped on her nose. She clutched the yellow plastic bag more tightly in her palm. It held two more boxes of granola bars.

She changed her course in the direction of the house, dreaming of a home-cooked meal instead of the same old granola bars, which didn't taste remotely similar to the ones Mamm used to make from scratch with marshmallows, oatmeal, chocolate, and other ingredients Shanna couldn't recall.

Hearing something beside her, she stopped and turned to see who was there. Her gaze met Matthew's steady gray eyes. She'd forgotten how incredibly gorgeous they were. Her stomach quivered. She couldn't tell if it felt better or worse than her hunger pangs.

He studied her silently for a moment, then turned and nodded toward the house. "They set a place for you at every meal."

They did? If that were true, then it would seem her exile had been self-imposed. Shanna's heart stuttered for a second, and then she remembered Daed's hard look when he'd caught her with the kittens. He'd called her a stray. If they fed her, it would be a cold meal on the porch, at best; at worst, a warm plate on a card table in another room, to keep up the guise of shunning. She'd rather eat hard boxed granola. "Nein, they don't."

One corner of Matthew's mouth quirked. "You'll never know unless you swallow your pride and go in there."

"I can't."

He shrugged and started moving toward the house. "You can't? Or you won't?"

Thunder rumbled again, and the spotty drizzle turned into a downpour. Matthew's steps quickened as he hurried toward the porch. Shanna stood in the yard, the rain stinging her cheeks and soaking her clothes, which began to cling to her body. Her hair was probably wet enough to form a lather with shampoo.

When Matthew reached the front door, he paused and looked back at her. Instantly, she felt like a fool for standing in the rain, watching him go. Still, she didn't move. The empty apartment held no appeal, but she didn't have the courage to follow him inside.

His gaze mocked her, and his words replayed in her mind: *They set a place for you at every meal.*

If only she could believe they wanted her.

"*You'll never know unless you swallow your pride....*"

She took one step toward the house, then glanced down at her clothes, now soaked through. After she'd kicked off her muddy shoes outside the door, Mamm might greet her with a big, fluffy bath towel and then shoo her upstairs to change into one of her old dresses, all of which probably still hung on hooks in her old bedroom.

Dry and appropriately dressed, she'd go back downstairs to the family meal, looking like an Amish woman but feeling the censure in Daed's eyes as she pretended to be someone she wasn't. And what would Matthew think?

It shouldn't matter. Still, she focused on him, waiting at the door. He made a motion with his hand, inviting her to come.

With a deep breath, she turned and fled inside the barn, to the warm, if lonely, apartment, to eat her bland, prepackaged meal.

"There's a towel on the hutch, if you need it." Deborah's words greeted Matthew when he came inside.

"I'm fine." His shoulders were a little damp, but he'd been under the protection of a big tree, and then the porch, when the downpour had hit.

The kitchen bustled with activity. Deborah stood at the stove mashing some potatoes with butter and milk, while the two little girls set the large farm table: Joy arranged the plates, and Joanna followed close behind with the silverware. A place was set for

Shanna, as it had been for every meal since she'd returned home. Too bad she didn't have the courage to come inside and see for herself.

He shook his head. Too bad Levi didn't have the courage to face his daughter and invite her to rejoin the family.

Both of them suffered due to a stubborn refusal to take the first step.

For a moment there, he'd thought that Shanna would come. He'd seen her take that step toward the house before she'd hesitated, her lip quivering. He'd almost gone after her when she'd turned and run for the barn, but then he'd stopped himself. She'd have to come on her own, when she was ready.

He hadn't had any contact with her since the day she'd come home. The day she'd flirted with him so outrageously, telling him she'd call him Matthew, because.... His face heated just thinking of it.

Matthew headed over to the sink, where he soaped up his hands and forearms, then rinsed them off. He was reaching for the towel when he heard a small, timid knock on the door. Deborah turned, the roast platter in her hands. "I wonder who that might be."

Levi stood up and took the few steps necessary to reach the door. He opened it wide, and Matthew saw Shanna standing there, dripping wet. Everyone froze, even the two little girls. The youngest one, Joanna, dropped the remaining silverware on the wooden table with a loud clatter.

For a long moment, Levi stood in silence. Matthew wished he could see his facial expression. Finally, Levi grunted. "Didn't think you'd have enough sense to come in out of the rain."

Hurt flickered across Shanna's face. Matthew saw the sting of rejection in her eyes. When she backed up a step, Deborah gathered the big, fluffy towel from the hutch, the one she'd offered to Matthew, and rushed to her oldest daughter. She moved so quickly, Matthew hadn't even seen her set down the platter. Apparently, she wasn't about to let Shanna leave so easily.

"Ach, you're soaking wet. Run upstairs and put some dry things on. We'll hold dinner for you. Your clothes are still hanging on the hooks."

Matthew dropped his gaze to the red shirt and black pants she wore. Her name tag was clipped to the left pocket of her shirt. She must have just gotten off work.

Levi grunted again and stepped aside. Shanna moved past him. "I don't want to pretend...."

Deborah waved her on. "Just go."

With another glance at Levi, Shanna scooted on by, pausing long enough to take her shoes off and leave them by the door. She made a wide arc around Matthew on the way to the stairs. The two little girls abandoned their jobs and ran after their older sister, chattering. With their daed having allowed her in, they must have felt free to follow her.

"It's the Englisch name." Levi turned around to face Deborah, his expression resigned. "I told you we should have gone with either Sara or Hannah. Or started the *J* theme earlier and named her Jubilee, instead of using that for her middle name."

"Jubilee" didn't sound very Amish, either, but Matthew kept his opinion to himself. He grabbed the hand towel and dried his arms.

Deborah frowned. "It doesn't matter at this point, Levi. What's done is done. And I don't think that her name has anything to do with her decisions. People with gut, solid biblical names leave, too."

One of the three boys lined up on the long bench on the far side of the table spoke up. "Jah. I heard that the Lehman boy left." Matthew glanced over to see which one had spoken. Thirteen-year-old Judah. Levi silenced him with a look.

His arms dry and reddened from the rubbing, Matthew hung the towel back on the rack and turned toward the table. He slid onto the bench next to seventeen-year-old Joseph as Shanna, Joy, and Joanna came back into the room.

Matthew sucked in a long breath, his heart thudding in his chest. He'd found her appealing before. But now.... Shanna wore a dark green Amish dress, complete with an apron and a white prayer kapp. The color of the dress reminded him of the pine trees in the woods back home. She entered the room quietly and took her place on the opposite side of the table, closer to her mamm than to her daed, he noticed. Ducking her head, she folded her hands in her lap.

She seemed an altogether different person from the Englisch woman he'd previously encountered. The boldness was gone.

Joy and Joanna quickly finished setting the table, then plopped down next to Shanna, one on each side. She scooted toward the middle of the bench to make room.

After the silent prayer, Levi started passing the food. Joy passed the potatoes to Shanna, who scooped a helping onto her plate. As she passed the bowl to Joanna, she bumped her cup of milk, which danced on edge almost in slow motion before starting to tip.

Matthew reached for it, but Joseph was quicker, grabbing it before it tilted completely. A small puddle of white pooled on the table. "Careful, Shanna," he said. "None of us wants a milk bath."

Shanna's face heated, and she dipped her head to avoid the smirks on her brothers' faces, and probably Matthew's, as well. She'd known better than to come over here for a meal, but it smelled so good. And the idea of having a warm, tasty, filling meal on a day like today had been too much temptation to resist.

She should have fought the lure.

Besides, she'd known that if she came here soaking wet, they would urge her to change clothes and have her back in Amish attire before she could blink an eye. Admittedly, she was the one who had chosen to include the apron and the prayer kapp. She would have felt undressed without them.

Her stomach churned. What did Matthew think of her now? Even more important, what did Daed think? She didn't risk looking up but continued to stare at her plate, afraid to see the censure on his face.

The clothes felt surprisingly comfortable, enveloping her in a warm hug that made her feel like she had come home. If only she could.

Well, technically, she supposed she could. All she'd have to do would be get rid of her Englisch things, drop out of college, and move back into the bedroom with her sisters, and all would be forgiven. She'd be welcomed back into the fold by both her family and the community.

But it wasn't that easy. Besides, she didn't want to. She enjoyed her freedom. Her choices. Her preferences.

Well, it didn't matter. She speared a slice of roast from the platter Joy held for her. She hesitated, then speared two more slices.

After all, who knew when she'd get another home-cooked meal?

With her plate filled, she forced herself to raise her eyes. Her gaze landed on Matthew, seated across the table. He openly studied her with a look of concern in his beautiful eyes.

Shanna studied him in return, just as openly. Why had this handsome man with such beautiful eyes chosen to move here? Didn't he have a girl back home? She straightened her posture and held his gaze. "So, Matthew. How did you come to be part of a man swap?"

Chapter 6

Matthew blinked. The question had come out of nowhere. Beside him, Shanna's brothers snickered, and Levi shifted in his chair. Without looking at him, Matthew knew the man's gaze had hardened and focused on Shanna. He could feel her discomfort. He supposed she had the right to know his reasons for coming here. After all, he'd already had the same conversation with others in the community.

He shrugged. "I have eleven brothers and sisters. I'm the baby of the family. My parents moved into the dawdi-haus several years ago, and my older brothers have taken over the farm. Daed had parceled out so much of it to my brothers that there wasn't much left for me. Daed and Mamm help out, and...." He set down his fork and picked up his glass to take a sip of water. "And there didn't seem to be room for one more. When I heard about the opportunity to move to Missouri in the exchange, I jumped at it. One of my best friends had already made the trip; another one had signed up."

Matthew looked down for a second and took another drink. He swallowed, then continued. "Besides, it was becoming unbearable at home. I was in my brothers' way, and I think they resented my presence. I decided to leave sooner rather than later."

He doubted he was even missed much. Mamm had cried when he'd gotten into the driver's van for the ride to the bus station. His brother Thomas had spoken only to ask if he could have Matthew's horse and buggy for his oldest son, who was beginning his rumschpringe.

Matthew had sold them to him and pocketed the money.

"So, now you've got to find yourself a frau."

He looked up in time to see her smirk. "All in God's time," Matthew said with a nod. But he couldn't deny the feeling he was looking at her—his frau. How that could be possible, he didn't know. It would depend entirely on the hand of God, that much was certain.

He took a bite of his food. Time to turn the tables. "My friend Jacob and I plan to fish this weekend. Think you can get some time off work to join us? We're going down to the pond." He jerked his finger in the direction of the large pond on their farm.

Her eyes widened, but the smirk remained. "Jah, if you'll go with me into Springfield when I take the kittens to the Humane Society."

Ach, nothing like laying his life on the line. He didn't want to ride with her into Seymour again, let alone go all the way to Springfield.

Levi cleared his throat. "Speaking of which, I saw Amos Kropf the other day. He told me he had his buggy at Daniel Troyer's shop for some repair work. Something about an Englischer running into it. You wouldn't know anything about that, would you, Shanna?"

Ignoring her brother Johnny's snicker, Shanna pursed her lips and looked down at her plate again, her appetite lost. But it'd come back. She couldn't let this food go to waste. "At least I didn't kill him or his horse."

"Jah, and that's gut, or you'd be in a heap more trouble. The question is, how do you plan to right this?"

Shanna frowned, mentally adding up her unexpected costs. Even with working through the summer, it would be tough to come up with enough money to cover her college expenses. She also had Onkel Micah's electric bill to pay for, plus the ticket for reckless driving. And, now, the cost of repairs to Amos Kropf's buggy. She needed to pay Matthew back, too, for what he'd given the driver Amos had called. She expelled her breath forcefully, then picked up her knife and fork and started cutting her meat into bite-sized pieces. "I don't know."

"I suggest you come up with some ideas, then."

She didn't have a clue where to begin. Her baking and cooking skills were rusty, not that they'd ever been worth mentioning. That distinction belonged to Becky Troyer, a quiet girl who spent every spare moment either in the kitchen or with her nose in a book. She was the last person Shanna would have expected to get pregnant during her rumschpringe, but apparently an Englisch boy had taken advantage of her, and now she had a boppli. But the community had always raved about Becky's pies and cobblers. So, really, Shanna had no hope of paving the way to forgiveness through Amos's stomach by offering to supplement his wife's cooking. Assuming they would even accept food from an Englischer.

Shanna shrugged. "What are his needs?" Probably a waste of time asking. She was still Englisch. He would still refuse.

Across the table, Joseph chortled. "A frau. His third one died."

"Ach. I hadn't heard."

"Maybe you should apply." Joseph laughed outright.

No one else did. Daed looked down and seemed to focus on cutting his meat. Meanwhile, a wistful gaze skittered across Mamm's face.

Their reactions sent Shanna's thoughts in directions they shouldn't go, because they tended toward gossip and curiosity. What would it be like to be an Amish man's fourth wife? She frowned. "How many kinner does he have now?"

Daed rearranged some of the food on his plate. "Seven, last I knew. All buwe."

"And nein frau?"

"Nein."

Shanna sat back. If she was allowed, she could do a lot to help Amos Kropf. She speared a piece of meat with her fork and took a bite.

Levi set his fork down firmly. "I don't like that look on your face. Explain yourself."

Shanna shifted her weight and frowned. "Nothing to explain. Just trying to think what I could do." That was a half-truth.

"I think you've done enough already," Daed grunted.

The words hit Shanna hard, like a slap in the face. She sat back in her chair, tears burning her eyes. "Jah. Jah, I guess I have." She yanked the cloth napkin from her lap and tossed it onto the table. So much for enjoying this home-cooked meal. She should have stuck with the granola bars. "May I be excused, please?"

Daed pointed his fork at her plate. "Sit. Eat. We're not feeding your gut food to the hogs. Besides, you need fattening up. Too skinny. What man wants a skinny frau? Matthew, you would like a little meat on her bones, ain't so?" He chuckled.

Matthew looked up, his eyes wide with unmistakable horror. His gaze darted to Shanna, and she felt her face heat. She averted her eyes and shifted uncomfortably. How could Daed ask him something like that? It wasn't even remotely funny.

When she chanced meeting his gaze again, she saw a look of sympathy suddenly light his features. He looked back at Daed. "She's gut."

Just "gut"? How did he define "gut"? Did he think she was pretty? Did he agree with Daed that she was too skinny but didn't want to hurt her feelings? Not fair for him to leave it with "gut."

On the other hand, maybe she didn't want to know what he meant.

Mamm got up from the table and began refilling the coffee cups. "So, how are the orders coming? You getting the work done?"

A deft change of topic. *Danki, Lord.* Shanna felt a lone tear escape her burning eyes, and she angrily brushed it away, unwilling to give the menfolk the satisfaction of seeing her cry. Well, if Daed wouldn't excuse her from the table.... She began shoveling food into her mouth, as if she hadn't eaten in a month.

Daed looked away from Shanna and toward Mamm. "Jah, the truck from the furniture store will kum Friday afternoon. Matthew and Joseph need to stain a couple of chairs, and that order will be complete. We got another one in. We'll stay busy."

"Gut. And the fields?" Mamm seemed determined to keep the focus off of Shanna. She retrieved two shoofly pies, which had been cooling on the counter.

"Had Judah and Johnny out there working the fields to get them ready for planting. Figured we'd start putting them in by next Monday."

"My seed order came in," Mamm said as she sliced a piece of pie, then transferred it to a plate, which she set down in front of Daed. "The girls and I will start getting that garden planted after school on Monday."

"I can help with the gardening, Mamm." Shanna heard the hoarseness of unshed tears in her voice, but she hoped no one else had noticed. She stood up and started collecting the dirty dishes from the table and carrying them over to the sink. Her two younger brothers dashed by her on their way out of the room, and her hands shook nervously, rattling the stack of plates. A fork slid off the top plate and clattered to the floor.

Shanna imagined the reprimands that probably hovered on the edge of Daed's tongue. Something about breaking all their dishes, maybe. Okay, her nerves were on overdrive. This stress was probably wreaking havoc on her blood pressure, though she'd never had a problem with it before. She placed the stack of plates on the counter, then picked up the fork and placed it in the sink before returning to the table.

Lightning flashed outside, followed by a deafening crack. The smell of charred wood drifted in through the window. She looked outside just in time to see the tree in front of the house split down the middle. Joanna wailed, then turned around and wrapped her chubby arms around Shanna's legs. Shanna picked her up and cuddled her close, taking in the fresh scent of her hair. Mamm must still use baby shampoo on her, though, at five years old, she was hardly a baby.

Daed got up and opened the front door to peer out. "Sky's turning green. Looks like it might be bad." He glanced over his shoulder at Shanna. "You might consider staying in the haus tonight."

Shanna opened her mouth to refuse, but the top part of the tree fell to the ground with such impact that the house shook. Daed turned from the doorway. "We have some sawing to do tomorrow, Matthew. God has given us some firewood."

Matthew nodded and reached for the coffee cup in front of him, cradling it in both hands, as if he was trying to warm his cold fingers. "Anyone up for a game of checkers?"

It wasn't that Matthew was really eager to play checkers. It was that…well, he was glad for anything to get his mind off of the storm brewing outside. The greenish tint to the sky made his stomach roil. Tornadoes. He hated them. And he probably should have considered the frequency with which they occurred in Missouri before moving here. Maybe he would have decided not to come. Maybe he ought to have abided his brothers' attitudes and the dearth of land in Lancaster, where such natural disasters were extremely rare.

Of course, he'd never met a girl at a singing in Pennsylvania who had attracted him enough to begin the courtship process. Well, except for Katie. He'd taken girls home from singings, but never the same girl twice. Truth be told, he hadn't had much luck here so far, either. His friend Jacob Miller had tried to set him up with Annie Beiler, who was best friends with his sweetheart, Becky Troyer. But Annie scared him. She was bossy and had somewhat obsessive tendencies. Matthew had seen her organize the desserts in alphabetical order at church socials.

Funny, the only girl he'd met who made him think of marriage was Shanna. And he barely knew her. He knew only that she was in her rumschpringe and very deep in the Englisch world. Which made her completely off-limits, especially considering he'd joined the Amish church.

"Looks like we might have some tornado activity tonight," Levi commented from his position at the open doorway. He frowned and shut the door. "We'll keep an eye on the sky at this point. Feel the heaviness in the air, Matthew? That's what tornado weather feels like. Do you ever have them in Pennsylvania?"

Matthew remembered one. It had torn their barn apart and reduced it to a pile of lumber yet left the buggy completely intact. Several of their cows had been killed. It'd been enough to put the fear of the Lord in him.

He opened his mouth to answer when a loud crash came from upstairs.

Deborah looked toward the ceiling. "What are those buwe up to?"

Chapter 7

Upstairs in her brothers' room, Shanna helped clean up the broken glass from the window that had been shattered by a tree branch, which now protruded through the opening. Daed and Matthew worked to saw off the branch, while Joseph went in search of a board to cover the window. Joanna clung to Mamm's skirt, her thumb stuck in her mouth the whole time. She sucked it only when she was scared.

When they finished, Shanna helped Mamm wash the supper dishes, enjoying their quiet conversation about her work in town and her schooling—topics they hadn't discussed until now. They kept their voices muted so that Daed wouldn't overhear. He'd probably make some hurtful comment. If only she knew how to improve her relationship with Daed. She glanced over her shoulder at him, seated again at the table, where he half watched Matthew and Joseph play checkers. The *Budget* was held open in front of him.

When the last dish had been dried and put away, Shanna grabbed a cookie from the bear-shaped jar on the counter, then pulled out a chair at the table and sat down next to Matthew. He grinned at her, then moved a round black piece one space to the right, blocking the path of his opponent. Shanna studied the board.

Joseph picked up one of his red pieces and jumped one of Matthew's.

Daed reached for his coffee cup, rustling the pages of the *Budget* as he did. "Says here that Leah Swartz died while visiting her cousin in Ohio. Did you know about that, Deborah?"

"Nein. Let me see." Mamm moved to peer over Daed's shoulder.

Matthew jumped two of Joseph's checkers. "King me."

Shanna grinned. "I'll play the winner."

"Ach, jah. And we'll mop you up." Joseph plopped a black piece atop Matthew's new king and then moved another of his own checkers. "Doubt your skills improved any."

Shanna scooted her chair a bit closer to Matthew's. "Well, maybe not. I haven't played since I left home. Monopoly's my new favorite. Have you ever played that? I brought the game with me. It's in the barn." She focused on the board and took a bite of the cookie. "Mmm. What kind of cookies are these, Mamm?"

"Applesauce. I need to make another batch tomorrow. Want to help?"

"Jah." She couldn't believe how her family was welcoming her back. Like she'd never gone. Well, except for Daed. Although he hadn't said a word about her being dressed as an Amish woman, she could feel his disapproval. Or maybe she imagined it.

"Careful. You might get domestic on us." Matthew leaned over and bumped her shoulder with his.

"Ach, you might be surprised by how domestic I can get," Shanna teased, then caught herself when Daed peered over the top of the newspaper at her.

"Aren't you the same one who used to burn the koffee and get her hair stuck in the wringer washer?" Daed pointed out.

Ouch, that hurt. Her laundry skills had improved since she had started using automatic washing machines, but her cooking abilities had probably suffered from the conveniences of a microwave and an automatic coffeemaker. And, since leaving home, borrowing a broom from the community supply closet to sweep out the dorm room had been the extent of her cleaning chores. Shanna frowned and pushed her chair away from the table. "You know, maybe the storm isn't that bad anymore. I'll go back over to the barn, and—"

Matthew pressed a hand on top of hers, and her breath lodged in her throat. Sparks sped up her arm, causing her heart rate to escalate. Her mouth dropped open, and she snapped her head to the side to look at the man sitting next to her. He had a skittish look in his eyes, like the buggy horse got when it was spooked.

He jerked his hand back. "Um, you might want to wait a bit." He pointed toward the window with his other hand. Rain and hail pinged off the glass.

"The electric will probably be out, anyway," Mamm put in. "Plan on staying here tonight. There's still an extra bed in your old room. Or, you can share with Joanna, if the storm is still bad."

"Better you than me," Joy said, ambling into the room with a book in her hands. "She kicks." She sat down at the table and pulled a lantern closer.

"I do not!" Joanna pulled her thumb out of her mouth.

"Jah, you do." Joy opened the book to a page she had marked with a torn piece of paper. "I need to do my homework."

Shanna relaxed. She'd missed her family, even the squabbles. She squirmed a bit in the chair, trying to find a comfortable position, but to no avail. These wooden chairs were nothing like the soft, overstuffed ones in the dorm lounge. She wished for a good fiction book, one by her favorite Amish author—funny how she wanted to read about the Amish but didn't want to be one—and a cozy chair by the window. She'd never cared much for watching television. That was an Englisch thing she could live without.

Joseph cackled, and she glanced back at the checkerboard, finding that it had changed while her thoughts had been focused elsewhere. Now, Joseph's remaining pieces were all kings, and Matthew had one left that hadn't been kinged yet.

Still, the game failed to hold her attention. She got up, wandered over to the window, and stared out at the trees, their branches whipped by the wind. A second later, she opened the door and stepped out on the porch. The rain and hail had stopped, leaving pea-sized pellets melting on the deck, like a late snow. They shifted and crunched under her bare feet. She shivered.

"What are you doing?" Matthew stepped outside and shut the door behind him. At the edge of the porch, he peered up at the sky. "Looks like the worst is over."

Shanna shrugged. "Not like it got bad, anyway."

Matthew lifted one shoulder. "Bad's debatable. I saw a tornado when I was little. Killed some of our cows and damaged some of our property. Do you have a storm cellar here? Just in case?"

"Not a storm cellar, exactly. It's more of an outside-entrance basement." She led the way around the corner, trying not to step in the mud—she'd always hated the feel of mud squishing up between her toes—and pointed to a trap door beside the house. "There. Mamm keeps her canning equipment and canned goods down there. There are some camping cots, all folded up, if we have to be down there overnight. Just have to watch for spiders. Brown recluses like it down there." She gave an exaggerated shudder. "They bite Johnny around his ankles, almost every year."

"Ugh." Matthew frowned at the sloped wooden door. A strong breeze blew past them, and he reached up and clamped his straw hat in place.

Shanna felt a couple of raindrops hit her cheek, and she looked up at the sky.

"We're going to get rained on again. Best get inside before you get that dress wet," Matthew advised.

"Jah." Shanna grinned and twirled as she followed him back to the porch. "So, what do you think?"

His face colored, and he looked away. "Um. You look like a very nice Amish girl."

Matthew thought they would go back inside, but Shanna stopped on the porch and leaned against the rail. It appeared that she wanted to stay out awhile. "Do you think you might take me for a buggy ride sometime?" she asked. "Do you go to singings or frolics?"

Matthew hoped that his facial expression didn't reveal his shock at her boldness. Hadn't anyone ever told her that men preferred to do the chasing? He shrugged. "Jah. I've been a time or two. You should go with your brother Joseph and see if anyone asks to give you a ride home. I think someone will." If it was someone other than he, though, he wasn't sure how he'd feel. "But then, you don't want to be Amish. You're returning to school and your Englisch world."

Shanna nodded. "Jah, I am. But I think it'd be fun to enjoy the Amish community while I'm home. I sometimes miss it."

"You do?" Why didn't she quit school and return home, then?

"Jah. Springfield is so busy. In the part of town where I live, there's a lot of crime. Occasionally, we receive text messages and e-mails from the school, telling us to stay locked inside our dorms because there's a gunman on campus. That's happened twice, so far. After dark, we have to walk in pairs, or call for security to give us a ride. Sometimes, I miss the quiet country. The safety. The comfort in knowing I can walk down the dirt road to my friend's haus and not worry."

Matthew looked around at the two neighboring homes they could see from the porch. One sat across the road, and the other was maybe half a mile farther. "Do you have friends near here?"

Shanna lifted one shoulder. "Jah, I did. They all married men in different districts. Probably have two or three boppli by now. Our lives have gone different ways."

"Jah. That happens." Matthew picked at a string on his sleeve. "My friend Jacob came down here first. His daed signed him up for the man swap but didn't tell Jacob; he thought he was just coming to his cousin's farm to help out for a while. Jacob ended up falling in love with Becky Troyer, and they're getting married in December. He needs to build a haus."

"Speaking of which, did you make up your mind about that farm?"

Matthew shook his head. "Nein. Been meaning to go out there and look around again."

"I work tomorrow morning. Maybe when I get off, I could drive you down to look at the farm, and you could help me take the kittens into Springfield."

"I...uh, I...." Matthew stepped back. "I'm thinking not."

Shanna had the grace to blush. "Seriously, my driving isn't normally that bad. I promise to be more careful. Bumping that buggy was the first accident I've had since I learned to drive. Cars get dinged a lot when you live in the city and have to park on the street. Trust me."

Trust me.

He'd heard it said that if someone needed to tell you to trust her, then you usually couldn't trust her. A skunk could be identified by its stripes.

"I'd still rather not." Maybe if she hired a driver. But saying that would be hurtful.

Shanna brushed past him. "Suit yourself. I just won't go fishing with you this weekend."

Matthew shook his head. Not that she could see him, with her back turned. It was just as well. If she came along, the fish wouldn't get much attention. Of course, that wouldn't be a bad thing.

Shanna walked two or three steps, then glanced over her shoulder. "Aren't you going to say anything?"

What? Did she expect him to give in? Matthew shook his head. "It won't hurt the fishes' feelings if you aren't there."

Shanna huffed.

Matthew grinned and followed her inside. He was surprised to see the unfinished checker game put away and a Monopoly game laid out in its place, with paper money distributed into four piles. He'd thought they'd finish the other game. He'd told Joseph he'd be right back.

Shanna gasped. "You have Monopoly?"

Joseph's eyes twinkled. "It's Daed's favorite game. We got one for Christmas last year. I'm the champ."

Levi started organizing his money, making neat piles according to denomination. "You'll be the champ when pigs turn down slop," he muttered good-humoredly.

Shanna plopped down in a chair and shuffled through the colorful stack of fake money. Whoever had doled it out had started with the one-dollar bills, so that they were at the bottom of the pile, and the $500 bills were on top. She re-sorted them in reverse order, though she wasn't sure they intended for her to play. She hoped they did, especially since the game had appeared after she'd mentioned it.

Matthew eyed the board warily, as if he expected some of the pieces to rise up and bite him. "This is the game where you buy properties and eventually add hotels? I think I've played once before."

"Properties, bah. Farms. They are farms. And the hotels will be upgraded to full-fledged Amish bed-and-breakfasts." Daed winked. "Have to make this materialistic game more palatable, ain't so?"

Shanna lowered her head and grinned. This was a side of Daed she'd rarely seen. She wasn't quite sure what to think.

Matthew shrugged and sat down on the edge of the seat next to Shanna. "Then, maybe we should find some horse-and-buggy-shaped playing pieces, ain't so?"

Joseph lifted the bag of pieces out of the box. "Hmm. We have a battleship, a hat, a cannon, a horse, a wheelbarrow, a flat iron, a thimble, a shoe, a car, and a dog. So, here's your horse, Matthew. Shanna, should we give you the car? I'll be the cannon, because I'm going to blow everyone out of the water."

"Ooh, violence from a peace-loving Amish man," Shanna teased.

"I'll be the shoe," Daed said, "because I'm going to walk all over you."

Shanna's eyes widened at the trash talk, something she never would have expected from Daed. "I'd rather be the wheelbarrow than the car."

Joseph nodded and put the extra pieces back in the box. Mamm set a plate of applesauce cookies on the table and settled down next to Daed with her knitting. Another pastime Shanna had never mastered, though Mamm had spent hours trying to teach her. To her credit, she had learned to crochet passably. Maybe she'd try one more time to learn how to knit. She could use a new scarf for winter.

"Let's roll to see who goes first." Daed picked up one of the pair of dice and gave it a toss. "I got a five. Beat that."

Matthew and Joseph both reached for a die at the same time, but Matthew rolled a three and Joseph a four. Shanna rolled a one.

"I start." Daed scooped up the dice and rolled. "Double six." He moved the shoe to the electric company and counted out the money to buy it. "What am I going to do with an electric company?"

Shanna's cell phone rang, the musical tone blaring out from her pocket. Everyone jumped and looked at her.

"Ach, you made me drop a stitch." Mamm unraveled a few stitches.

Shanna reached into her pocket and pulled out her cell phone. The caller was Nate, a guy she casually dated in Springfield. She wanted to talk with him, but did he have to call while she was enjoying time with her family? She deliberated a moment, studying the phone, then the game. Well, maybe she could play a game later. She'd be here all summer. "I won't be playing this time." She got up and headed for the door. On the porch, she opened the phone and held it to her ear. "Hey, Nate. What's happening?"

Chapter 8

The next morning, Matthew crawled out of bed before the rooster crowed. He glanced across the room at the other twin bed, where Joseph was still sprawled, sound asleep. Matthew dressed quietly, then went downstairs.

Deborah was already in the kitchen, starting the breakfast preparations. She looked up from her task of measuring coffee and smiled. "You're up early, Matthew."

"Not so much. I'll get a head start on the chores." At the door, he pulled on his shoes and shoved his hat on his head. Then, he stepped outside and took a deep breath of the fresh spring air. He paused for a moment to listen to the chorus of birds before striding toward the barn.

When he had slid the big barn doors open, Matthew's gaze wandered to the closed apartment door, and he wondered—not for the first time—who Nate was. Shanna hadn't bothered to come back into the house last night after his phone call. Instead, she'd padded barefoot over to the barn, leaving her shoes and wet clothes behind. He could only assume she'd stayed there. He hadn't seen or heard her car leave the property.

He milked the cows and led them to the pasture. After that job was complete, he hiked back to the barn to clean out the stalls. He'd just started the first one when he felt a presence. Turning, he saw Shanna grab a shovel and move to another stall. "You're up early" was all he could think to say.

She grinned at him. "It's about time I started pulling my weight around here, ain't so?"

"Jah, but Judah usually helps with the stalls."

Shanna nudged a gate open. "I know. I wanted to do something."

Matthew supposed she could have gone to the house to help her mamm prepare breakfast, but since that thought hadn't occurred to her, maybe it wasn't his place to bring it up.

"I have to work eight till noon today. I thought maybe I'd help Mamm when I got home."

It was good to see that she'd apparently swallowed her pride and was ready to try reconciling with her family. But he wouldn't mention that, either. Nor would he remark about the Amish clothes she wore this morning, though he was surprised to see her in them. He'd figured she'd go back to her Englisch attire, since she'd put on plain clothes last night only because her other clothes had gotten wet. Soaked, really.

It wasn't raining today. Just a bit drizzly. Misty. He grinned, remembering a nursery rhyme from childhood. *"One misty, moisty morning...."* It seemed to fit.

Shanna sucked in a deep breath. "I need to leave for work in an hour. You sure you don't want to go into Springfield with me this afternoon?"

"Jah, I'm sure."

"I need to get those kittens out of here before they wear out their welkum."

"I haven't heard Levi complain." And he doubted he would. After all, Shanna had brought them. He was so happy to have her home, she could have come with a dozen extra mouse catchers and not worried about him drowning them.

She exhaled with a whoosh of air. "Well, that's gut." She paused. "I have a date tonight. Maybe Nate will come out a little early so we can take care of the kittens before the Humane Society closes for the evening."

A date? Tonight? With Nate? The air left him so unexpectedly, his insides felt hollow. Nate. He would be her boyfriend, then. An Englisch man, no doubt.

Which meant that she was taken. And all his foolish thoughts about her being his future frau evaporated. No matter. They'd been pure craziness, for more reasons than one. He would never consider marrying someone who was not a member of the church, and he would certainly never court a woman who was someone else's girl. Even if that someone else was Englisch.

They worked in companionable silence for a few more minutes, until the barn doors burst open and Judah darted in. "Sorry I'm late. I overslept. Mamm woke me up and told me to get out here so we could finish in time to eat breakfast before it got cold."

Shanna thrust the shovel she'd been using at Judah. "We're almost finished. I need to get ready for work anyway, so you're just in time."

"Danki, Shanna. Glad you're home."

Shanna stood rooted there a moment. Then, she reached out and pulled her brother into an embrace. He hugged her back.

Matthew turned away. He didn't need to watch this display of emotions, normal as they were between siblings. He still remembered the feel of her in his arms. The softness. The rightness of her body against his chest.

And that was something he didn't want to dwell on further.

After work, Shanna changed out of her uniform and into Amish clothes again. She didn't want to disrespect her parents by dressing as an Englischer while she lived at home. Funny, because when she'd arrived, she would have sworn she would never put on another plain dress and apron. Maybe it was more because of the way Matthew had looked at her that night when he'd seen her with her old dress on. Like she had suddenly turned into the most beautiful girl he'd ever laid eyes on. He'd never said those words, of course.

She hurried into the house, the strings on her prayer kapp bouncing with each step. In the kitchen, Mamm stood over a large mixing bowl, studying a recipe card on the table. Canisters of flour and sugar, eggs, and other ingredients were spread around her.

"What are you making?" Shanna asked, glancing down at the recipe card.

Mamm looked up. "Ach, it's the third weekend. Daed allows me to sell baked goods here at the haus once a month. I'm trying to get the baking done for it. This will be pecan pies." She waved her hands at the messy table.

"May I help?"

Mamm looked at Shanna with a smile. "Jah. That would be wunderbaar. I'm getting the pie crusts made now. You could start on the fillings." She moved the recipe so that Shanna could see it, too. "You re-member where everything is kept?"

Shanna gazed around the room—spotless, ex-cept for the table. "Jah, unless you rearranged."

Mamm shook her head. "We'll make six pecan pies, and about the same of apple and cherry. Plus extra bread and cookies."

Shanna tilted her head. "How much have you done already?"

Mamm gestured at the table again. "I've bare-ly started. I'm going to be baking all week." She hesitated and moved the recipe away. "On second thought, you never were able to get the fillings to set right. I'll let you try on a day when they're not for the sale."

"Wise." At least Matthew wasn't in the house to overhear Mamm talk about her lack of culinary skills. She could manage some recipes well enough, but pies were something she'd never mastered. "Then, I'll get started on the cookies. What kinds do you want?" She hadn't made cookies since leaving home. Hadn't baked at all, really, unless she counted the Duncan Hines brownies she made in the microwave whenever she craved chocolate. But that powdered stuff wasn't real chocolate. Scary, if she stopped to think about it. She usually tried not to.

"Whatever kind sounds gut to you. We'll need to replenish our cookie jar, too. That Matthew, he likes his cookies."

Daed preferred pies. That never kept Mamm from keeping cookies on hand.

"We have plenty of peanut butter, oatmeal, rai-sins, chocolate chips, and molasses," Mamm said, working her wooden spoon around the bowl.

Shanna retrieved a mixing bowl and Mamm's recipe box. "Oatmeal raisin sounds gut."

"Englischers like their chocolate." Mamm dumped the contents of her bowl on a faded floured towel and then reached for the rolling pin.

"I'll make chocolate chip, too, if I have time. I have a date tonight. Nate is supposed to pick me up around three so we can go into the city."

Mamm peered at the battery-operated clock. "You won't have time for both, then. But I appreciate the help you can give me."

"I need to refresh my baking skills, anyway." Shanna started thumbing through the recipe box and pulled out the card for peanut butter cookies. Maybe she'd make those first.

"Just be careful you don't burn them. No one likes black cookies."

Shanna grimaced at the gentle reminder of the last time she'd helped Mamm bake. Hopefully, she had matured since then and could be counted on to focus.

Focusing shouldn't be too hard, as long as Matthew stayed out of the kitchen.

She glanced out the window toward the shop, where Daed, her brothers, and Matthew would be working on furniture. Nothing moved. All she saw was the barn, the shop, and the fields beyond. She turned her attention back to the recipe and reached for the flour.

Two hours later, Shanna tucked a few strands of hair back beneath her kapp, then used the oven mitts to pull the last sheet of cookies out of the oven. She carried it over to the table to cool for a moment, then began using a spatula to transfer the cookies to the wire rack.

Mamm peered out the window. "A blue car just pulled in. Ach, that must be your friend. Nate, you said?"

Shanna looked down at her Amish clothes, and the black apron covered in flour. She'd meant to be done earlier so she could shower before Nate arrived. He'd never let her live this down.

She straightened her shoulders when she heard the car door shut. A few seconds later, the porch steps creaked, followed by the sound of a hesitant knock on the door.

Shanna lifted the last cookie from the tray.

Mamm wiped her hands on her apron. "Come in!"

After a moment, the door slowly opened. Nate peered in, his eyes going to Shanna. They widened. Then, he smirked, and his gaze darted to Mamm and the table as he stepped inside. "Oh, you're baking. I haven't had cookies in I don't know how long." He glanced at his watch. "I am a bit early, but you said something about kittens?"

Shanna gestured to Mamm. "Mamm, this is Nate. He's a friend from school. Nate, this is my mamm, um, mom."

"Sit down and help yourself." Mamm headed for the gas-powered refrigerator. "Care for some milk with your cookies, or would you rather have koffee?"

"Uh...." Nate's brow lifted questioningly, and he glanced at Shanna.

"I need to get ready." Shanna indicated her clothes. "I'll be right back." She darted out the door and ran toward the barn. She needed to take a shower and put some normal clothes on. Maybe jeans and a T-shirt. Nate had said something about going to the movies. She'd been so out of the loop that she had no clue what was playing. And it wasn't just because she'd moved out here or because she had barely any cash to spare. Even in Springfield, she'd been so busy with school, studying, dating, and trying to get at least a little more involved in a church. She'd started attending the college-age Bible study, at least. But she pushed the thought away. Her parents would never believe her recent lack of attention to God.

If they went to the movies, Nate would probably let her choose, unless there was something he wanted to see and would prefer not watching alone.

Chances of it being a romantic comedy?

Not good.

A shadow moved in the dark recesses of the barn, and Shanna jumped. The next moment, a form stepped into the dim light.

"I caught the kittens for you." Matthew held out a box, and Shanna could hear the kittens mewing inside.

"You scared me."

Matthew chuckled in a short, abbreviated way. Actually, it was more of a bark. "Sorry."

He didn't sound sorry. "Nate's waiting. I need to get ready to go. I'll be right down."

Matthew nodded. "I'll take this box to the workshop, then, and make sure they don't escape."

"Danki." She turned toward the apartment door.

He moved a step closer. "You smell gut. Like peanut butter cookies."

Her breath caught. How he'd managed to detect that aroma in a barn full of animal smells, Shanna didn't care to figure. She waved a hand toward the house. "Go help yourself. I made plenty."

"For Deborah's bake sale?"

"Extra. For the family."

His grin could have lit the barn. "Guess there's some hope for you, after all."

Hope? For what? She frowned and reached for the doorknob. "Maybe you'd better wait until you taste them to make a final opinion." With that, she opened the door and hurried up the stairs.

Matthew peered out the upstairs window at the car turning into the driveway. Shanna and Nate had been out later than he'd expected them to be, though why he'd had expectations, he didn't know. She had the right to date, even if it meant that he suffered through visits from the green-eyed monster.

Nate seemed to be the perfect gentleman. He got out of the car and came around to the passenger side to open the door for Shanna. She accepted his hand as he helped her out and then stood there beside the car, talking with him. And then he leaned in for what appeared to be a kiss.

Matthew clenched his fists. It was a quick kiss, an innocent peck. They were saying good-bye and thought no one was watching.

Matthew didn't mean to see their kiss. He hadn't expected there to be a kiss, or he would have moved away sooner. He wished he had, not only out of guilt for spying, but also because it added to this strange sense of jealousy that haunted him.

Shanna eased away, then shut the car door. Her lips moved, but it didn't appear as if she was scolding Nate for taking such liberties. Then, with a smile, she turned and walked toward the barn.

A smile. Nein, she hadn't been scolding him.

Nate called to her as he jogged around the car. She turned around to look at him, but her gaze traveled upward, to the second-floor window where Matthew stood. They made eye contact. For a moment, neither one moved. Then, out of the corner of his eye, Matthew noticed Nate's head lift.

To his shame, he ducked to the side, away from the window.

"She's home, then." Joseph ambled barefoot across the room and peered out the window.

"Jah."

"Gut." Joseph turned away and crawled back into bed.

Minutes later, Matthew heard the car engine start and the tires crunch over the gravel.

"You should go talk to her."

Matthew leaned to the side and glanced out the window. All clear. "About what?" He turned around and looked at Joseph.

Joseph shook his head but didn't answer.

Matthew slid his suspender straps off his shoulders. "I'm going to bed. Morning comes early."

"Jah. No wonder you haven't got a frau. You don't even try."

"With Shanna? She's not Amish."

"She might be, if you get her to fall in love with you."

"Ach. That'd be setting myself up for a heartbreak. Besides, what makes you think I'm even interested in your sister?"

"Why else would you be spying on her?" Joseph shrugged and extinguished the gas lamp beside his bed. "Suit yourself. Gut nacht."

Matthew hesitated, his face heating. He pulled his straps back up, turned off the other gas lamp, and left the room. As he padded downstairs, he could hear Levi and Deborah's voices coming from their bedroom but couldn't make out what they were saying. He opened the front door and slipped outside.

An owl hooted, and a dark form flew past the barn. Matthew glanced up at the star-studded sky. Not a cloud in sight. He picked out the Big Dipper.

The porch swing creaked. "I've been expecting you."

Chapter 9

Shanna gazed at Matthew, who stood at the far side of the porch. He stared out in the direction of the barn and made only a slight twitch when she spoke.

Maybe "expecting" had been the wrong word. Maybe she should have said she'd hoped he'd join her instead of implying that she'd figured he would.

Still, he'd been spying on her. She hadn't noticed him at first, but when Nate had called to her and she'd turned back, she'd seen his face, framed by the bedroom window.

Had he seen Nate kiss her? Was he jealous?

Ach, that was presumptuous of her. Nothing about Matthew's actions indicated any interest in her. At least, nothing beyond curiosity, or maybe friendship.

Matthew remained silent.

She patted the space next to her on the swing. "Want to kum sit?"

He shook his head. "Nein. Let's walk."

Shanna stretched, then pulled herself up off the swing. "Okay." She followed him down the steps.

He turned toward the road, not the fields. "Did you get rid of the kittens?"

Ach, a sore spot. She hadn't anticipated being asked to make a donation to the Humane Society. She'd borrowed the money from Nate, promising to reimburse him after she received her first paycheck from McDonald's.

She needed money for school, not for all these miscellaneous expenses that seemed determined to eat away at her earnings.

"Jah, they're gone. Nate is keeping one. We left the other four." They'd chased her to the door, mewing. One had even jumped on the screen door, seeming to plead with her to come back. She blinked at the tears burning her eyes. Who knew that getting rid of a few stray kittens would hurt so much?

Matthew moved a little closer. "They'll find gut homes."

"Maybe." She struggled to find a new topic of discussion and soon settled on her evening with Nate. Maybe then, she would be able to tell whether Matthew was truly a little jealous, as she suspected. "Nate and I went to a movie, one that he'd wanted to see. It was kind of scary. Lots of graphic images...." She shuddered. If only she'd insisted on a romantic comedy, instead.

She could understand the wisdom in not having a television and in staying away from movie theaters. Now, she had all this garbage filling her mind, taking up space that should have been filled with God and His goodness. Her spiritual life needed work. Lots of work. She smiled. Well, her mind definitely should have been filled with less scary stuff.

Matthew came even closer but still said nothing.

Shanna lifted her shoulder. "We shared a large popcorn, and he bought me a drink. Before that, we ate pizza."

"I haven't had a pizza in a while."

At least he hadn't been struck mute. "I can make one for supper sometime. Maybe Mamm will let me."

"Mmm. Sounds gut."

Shanna smiled. "Then, he brought me home."

Home. To the farm she'd dreamed of escaping. Ironic that once she'd left, she'd wanted to go back. To the quiet, the safety, the community of friends and family. The sameness that used to drive her insane now beckoned her.

Yet she couldn't stay.

"You'll see him again." Matthew's voice held a measure of comfort.

"Jah. He wants to go to the movies again soon. There's another one he wants to see."

She didn't think she did, though. If only she had Internet access here to search for reviews and see if it was as bad as the previews had seemed to indicate.

If only she could decline Nate's invitation and maybe do something with Matthew, instead. If only he were interested. She didn't see any sign of jealousy in his quiet, calm answers.

Well, she could say no to Nate and suggest he find another date for that movie. But Matthew.... She was doing something with him. Right now. Whether he wanted to or not.

Was there anything more romantic than a walk down a moonlit dirt road?

It took a while, but Matthew finally figured out what bothered him about the kiss. It'd been too casual, suggesting that this Nate person had kissed Shanna before. It was bad enough that he'd seen this one. And now, to imagine all those that had come before.... Matthew squinted through the darkness at the dirt road. At least the moon lit the way enough for him to avoid stubbing his bare toes.

If only he dared tell her the things her mamm should have. Like the fact that first kisses were special and shouldn't be given away casually. That boys liked to do the chasing. That the purpose of dating was to find a spouse, not simply to go on outings that seemed to be the equivalent of setting a mousetrap. In his experience, the mice ate the peanut butter and escaped anyway. Unscathed.

That was why God had made cats and owls. Why had He made mice? Matthew pondered that for a moment. To feed the cats and owls. Must be.

His mind rambled worse than a nervous woman's mouth. What did any of this have to do with Shanna? He struggled to straighten out his train of thought.

"I'm glad I came home."

"You are?"

She laughed. "Well, except for Daed. He and I... it's like trying to mix salmon and chocolate."

Matthew couldn't hold back his soft chuckle. "That's a combination I don't even want to consider."

"Exactly."

He shook his head. "Nein, Shanna. He loves you. Someday, you two will reach each other. It might help if you tried a little harder. You've left his faith and his community for a lifestyle that he doesn't understand, that goes against everything we—uh, he believes." He hesitated, regretting having to bring up the next point, but it needed to be said. "Not to mention, you love a man who will hinder you from ever returning."

"Love? I'm not in love with Nate."

"You're not? Then, why—"

"We're friends. That's all. Friends do things together. Like you and that Jacob you mentioned."

"Maybe so. But I've never kissed Jacob. And never will."

She exhaled loudly. "I don't even want to imagine that. Nate's going to somewhere in Europe to study. Required for his major. He's leaving in August."

Matthew couldn't think of anything to say. Relief flooded through him. Nate would be out of the picture in a short time. On the other hand, so would Shanna. She'd be returning to her Englisch world in mere months. He fell silent, hearing the wings of an owl as it flew overhead.

Shanna glanced up. "I've missed that."

Matthew must be a little jealous, or he never would have mentioned the kiss. Though why a little peck would merit a mention by him, Shanna didn't know. Unless he wished it had been he, not Nate, kissing her....

A thrill shot through her. What would it be like to kiss Matthew? Maybe she'd find out tonight. She moved a little closer to his side. He glanced at her, maybe out of alarm, but didn't try to increase the distance between them. Nor did he reach for her hand.

They must have hiked for miles. The blacktop was two miles down the dirt road, based on what her car odometer always read, and they'd reached that point and kept going. Mostly in companionable quiet.

She didn't feel inclined to break the silence, either. They walked down to the Amish grocery store, closed at this hour of the night.

A car drove slowly by in the darkness. The headlights blinded Shanna for a few moments, and she stumbled over something in the road. A hand closed around her elbow, steadying her. Matthew. She smiled with gratitude but doubted he saw it.

He released her and moved away. "We need to get back." He stopped and turned around.

Shanna pulled in a long breath, letting her diaphragm expand. "Jah, I guess you're right. Morning will be here before I'm ready. I have to open at the restaurant tomorrow."

"What do you do there?"

"Depends on the day. Breakfast, they usually have me up front, taking orders and filling them. In the afternoons and evenings, they put me at the drive-through window. Same job, different location."

"Do you like it?"

Shanna shrugged. "It's a job. I need the money. It isn't something I want to do for the rest of my life."

"Do you want to be a nurse for the rest of your life?"

Did she? She pondered that for a bit. She imagined herself working for a while, then marrying and settling down, raising young ones with a good man—an Amish man was what she pictured, surprisingly. Funny how that was what came to mind when she thought of marriage. Being home. Being Amish. Probably due to how she'd been raised.

It certainly didn't correspond to her plan of becoming a registered nurse.

She couldn't discuss questions for which she had no answers. "I don't know. What do you want to do for the rest of your life?"

Matthew hesitated. "I want to raise blueberries."

"Yum."

"Not sure how they'd do around here. I noticed most of the Englisch farms are cattle. The place I'm considering was a cattle ranch. Owner died. Son didn't want the property. He auctioned off all the cows already."

"The Amish raise more than cattle."

He made a movement with his hand, but the dimness and the distance between them made it difficult for her to make out the gesture. "I know. I'm still studying up on it."

Studying? On what to raise? Shanna scratched an itch on the left side of her nose, then brushed the left side of her mouth when the itchy spot moved. "So, why blueberries?"

Matthew chuckled. "Long story. The short version is, I love them. They're my favorite fruit. And I know blueberries. My parents grew some."

"Some?"

"Jah. Not a lot, just some. Mostly, they raised wheat. That's another reason I signed up for the man swap. I wanted to raise blueberries on my own patch of ground. My brothers wanted to specialize. All wheat. They ripped out the berry patch last fall."

Shanna touched his arm. She intended it to be a compassionate gesture, but those unexpected sparks flared again. Still, she didn't pull back.

After a moment, Matthew did.

Shanna swallowed her disappointment.

They remained silent the rest of the way home. Matthew walked with her to the barn door and opened it for her. The scent of warm hay wafted out, mingled with the more earthy smells of the animals. Still, it was comforting. For a moment, she let herself think about what it might be like to come home to things so familiar.

And then a shadow moved in the darkness.

Chapter 10

S hanna shrieked and stepped back against Matthew's chest. Instinctively, his hands rose to grip her shoulders. He was trying to be supportive, but in reality, he felt as nervous as she seemed. Maybe he should shove her behind him and face whoever it was.

"Hey! Sorry, Shanna. It's me. Nate. My car broke down on the road. I think I turned the wrong way, because I drove and drove and never got to the highway, so I walked back. Could you take me to Springfield?"

Ach, Nate. Matthew released Shanna and moved away. They hadn't passed a car stranded on the road while they'd been walking, he realized. He hesitated, trying to study the other man's expression, what he could see of it in the moonlight.

"I have to open tomorrow at—" Shanna stopped. "Jah, um, yeah. I can do that. Just give me a moment, okay?"

That would make a late night for her. She wouldn't get back until the wee hours of the morning. Matthew frowned and slipped his hand into his pocket, feeling for his cell phone. Maybe Nate could call another friend for a ride.

Didn't Nate have his own cell phone? Surely, he did; he was an Englischer. Why hadn't he used it to call for help? That made Matthew even more curious.

Shanna pushed past Nate and disappeared into the barn.

Without a single word to Matthew. Not a "Gut nacht," not a "Good-bye," not anything.

Matthew turned and started toward the house. He was almost across the yard when she called after him. "Hey, Matthew. Want to go with us to Springfield?"

Matthew turned to her and waved his hand in dismissal. "That's the stuff nightmares are made of." Yet, in a way, he wanted to be there for her. To keep her from being alone with Nate.

Nate, who wasn't being entirely truthful about something.

She laughed, not sounding at all upset, even though he'd been serious. "Please? I don't want to go alone. I promise the traffic won't be as bad as it was when you went through. It kind of dies down after a time."

Matthew frowned. Seeing Nate standing behind Shanna, he almost refused again. After all, he would be with her. But only for the trip there. After she dropped him off, she would be alone for the drive back. And she'd said that part of town was dangerous.

The silence stretched between them for a moment longer, and then he nodded. "Jah. I'll go. Give me a moment to get my shoes." And wash his muddy feet. No way would he stick them into clean socks. Besides, he hated to go to bed filthy. He'd washed up already that night, but that had been before his barefoot walk down the dirt road.

Clean was a distant memory.

"Gut. Danki." Shanna turned and darted back into the barn, leaving him and Nate standing there in the yard, staring at each other through the darkness, dimly lit by the bright moon.

Matthew moved first. "Give me a moment. I'll be right back."

"Take your time," Nate said. His displeasure with the plan was clear by the disdain in his voice.

And that made Matthew glad he'd agreed to go. He didn't trust Nate.

Shanna drove the car around the barn. In the glow of the headlights, she saw Matthew and Nate waiting next to a row of poplars. A considerable distance, and Daed, separated them. He stood a little closer to Matthew than to Nate, and his arms were crossed over his chest. He held a flashlight in one hand.

Shanna pulled in a breath. She didn't want Daed to join them on her excursion, but why else would he be standing there? Hoping to judge her in the Englisch world, no doubt. Ach, she would be so much more nervous if he started criticizing her driving, the city, the traffic, and her friends.

Should she get out of the car and go to him? Or wait until he forged the narrow drive? Shanna shifted into park and pressed a button beside her to unlock the doors.

Daed crossed around in front of the car and waited as she pressed another button to lower the window. He peered inside and frowned at the car door handle. "They make everything so easy for the Englischers. I remember the day when they had handles that needed to be turned manually. Some even had little triangle-shaped air vents that pushed out. Manually."

Shanna considered her car, then looked up at Daed. Surely, he hadn't come out here to comment on the evolution of automobile technology.

He leaned closer and lowered his voice. "Your mamm says I was too harsh on you yesterday and said some unkind things. I was wrong, and I say I was wrong."

Shanna blinked, surprised to receive an olive branch instead of a lecture. "Jah. I'm sorry about my part, too." Not that she knew exactly what her part was. But Matthew had said she wasn't really trying to connect with Daed. If a complete stranger could see that, then it must be true.

Daed nodded and straightened a bit, frowning at the car. He pulled out his pocket watch and glanced at it, and his frown deepened.

"Nate's car broke down." Shanna didn't know why she felt obligated to explain. "I need to take him to Springfield."

"Hmm." Daed turned to look at Nate. "Where's the car?"

Nate stepped closer and pointed toward the road. "About half a mile down, on the left."

"You were headed the wrong way to town, ain't so?" Daed speared him with a sharp look, then glanced back at Shanna. "Did you call a tow truck?"

"Nein. Didn't consider it. It's kind of late now, anyway. Nate can call for one tomorrow."

Daed nodded. "Give me a minute, and we'll tow the car here. It isn't safe to leave vehicles unattended beside the road for long. In the morning, I'll take a look and maybe find out what's wrong with it."

"You can fix cars?" Nate's voice squeaked in surprise.

Daed shrugged. "Maybe. Matthew, kum with me. We'll be right back." They disappeared into the barn. A minute later, they returned, Matthew carrying a tow rope, Daed hefting something else Shanna couldn't identify. She opened the trunk of her car, and Daed and Matthew loaded the items before crawling into the backseat.

Nate settled next to Shanna in the front, and she pressed the gas pedal. "Left at the road and about half a mile," Nate instructed her. "You'll see it."

Shanna drove down the driveway and turned left.

"I used the horses last time I had to pull a car out of the ditch," Daed said, leaning forward. "Driver had slid off in the twelve inches of snow we got last winter. Don't get accumulation all that often around these parts, so no one knows how to drive in it."

"I'm not exactly in the ditch." Nate glanced back at Daed, then faced forward again. "It's kind of half on, half off the road. So, no, it isn't safe, but I didn't know what to do." He pointed ahead at a dark shape. "There it is."

Shanna passed the car and turned into the next farmhouse drive, then backed out into the road. She came to a stop in front of Nate's car. "Okay, now what?"

Daed opened the back door. "You hold the flashlight. Matthew and I will get this hooked up in no time."

When she stepped out of the car and joined him on the road, he handed the light to her.

"Can I help?" Nate came around the front.

Daed gave Nate a dubious stare. "I'm guessing not. Unless you want to hold the light."

Nate took the flashlight from Shanna as Matthew went around to the trunk of the car and got the rope. "Where do you want me, then?"

"Matthew will hook up under the car. You could shine the light under there so he can see what he's doing."

Shanna wasn't sure if Matthew had heard or not, since he remained silent, but he worked as if he knew exactly what to do and how to do it. Without asking any questions, he slid under Nate's car. Maybe Amish men knew instinctively how to hook up cars for transport. She grinned. Could be from having to hook up horses or oxen to buggies and farm equipment.

Daed attached the rope to Shanna's vehicle as Matthew shimmied out from under Nate's car. Then, Matthew leaned close and whispered something to Daed as he double-checked the ropes. Her father straightened, gave Shanna a look she couldn't identify, and whispered something back to Matthew. Finally, they moved away from the cars. "Okay, we're ready now. Nate, you want to shift into neutral? Make sure the brake's off."

Nate slid in behind the wheel of his car, while Shanna scampered over to hers and got back in the driver's seat. Ten minutes later, she pulled to a stop in front of the barn.

While Matthew got to work disconnecting the cars, Daed turned to Shanna. "If you want to go down to the basement and get one of the cots, your friend can sleep inside the haus tonight. I'll send him home tomorrow in his own car."

Shanna hesitated, not sure how she felt about Nate spending the night. Not that she wanted to be antisocial, but, well…. She didn't trust him, she realized.

"Wait a minute." Nate scratched his head. "You're Amish. How would you know how to fix a car?"

Daed grunted. "Jah, I'm Amish. Not stupid." He paused. "Will it be all right with you to sleep here?"

Nate hesitated, fixing his gaze on Shanna. "I guess. I have to work tomorrow, but I don't have to be in until eleven."

"If I can't fix it, or haven't finished by the time you need to leave, I'll call a driver for you." Daed strode away. "Shanna, the cot."

She started to move, but she wasn't out of hearing when Daed turned back to Nate. "Don't for a moment think that because the haus isn't locked, the barn will be open, too. It will be securely bolted. Not much is more valuable than a daughter."

A grin spread across Shanna's face. Daed still considered her his daughter? And he valued her?

Levi turned and disappeared inside the house, leaving Matthew to take care of the towing equipment. Nate trailed him into the barn. "If daughters are so important, why is he making Shanna sleep in the barn?"

"He's not making her. She has the option of sleeping inside, but she'd have to share a bed with her sisters, and they thought she'd be more comfortable in the apartment. It has electric."

"You don't have electricity?"

Matthew didn't answer. He picked up a lantern and lit it.

Nate looked at the buggy, illuminated in the flickering light, and his eyes widened. "And you drive buggies! Why would you want to do that? You have choices! There's a whole world out there."

Matthew set the lantern on a shelf and began coiling the rope. He didn't bother responding to Nate's questions. It would be impossible to explain his beliefs and lifestyle to a city-dwelling Englischer. If he wanted to know the reasons, he could always ask Shanna later.

"And you guys dress like you just came off the *Mayflower*."

Matthew forced a smile. He'd seen pictures of Pilgrims. Their clothes didn't remotely resemble Amish dress.

"Why would you want to do that? They make belts to hold pants up, so you don't have to wear suspenders."

"Jah. I know." Matthew picked up the lantern and turned toward the door. He considered mimicking Levi's curt *"I'm Amish, not stupid"* comment. "Kum. We'll get you settled in the haus."

"So, are you one of Shanna's brothers?" Nate followed him out of the barn and across the yard.

Matthew sighed. Those who said that northerners were nosey had obviously never met Nate. "Nein. Not her brother. I'm...." What? Slightly more than an acquaintance, slightly less than a friend. "I'm a boarder."

Shanna came around the corner, dragging a cot and smiling. Was she that happy Nate would be sleeping here? If only she knew what Matthew thought. It had been too dark to be absolutely positive, but it had appeared Nate had disconnected a wire to the alternator. Matthew had definitely noticed something dangling in that area. He'd told Levi as much.

Shanna touched Matthew's arm lightly, then pulled her hand away, probably because he had done the same so quickly before. "You're more than a boarder, Matthew. You're a friend."

A friend? Maybe. The temptation was there to be more. Much more.

Chapter 11

T he next morning, Shanna woke up to realize she had overslept by half an hour. She needed to hurry to get to work on time, so she didn't have time to help with the morning chores in the barn. Daed and Matthew were already tinkering with Nate's car when she drove past them on her way down the driveway. At least, they appeared to be. Matthew sat on the ground in front of the car, like he'd been fixing to slide underneath or had just slid out. He raised his hand in a wave.

She waved back. She didn't see any sign of Nate. Of course, she'd never known him to get up before ten in the morning. He always managed to schedule his classes around his penchant for sleeping late. Englisch were funny that way. She'd been raised to be up before the sun.

When she returned home four hours later, Nate was gone. Daed must have been able to fix his car. Shanna ran upstairs to her apartment and changed out of her uniform into a blue dress. She'd retrieved all of her old clothes from her sisters' bedroom. Good thing they still fit.

She was on her way to the house when Matthew came out of the shop. He grinned at her. "Shanna. You got a minute? We need to talk."

"Jah. What's up?"

He hesitated, the expression on his face changing from pleasure to trepidation. He gestured toward the fields. "Let's walk."

A walk sounded nice, but Matthew looked too serious. Troubled. Like she'd done something wrong. She couldn't think of what she might have done to bother him. And she hated getting into trouble. Shame, since she seemed to be good at it. She didn't even have to try.

"I planned to help Mamm with the baking. Cookies, again." She forced a smile, but he didn't return it. In fact, his eyes turned even more serious. She sighed. "Will this take long?" Might as well get it over with. Then, she could apologize and go her way.

"That depends on how blunt I am. If you'd prefer, I can get your daed. He thought maybe you'd take this better from me."

Shanna tensed. Daed was using Matthew to pass along criticism? Anger flashed through her, and she glared at him. "Just spit it out."

Matthew frowned, his eyes narrowing in confusion. "Spit it out?"

"Say what you're going to say, okay? And in the future, if you want to keep being my friend, maybe you shouldn't get involved in Daed's never-ending issues with me. He can yell at me himself."

Matthew's eyes widened. "Whoa. Maybe you shouldn't jump to conclusions so fast."

She fixed him with a hard stare and straightened her shoulders defensively.

Matthew pulled his shoulders back, as well. Not to mention, his jaw tightened, and a muscle flexed in his neck. Stubborn, was he?

"I'm not going to stand here and blurt out things where others might overhear."

Shanna lifted her arm and massaged her neck muscles for a moment. Then, she dropped her hand to her side, ready to give in.

The shop door opened, and Daed strode toward them. "Matthew. Never mind. Furniture truck should be here in a short while. Why don't you help Joseph get the order together?"

Though he'd phrased it like a question, it was an order. Matthew glanced at Daed and nodded, then gave Shanna a long, pointed look before he turned and headed into the shop.

His expression had shifted from anger to concern, perhaps even pity.

Maybe she would rather have heard whatever it was from Matthew. Daed's expression almost terrified her. His eyebrows drew together as he studied her with obvious assessment. She stiffened.

"Kum."

She hesitated and glanced toward the house, then the shop, hoping for something urgent that needed her attention. A fire, maybe. Or a roof that was about to collapse.

Not seeing anything, she followed Daed out behind the barn.

"I'm not going to sugarcoat this, Shanna. The bu had disconnected his alternator. Those don't come detached by themselves. He had deliberate car trouble."

Shanna stared at him. "Deliberate?"

"Jah. Maybe you should choose your friends more wisely. He isn't a gut choice."

"Nate?" She scratched her head, forgetting about the prayer kapp she wore, and stabbed a pin into her scalp. So, she chewed her lower lip, instead. The wire *must* have become detached on its own. While she'd realized she didn't fully trust Nate, she didn't believe he'd deliberately disable his car. That didn't make any sense. "I think I know him a lot better than you do."

Daed frowned. "Maybe so. But it's clear that bu has designs on you, and they don't include marriage."

Withholding a snort, Shanna looked away. "If that's true, he's had ample opportunity. I went on a date with him. To the movies and out for pizza. Seriously, Daed." She shouldn't have to describe their date to him. Anger flared within her. "Maybe you should leave my choice of friends alone. Just because he isn't Amish doesn't mean he's bad."

Daed's green eyes hardened. "And just because he's Englisch doesn't mean he's gut. You won't take my word for it. You have to find these things out for yourself, ain't so? Always have. When will you ever learn to listen?" He flung his hands in the air. "Go on, 'do your own thing.' But don't come crying to me." He turned and stalked off.

Shanna growled in frustration. With tears burning her eyes, she rushed through the weeds behind the barn to her car. She flung herself into the driver's seat, slammed the door, and reached inside the console for her keys.

When her hand came up empty, she realized she'd left them in the apartment. She pressed her forehead against the steering wheel as a couple of tears made tracks down her cheeks. Why couldn't he leave her alone? Why did he have to ruin everything?

The passenger door opened.

Shanna straightened, hastily wiped her face, and fixed a glare on—Matthew?

Matthew slid into the passenger seat of Shanna's car and closed the door. Levi had told him to go check on her, but that hadn't been necessary. When he'd stomped into the shop, steam almost visibly rising from his head, Matthew had set down the glider rocker he'd been carrying. What Levi had needed to tell Shanna must not have gone over well. Of course, their talk had been doomed to fail from the start, considering how defensive she'd gotten with Matthew.

He wondered how he could have worded things differently so that she wouldn't have reacted so strongly.

Matthew hadn't wanted to be involved in this at all. It wasn't his place.

Besides, he couldn't quite grasp Levi's insistence on telling Shanna the "truth" about Nate. Yes, Matthew had pointed out that the wire had been disconnected, but Levi was the one who had jumped to conclusions about what that meant. He'd called Nate out about it, too, pointing at the wire and accusing him of having ulterior motives.

Nate had stared at Levi, his eyes wide with shock—whether from simply being accused, or being accused of something he was guilty of, or even not having expected an Amish man to know so much about a car, Matthew didn't know. Still, Nate hadn't denied the charges. He hadn't thanked them for reconnecting the alternator. He'd merely jumped into his car, gunned the motor, and roared off.

All this had cemented Levi's belief that Nate had been up to no good, and he'd confided this to Matthew. To be honest, Nate's actions had disturbed him, too. Why would anyone go to such lengths?

He couldn't wrap his mind around it. Englischers were confusing creatures.

Matthew turned to face Shanna. He could still read the anger in her eyes, but now it was mixed with hurt.

He didn't know what to say. How had he gotten himself appointed to the cleanup crew?

"He was trying to dictate my friendships! I knew this wouldn't work. Daed doesn't love me, and he wants me to be unhappy."

"Ach, Shanna. That's not—" Saying it wasn't true wouldn't go over so well. *Lord, help me know what to say.* Prayer. Always a good place to start. "You want to pray?"

Shanna gave him a blank look. "Pray?"

"Jah. Why not?"

She gave a harsh laugh. "Nein. Prayer won't help me. God is on Daed's side. Always has been."

"God doesn't choose sides. He loves you. Just like your daed loves you."

"I don't want to talk about this." She folded her arms across her chest. "In fact, I'd rather just make out."

Make out? She couldn't believe she'd just suggested that to Matthew. Come to think of it, though, that might make her feel better. Especially considering the sparks she felt around this man.

"I think I know what that means." Matthew stared at her as color crept up his neck. Then, he reached for her, his gaze flitting to her lips.

Anticipation shivered through her. She waited while he shifted a bit closer, and she thought she saw mischief gleaming in those beautiful eyes.

Mischief?

Tenderly, he grasped the back of her head with his hand, and then, to her surprise, he gently pushed her head down. "Let's pray."

Prayer. Maybe that was the answer, after all. She closed her eyes, letting the silence sink in before she even attempted to put her thoughts into words. Enjoying the weight of his hand against the back of her head, holding it down. His fingers moved, caressing the strands of hair against her neck.

Ach, Lord, I want this man in my future. That wasn't what she was supposed to pray about. She dipped her head further in shame. Her attitude toward her father, and the whole situation with Nate.... He wouldn't.... Would he?

A memory surfaced. Right after Shanna had left home, Nate had invited her to move in with him, to share expenses. He already lived with another guy, who, like Nate, was into cars. Posters of hot rods with bikini-clad women posing on the hoods lined their living room walls. Shanna had been uncomfortable when she'd been in his house. Oddly, when she'd prepared to leave that night, she hadn't been able to get her car to start.

Instead of offering to take her back to campus, he'd asked her to spend the night, to experience what it might be like living together. She'd called a friend to pick her up. The next day, she'd found another guy who was willing to look at her car. Strangely enough, it had started fine then. He'd figured she'd flooded it.

If she'd taken Nate home last night, would she have found herself stranded with no way to call for help? It was good she'd asked Matthew to come along. Better yet, that Daed had intervened before they'd left for Springfield. *Ach, Daed,* she thought. *Maybe you weren't completely off base.*

But how could Daed have picked up on Nate's intentions immediately after meeting him?

Matthew's fingers moved down to her shoulder. He caressed it briefly, then pulled away. "You're not so tense now. Gut." His voice conveyed peace.

How could he always be so calm?

"You're gut for me, Matthew."

He settled back in the seat, his smile reaching his eyes. A dimple flashed on the right side of his mouth. "God is gut, ain't so?"

She nodded. "I'm sorry for my attitude. Didn't mean to take it out on you. I probably need to apologize to Daed, too."

"Might be a gut idea, but he's kind of sidetracked now, if that truck was on time. Should probably wait until it's gone."

"If the truck's here now, shouldn't you be there helping?" Shanna straightened.

Matthew shrugged. "He wanted you cared for first. Not much is more important to him than his daughters."

Chapter 12

S ince Shanna seemed to be doing better, Matthew left her in her car and walked to the shop to help. On his way, he noticed the white furniture truck parked outside. Its back door was wide open, and the ramp had been pulled out. Levi stood beside the truck, studying a sheet of white paper. When Matthew came closer, he lifted his head and raised his eyebrows in a silent question. Matthew nodded in reply.

Levi exhaled, a smile flickering briefly across his lips, then shifted his gaze back to the page.

Matthew walked into the shop and stood there for a moment, wanting to bask in Levi's approval. Soon, he turned his attention to the order. He glanced around the room and saw Joseph balancing on the second highest rung of a tall ladder on the other side of the room and lowering a wooden chair from a hook on the ceiling. When he stepped down to the next rung, still carrying the chair, Matthew hurried over. "Let me help. Is this for the shipment?"

"Jah. Daed said this shop ordered twenty chairs, five tables, a couple of rolltop desks...don't remember what else. Figured I'd get started on these."

Matthew took the chair from Joseph and set it off to the side, then waited for the next one to be handed down. He breathed in the familiar smells of sawdust, wood stain, and furniture polish.

"Shanna and Daed have another go-around?" Joseph glanced at him.

Matthew grimaced. "Jah, but I think they're both learning how to relate to the other. They might get it right before she goes back to Springfield."

"Maybe she won't go back." Joseph handed Matthew another chair and gave him a measured look.

With a lift of one shoulder, Matthew set the chair beside the other one. "Guess we'll see."

"Or maybe you could give her a gut reason to stay. Propose, if necessary."

Matthew's heart leaped at the thought, but he laughed, trying to downplay his interest. Yet he didn't find that suggestion even remotely funny. "That'd be putting the buggy before the horse. Whoever marries her needs to do some courting first, ain't so?"

"You might want to get busy, then."

For a second, Matthew froze. The words *Me? Why me?* hovered on the end of his tongue. He tried to think of what he might have done to make Joseph think he was interested in Shanna in *that way*. Joseph had caught him spying on her from the bedroom window last night. And then, there was that talk he and Shanna had had. The one that had stretched into the wee hours of the morning. That had been nice. Talking. Getting to know each other better.

Matthew sighed and shook his head. "Not me. We're new friends. *Friends*, Joseph. And I'm not going to marry an outsider."

Marrying outside the faith was not an option. No matter how much he was attracted to her.

God have mercy, he was drawn to her. Beautiful. Friendly. Kind. And somehow she spoke to his heart. Had, from the first moment he'd seen her.

No other woman had ever affected him that way. Not even Katie. And he'd almost asked her to marry him.

Jah, truth be told, he wanted Shanna to be his frau. Wanted to watch her grow big with his children. Wanted to live to an old age with her by his side.

Matthew took the last chair and set it with the others as Joseph clambered down the ladder. "That should be twenty. Want to help me get them out to the truck? Then, we'll carry the tables out."

An hour later, the loaded truck left, headed for a store in Branson that specialized in handcrafted wood furniture. Levi pulled out his pocket watch and glanced at it. "It's after one. I'm hungry. Kum, let's go see if they have lunch waiting for us. It should be ready."

Matthew's stomach rumbled in reply.

He hurried with Levi and Joseph across the yard and followed them into the quiet house. The four younger children were in school. The scent of fresh-baked bread filled the air, and a kettle of soup simmered on the stove. Deborah and Shanna stood at the far end of the table, Deborah filling a pie crust with sliced apples, Shanna mixing up some sort of dough in a big silver bowl.

Several strands of hair had escaped from her kapp, and one of her cheeks was dusted with flour. Matthew ached to brush it away. And as much as he wanted to keep his distance, he was drawn to her like a magnet.

When Levi and Joseph had finished at the sink, Matthew washed up, then wandered over to Shanna, his attention still on the loose hair brushing her neck and the streak of white on her lovely face. He was too close, really, since his chest brushed her arm. Yet he stepped nearer still. His heart rate increased when he heard her inhale sharply. Fighting the grin that threatened to appear, he glanced down into the bowl. Chocolate chip cookie dough. His favorite.

He couldn't resist reaching down for a scoop with his finger. He'd already licked it off when Shanna slapped his arm.

Matthew swallowed. "You're a bit slow. My mamm would have slapped my hand when I was reaching for it." He winked at her.

"*My* mamm raised me better. I wasn't prepared for a stunt like that," Shanna retorted.

"Well, then, consider yourself forewarned. And 'Forewarned is forearmed.'" He winked again and poked his finger into the dough once more, then pretended to study his prize. "It could use some chopped walnuts."

"Matthew Yoder." Shanna planted a fist on her hips and backed away from the table, away from him, the wooden spoon still clasped in her other hand.

"You look so domesticated that way," he teased. "Like some frau correcting an errant child." He turned away and plopped the second scoop of cookie dough into his mouth. Then, he met the amused stares of Levi, Deborah, and Joseph. He'd forgotten they were in the room. He couldn't help but grin, even as he felt the warmth of a blush on his neck. He hadn't meant to make his attentions so public. He wouldn't have crowded her space so much if he'd remembered his audience.

How awkward. What would Levi think about this latest indication of his interest in Shanna? Would he make efforts to keep them separate, or would he "discover" opportunities to put them together?

Matthew hoped for the latter, even as he feared it. Too little effort was required to fall in love with Shanna Stoltzfus.

Shanna's breathing was still a bit erratic as she set the bowl of cookie dough aside and went to the cupboard to retrieve five white bowls and salad plates for lunch. Mamm had guided her through preparing her creamy broccoli soup, which still simmered on the stove. Shanna fretted over how it would taste. Would Matthew like it?

It didn't matter if he did or didn't. Her cooking skills, or the lack thereof, would mean nothing to him.

He probably hadn't even noticed his body pressing up against hers, so close that she could feel his heartbeat. Or maybe the thundering pulse had been her own, in response to his nearness. It'd taken a huge effort to keep from turning into his arms. Only the fact that they hadn't been alone had kept her from doing so.

Mamm began slicing the still-warm loaf of bread on the cutting board. Daed left the room for a moment, while Joseph collected the silverware. "Don't know what you have been doing all day, leaving me to do women's work," he complained good-naturedly.

"How can I help?" Matthew seemed to take his cue from Joseph.

Shanna was glad for the assistance. Mamm had been baking all day to get ready for the sale tomorrow, and Shanna had jumped into the fray when she'd come inside after the disturbing encounters with Matthew and then Daed, followed by the peaceful time of prayer with Matthew.

Her face heated as she recalled how she'd brazenly tempted Matthew by suggesting they make out. What must he think of her? It was fortunate that he hadn't taken her up on her entirely too forward comment. Of course, his refusal also made it clear that any attraction between them was one-sided. If he were interested in her, he would have....

Then again, he belonged to the church. He held to more traditional values than the world she'd embraced when she'd run away from home.

It was probably a good thing she hadn't thrown herself into his arms moments ago. He wouldn't have known what to do with her. Or would he? Her mind flashed back to the awkward hug after her accident, mere days ago.

Deborah looked up at Matthew. "You can get the butter from the refrigerator, if you'd like."

"Get the cheese, too, please," Shanna added. "I need to shred some." She reached for a stainless-steel grater, but her senses screamed with Matthew's every move. He wouldn't marry outside the faith. But why couldn't he be interested in her?

If only she could have it both ways.

Joseph left the room and returned shortly with canning jars full of jam, chowchow, and fruit. Matthew also returned with his arms loaded. He handed the cheese to Shanna, then placed the butter in the middle of the table.

"Sorry we didn't have lunch ready for you. We didn't notice the truck leave." Shanna opened the package of cheese, laid the plastic wrapper on the table, and started grating the cheese into a bowl. "Do you still order your cheese from Mary-Beth Schmidt?" She glanced over at Mamm.

Mamm placed the platter of bread on the table. "Jah. She said this one didn't set up right, so she gave it to me. I don't see anything wrong with it, but maybe she felt guilty for being nosy and asking so many questions about you."

Shanna froze. "Me?"

"You have to know you're what a lot of people talk about now."

She supposed that was to be expected, yet the idea of others snooping on her family and asking questions because she'd come home for a couple of months hadn't crossed her mind. "I'm sorry. I didn't mean to make things uncomfortable." Not for her family. She'd never wanted to hurt them.

But she had to leave soon to return to school. And that would cause them even more pain.

She closed her eyes briefly but snapped them open again when she felt a soft touch on her arm.

Mamm pulled away. "We are glad you're back, even if it's for just a short while. If they want to know more, they can talk to you."

No one would dare. The Amish she saw in town eyed her with distrust and kept their distance. As if her Englischness would rub off on them like a contagious disease.

Her eyes flickered to Matthew. He caught her gaze and held it as he moved closer. His focus shifted to her cheek and then to her mouth, but it immediately shot back up to her eyes, as if he thought he'd done something inappropriate. She was still recovering from that too-brief look when he reached over and grabbed a handful of shredded cheese.

"What's gotten into you today?" Shanna pretended to glare at him. "Did you swallow a mischief pill or something?"

"Or something." He winked and slid onto the bench next to Joseph as Daed entered the room. Matthew's gray eyes sparkled up at her like the diamond earrings she'd seen once at the mall.

Space. She needed space. Shanna's mind scrambled to find a new topic of conversation, one that wouldn't involve Matthew or this sudden flirtatious trend that had flared up unexpectedly between them. Not that she didn't like it. She did. Maybe too much. She turned to Mamm. "Is this a church Sunday coming up?"

"Jah. It's at the Lapps' haus." Mamm put the kettle of soup on the table near Daed's place. "The Zooks are hosting the singing, ain't so?" She glanced at Joseph.

Joseph nodded, then looked at Shanna. "Want to ride over with me?"

She'd prefer to ride there and back with Matthew—and take the long way. But he didn't seem inclined to ask. Then, she remembered that he'd even told her she'd have to ride with her brother. "Jah. Danki."

"I'll take you home, too, if need be. Just not right away, maybe." Joseph blushed.

Shanna stared at him a moment before comprehension kicked in. Her younger brother was courting someone. Either that, or he was trying to work up the courage to begin doing so.

Shanna couldn't imagine that anyone would ask her to ride home with him. Well, except for Matthew, maybe. It'd be nice, but unlikely. How awkward would it be to ride home perched on the buggy seat with Joseph's girl squeezed in between them?

"Maybe it'd be best if I didn't go." Shanna tried to keep the disappointment out of her voice. She'd been looking forward to an outing with other young people. Pretending not to notice the buwe watching the girls as they walked into the building. Feeling the thrill of suspecting that a certain bu had his eye on her.

Guess that probably wouldn't happen to her, though. She'd made the decision to jump the fence. Returning wasn't in her immediate plans. Maybe not even in her future plans.

"You should go." Daed folded his hands in front of him, indicating the conversation was finished, and it was time to ask God's blessing on the meal. "Go and have fun. Don't worry about how you'll get home until the time comes." He cleared his throat. "Shall we pray?"

When lunch was over, Matthew pushed his dishes away. He'd had three helpings of soup and two slices of warm wheat bread. "It was wunderbaar, Deborah."

She smiled. "Shanna prepared the soup."

Matthew glanced at Shanna and gave a nod of recognition. "Really gut." He wished he could think of something else to say, but his forwardness had disappeared almost entirely once he'd realized her family had watched the flirtatious exchange and formed opinions. Not that any of them seemed to be opposed to the idea of him courting Shanna.

"Danki." Shanna seemed equally shy. She avoided his gaze and dipped her head as she scooted out of the chair to collect the dishes. "Koffee?"

"Jah." Matthew swallowed the lump in his throat.

Levi nudged his mug closer to the edge of the table. "I'd like some too, please." He turned to Matthew. "What are your plans for this afternoon?"

"I made an appointment to go take a look at that ranch again. The realtor's supposed to meet me there around three."

Levi nodded. He'd already offered to come along and give his opinion, but Matthew didn't think he wanted the older man there. At least, not yet. It would imply that he was serious about the property, an impression he wasn't prepared to give right now. When he made his decision, or when he was close to making one, he would certainly value Levi's opinion.

"I have some paperwork to do, so I'll be working on that." Levi stretched his legs out.

Shanna brought over the coffeepot and filled her daed's mug, then Matthew's when he held it out.

"If it's okay, Daed, I thought I'd get some fishing in this afternoon." Joseph shook his head when Shanna started to fill his mug. "Nein, danki."

Matthew watched her place the coffeepot on the back of the stove and then begin piling dirty dishes in the sink.

He mustered up some courage. "Shanna, would you like to see the ranch?" He hoped she'd say "Jah." At the same time, he expected a "Nein, danki."

Levi set his mug down and turned in his seat. Matthew cringed under the sharp assessment. It reminded him of when he'd first arrived, accompanied by the bishop. The man seemed able to see clear into his soul.

He wanted to tell Levi he had nothing to worry about. But maybe he did.

His intentions toward Shanna? Undecided.

Until he did decide, he needed to keep their relationship at the friend level. That would be difficult. He wanted to push past that stage.

He looked in Shanna's direction, watching the sway of her skirt as she scrubbed the dishes. Ach, why did she have to make it so clear she'd be leaving? That meant the decision had already been made.

He fought the disappointment that washed over him and opened his mouth to take back his invitation. She'd have no need to see the ranch. It would never be her home.

Levi picked up his mug and took another sip of coffee, apparently satisfied by whatever he'd seen in Matthew's expression. Yet, which expression had satisfied him? Matthew's wistful smile to think that Shanna might be the one for him? Or the frown of disappointment when the unlikelihood of that reality sank in?

"Actually, Shanna—"

Shanna turned away from the sink, wiping her hands on her black apron. "I have baking to do. Mamm needs me. Danki, anyway."

"Do the baking when you get home," Mamm said, picking up a dish towel and joining her at the sink. "It'll keep. Or, I could have the girls help when they get home from school. We've nearly finished everything, so go and have fun. It helped to have both of us working. Danki." She wrapped Shanna in a hug.

Matthew looked away. He pulled his watch out of his pocket and glanced at it. "I need to go. By the time I get the horse hitched up to the buggy and get out there, it'll be time to meet the realtor."

"I guess I can go. If you want, I'll drive you." Shanna came up beside him and touched his hand.

He looked up and to the side, not quite meeting her eyes. "Nein, we'll take the buggy. I'll get it ready."

"Okay. That'll give me time to finish the dishes and get the kitchen cleaned up. Danki for inviting me. I love going through houses. Sometimes, my girlfriend and I go to open houses in Springfield. It's fun."

Matthew blinked. "Fun" wasn't at all how he would describe going through buildings. It was just a necessary step when one was looking to buy. "I'll be right back. Give me a moment."

Shanna waved him off, then scampered back across the room and plunged her hands into the soapy water in the sink.

For a few seconds, Matthew couldn't stop watching her. He finally forced himself to turn and follow Levi out of the house.

"I'm willing to take a look anytime you want," Levi reminded him, a hint of teasing in his tone, as if Matthew was courting Shanna and wouldn't want him to intrude on their outing.

Matthew ignored the implication. "I know. I'm not sure I'm that serious about this particular piece of property." He shrugged. "When I decide, I'll certainly ask you to kum."

Levi nodded and pulled a key out of his pocket. "I'll see you later, then. You and Shanna have fun."

Matthew couldn't imagine being in Shanna's company and not having a good time. Unless she became defensive about something. He'd do what he could to keep the conversation pleasant.

Taking a long drive through the district, talking and getting to know each other better, would be nice. Maybe on the way back, they could take the scenic route.

Or maybe not.

Matthew straightened, reminding himself that Shanna was home for only a season. Not forever. And definitely not for him.

Unless there was something he could do to tip the scales in his favor.

Chapter 13

By the time Shanna finished the dishes, put her socks and shoes on, and went outside, Matthew had the buggy ready. Shyness hit, making it feel like she was being courted by her first bu. She tried to control a shiver, reminding herself that going with him to look at a house didn't constitute a date. They were friends. Just friends.

She would be going back to Springfield.

But she wanted it to be a date. She wanted to pretend she'd be looking at this property with her future husband.

Ach! Shanna reined in her thoughts.

Matthew came around the front of the buggy to offer his assistance. Whether she needed it or not didn't matter; accepting help would mean physical contact, and that definitely sounded appealing. She took his outstretched hand and climbed up on the step, wincing when the buggy sagged slightly under her weight. It'd been so long since she'd ridden in one, she'd forgotten that part.

She slid onto the seat, while Matthew jogged around to the other side and climbed up next to her. He grabbed the reins and made a clicking sound with his tongue, and they were on their way down the lane. Shanna waited until they had turned onto the road before scooting closer to him. Close enough so that their arms brushed or bumped with every jostling motion of the buggy.

Any nearer would be entirely inappropriate, but she wanted to be closer. It would make it easier for her to pretend that this was a date. Especially if he put his arm around her.

He turned and glanced at her, the corners of his mouth lifting with the hint of a smile.

Shanna grinned back at him. "Maybe I would like to go fishing with you tomorrow."

His smile deepened, and the right dimple flashed. "Maybe so?"

"Jah. Maybe so."

His shoulders twitched, and he faced forward again. "Then, maybe I will take you."

Shanna settled back against the seat. The sway of the buggy soothed her. "You know, some of my friends in Springfield would think this is so romantic."

"What is?" Matthew shifted a bit. Now, his upper arm rested against her shoulder rather than just brushing it occasionally. And his right thigh pressed against her skirt. She imagined she could feel its warmth. But he didn't put his arm around her.

She scooted a bit closer, so that her shoulder was behind his, hoping he'd get the hint. So much for being inappropriate. If anyone saw them, they'd think they were courting. And courtship was supposed to be a private matter.

But they weren't courting. Even so, she wanted his arm around her.

She struggled to remember what they'd been talking about. "Riding in a buggy," she said, to answer his question. "You can take carriage rides in the old parts of Springfield, where there are cobblestone roads. My friend Carly and her boyfriend rented one. They dressed up in evening clothes and had dinner at a fancy restaurant, went to the opera, and then went for a carriage ride. And that's where he proposed."

"He proposed in a buggy?" Matthew glanced at her, his eyes wide.

Shanna nodded. "It was so romantic. All my friends were swooning over it."

"Did you?"

Was it her imagination, or had his voice dropped a little in pitch? Shanna suppressed another shiver. "When she gushed about how poetic Bill is? Nein. A buggy ride is a buggy ride." Though, with Matthew, it seemed so much dreamier.

"Maybe it depends more on the company, ain't so?"

Heat rushed to her cheeks. His voice *had* deepened to a sexy rumble. Did guys do that on purpose? She looked away and didn't answer. Apparently, he already knew how she felt, anyway.

"So, Shanna." He shifted again and lifted his arm, letting it drop carelessly around her shoulder, as she'd wanted him to do. Except maybe not the "carelessly" part. "Do you want to be proposed to in a buggy? After a fancy dinner and an opera?"

Proposed to? She hadn't meant to bring up that topic, just the romantic reputation of buggy rides. Time to change the subject. Shanna shook her head. "Nein. I've been to an opera, once. It wasn't my thing. I mean, it was gut, but it isn't something I ever really want to do again. Eating out is nice, too, but—and I guess this is my Amish upbringing—a gut home-cooked meal is better. Mamm can outcook any restaurant chef."

"Your mamm is a gut cook, but I like your cooking, too. So far." He lifted his arm again and put it back at his side.

She wished for the weight of his arm to return. At least he had done what she'd wanted, if only briefly.

"This is it." Matthew gestured to the right. "Think they said it was five hundred acres right now. They've sold off some acreage already. The barn you can't even see from the haus. I guess, with cattle, you don't want them so close. I don't know. There's a pond the previous owners kept stocked, like your daed does." He pointed down the road. "And the haus, it's a two-story with a basement. It has two and a half bathrooms and four bedrooms. There are big walk-in closets in all four bedrooms, but I guess Englischers have need of lots of clothes." He shook his head, as if trying to imagine what that would be like.

Shanna knew firsthand how quickly clothes could accumulate. And shoes. Ach, when she'd first moved to Springfield and discovered heels.... It had taken a bit of practice to toddle around on four-inch spikes without falling. The guys liked it, though. Would Matthew? She'd probably never know. Heels were not appropriate footwear for an Amish farm. Still, he was tall enough that she could wear heels and not tower over him.

They weren't talking about shoes.

"Can you afford something like that?" Shanna asked, then clamped her hand over her mouth. That kind of question was way too nosy. "Never mind."

He chuckled. "Land is cheaper here than in Pennsylvania. My brothers bought my share of the family farm. Plus, I have money I've saved up, working. Daed took my paychecks and deposited them for me so I'd have a head start. I didn't have much to spend my money on, anyway."

"Nein girl?" Oops. She had a talent for bringing up subjects she shouldn't discuss. Yet she wanted to know if he had left someone behind.

He laughed. "Fishing for information, Shanna?"

Of course, he would see right through her. "You don't have to answer that," she muttered.

He tugged on the reins and turned the buggy into a driveway. The house did appear fancier than most Amish homes, but it was plainer than some Englisch ones. It had no garage but a carport.

The real estate agent must not have arrived yet, as there was no car parked in the driveway.

Matthew wrapped his arm around her, this time in a loose hug. She snuggled against his side. "Nein. I'm not courting anyone. Yet."

Yet. There were mountains of meaning in that simple three-letter word. The unspoken implications. She pressed herself nearer to his side. His embrace tightened in response.

"I meant back in Pennsylvania. Did you break some girl's heart when you moved down here?" She looked up at him.

Matthew frowned. "Break a heart? Nein. I gave a couple of girls a ride home from singing. I courted one. Briefly. We mutually decided we weren't right for each other. She's married now." He glanced at her. "So, what about you? Anyone other than Nate?" His arm fell back along the edge of the seat. She missed the contact, the warmth, the sparks.

"Just a bunch of guys who fall into the same category as Nate: casual friends. No one I have dreams of marrying."

At the sound of crunching gravel, they both turned and saw a car approaching. When Matthew looked back at Shanna, his expression had changed. A teasing grin had replaced his frown. "Gut. Because you're going to marry me."

Talk about a comment out of left field. Her breath caught, but before she could think of an appropriate reply, something similarly flippant, the real estate agent opened her car door and stepped out.

She'd never thought Matthew would be the type to kid around about marriage. The Amish didn't treat it as a joking matter.

Wouldn't it be fun to pretend?

She returned her attention to the realtor, an older lady, maybe middle-aged, dressed in brown slacks and a cream-colored top with a plunging neckline that showed way too much skin. Her hair was dyed a mahogany red—straight from a bottle, no doubt. Shanna's roommate had tried the same color last semester, with similarly disastrous results.

Matthew pulled his arm away. As he did, his fingers trailed along the back of Shanna's neck. Whether it was on purpose or by accident, she didn't know. Awareness sprang to life. He jumped out of the buggy, then came around to help Shanna out.

"Matthew, hi," the realtor said. "Sorry I'm a little late. Oh, you brought your girl. Well, let me open the door and I'll let you look around. I'll be in the living room if you have any questions." She glanced at Shanna. "I'm Terri Mayberry. Really nice to meet you."

"Shanna Stoltzfus. It's nice to meet you, too."

Matthew and she followed Terri to the front door. She unlocked it and then stood aside to allow Shanna and Matthew to enter first. "I told Matthew this, but the previous owner died, and the son is looking to unload the property fast. He has it listed way below its value, which is good, because I know the house doesn't meet Amish standards."

Shanna nodded. She'd heard at least a partial list of necessary "de-improvements" firsthand from Matthew.

She entered the living room. It was big and inviting, with a large stone fireplace and beautiful, built-in, floor-to-ceiling bookcases flanking the mantel. A bay window overlooked the road. Lovely, really. But Shanna wasn't sure what the bishop would say about it. She wasn't familiar with the procedure of buying new property.

A ring tone split the silence. Shanna glanced at the realtor.

"Excuse me." Terri held her cell phone to her ear and stepped outside on the porch.

Leaving Matthew and Shanna alone in the house. And making it so much easier for Shanna to pretend that she was here with her fiancé. That he was serious about marriage.

Shanna glanced around the living room. The house was definitely fancy. Nobody she knew had a home like this. Her family and her Amish friends all had turn-of-the-century—and not this century— farmhouses. Similar to the ones that lined the streets of the inner city, the bad part of town. Maybe the Amish kept their homes in better condition. Or maybe not. Depended on the homeowner.

When it came to Amish families, their barns tended to get more care than their houses.

Shanna followed Matthew through a set of doors, noticing a half bath they passed, into a big country kitchen with a built-in breakfast nook. A screened-in back porch beckoned through the window. "Ooh, this is lovely. Can you imagine canning and baking in here?"

Matthew shook his head. "Nein. It's all electric. Did you catch that? Completely unacceptable. Might as well start from scratch."

Shanna faced him. "Then, do that. You could buy the land, rent out the haus, and build a new one closer to the barns. It would save having a barn raising, but you'd have to build a haus yourself; it wouldn't be a community thing. At least you'd have the haus of your dreams."

"The haus of my dreams would have you in it."

Her lips parted, and she stared at him, hunting for the teasing look she'd seen earlier. She didn't find it. Instead, he appeared to be in shock himself at his words. Still, the jolt of electricity that ran through her could have lit up the kitchen.

His eyes dropped to her lips, where they lingered for a long, searing moment before he met her gaze again.

What was he doing? The Old Order Amish community forbade kissing on the lips until marriage. Well, at least until you were courting. Matthew shouldn't be looking at her like that. She swallowed hard. She'd probably goaded him into it with her shameless flirting, treating him as she would an Englisch boyfriend. Tempting him by suggesting they make out. Her face heated. She turned away and went into the next room, a dining room, ignoring him when he whispered her name.

Shanna massaged her neck, trying to work up the courage to face Matthew. He'd spouted so many things today that were nonsensical. Meaningless. He'd probably wanted to throw her for a loop. He'd succeeded.

Hearing his footfall behind her, she turned and watched him enter the dining room. He stopped and stood in silence, studying her. Shanna shut her eyes. Maybe she shouldn't have led him on like she had. But he seemed equally guilty of that. Now, she was the one who had to find her footing.

He sighed. "I guess I'll ask your daed to kum and check out the barns and outbuildings with me. And I'll ask what he thinks about subletting the haus. Do you want to see the upstairs?"

Upstairs, where the bedrooms were? With him? Ach, that'd be asking for trouble. Those areas were much too private to see with a man. Especially this man.

He probably shouldn't have told her earlier that she'd marry him, but the words had escaped before he'd thought much about them. Uncharacteristic of him. He usually mulled things over for a while before voicing them. His heart had recognized Shanna from the start, but he knew she wasn't prepared—mentally, spiritually, or emotionally—to come home to the Amish faith. Especially not for him, a man she barely knew.

He needed to control himself. His tongue had issued two invitations for heartbreak this afternoon. *God, don't let there be an outright rejection to my too-forward comments.* "You're going to marry me," he muttered to himself, shaking his head. How could he have said that? He may have wished it to be true, but—

"Oh, I am, am I?" Shanna spun around and marched past him, back into the kitchen, then turned to face him. "And you're going to become Englisch, then? You might need that big closet, after all."

He hadn't meant for her to hear him. It seemed he had two choices: ignore her and let it go, or make some foolish comment that would make her laugh and get him off the hook.

"You're going to return to the Amish." He winced, even as the words left his mouth. His tongue apparently had a mind of its own.

Shanna made some kind of noise his stunned brain couldn't interpret. A snort, maybe.

Time for damage control.

He stepped into the kitchen and grabbed her arm, gently pulling her back toward him. "Listen, I'm sorry." He'd taken it too far. "Don't be mad at me for keeps."

Shanna swayed on her feet. Not wanting her to fall, he drew her against him and wrapped his arms around her.

"Matthew...." She raised her head, her mouth parting as she formed whatever words she planned to say. "Don't make any assump—"

Before she could finish, he leaned down and brushed his lips tenderly against hers.

Shanna's breath caught in her throat, and her hands gripped Matthew's upper arms when he lifted his head. He gazed into her eyes for a moment, and then his lips found hers again, settling in firmly, as if they belonged there. He tasted of cinnamon, as if he'd just chewed a stick of a strong-flavored gum. Or maybe swallowed a breath mint.

He shifted and eased her back against the kitchen counter, while his mouth moved over hers, exploring, prodding, teasing.

Sighing with pleasure, Shanna slid her arms around his neck and surrendered to his masterful touch. Her toes curled spontaneously, and she felt her knees weaken beneath her. She groaned and pulled him more tightly against her, responding to him with all of her pent-up passion and longing, giving him everything she could in return.

"Shanna..." he whispered against her mouth. "Ach, Shanna." His kiss deepened as his hands moved over her back, down to her ribs and her waist, then up to her shoulders. He gripped them for a second and then pushed away. "Ach, nein." He backed up quickly, as if he was trying to get away from a dangerous animal. "Nein, Shanna. I'm so sorry."

He stopped against the opposite counter, staring at her with a mixture of longing and horror, as she fought for control, for air. She dragged in a deep breath, but her lungs didn't seem capable of holding more than a thimbleful of oxygen. Her pulse beat erratically, pounding inside her temples.

A kiss wasn't supposed to affect her this way. What kind of power did this man possess?

She wanted to find out. But then, why was he looking at her with that expression of horror?

Chapter 14

S omewhere in the dark recesses of Matthew's mind, he heard the sound of heels clicking down the hall toward the kitchen. He glanced at Shanna, worried that she might think he was no better than Nate, trying to get her alone and have his way with her.

He fought to regain control of his breathing as the realtor entered the room.

Terri looked from him to Shanna. "What do you think?"

Pretty sure she wouldn't be interested in his present thoughts, he cleared his throat a couple of times and glanced at Shanna again. Seeing confusion and hurt in her eyes, he quickly looked away and felt his stomach clench. "I'm going to, um, take Shanna home and get Levi. I'd like his opinion on a few things. Do you have time to wait?"

Terri nodded. "I have a few phone calls to make, anyway." She reached inside her pocket and pulled out a phone. "Aren't cell phones wonderful?" Her smile was huge at first, but it faded quickly. "Maybe you wouldn't know that. Handy for me, at least...."

There was no point in mentioning that he owned a cell phone. It would only provoke questions.

Matthew pushed away from the counter and wobbled a moment before he found his center of balance. He'd kissed before, and been kissed back, but like that? Never.

Jah, he would definitely marry Shanna Stoltzfus.

Somehow, he made his way across the room to Shanna, reached out, and clasped her hand. Never mind that it wasn't an Amish gesture, especially outside of courtship. Right now, he needed it. Thankfully, she didn't resist but quietly allowed him to lead her out of the house.

After the supercharged moment they'd experienced in the kitchen, he wasn't sure what to expect on the drive home. He wanted to go straight to the bishop—or even the Englisch Justice of the Peace—and marry her. Now. As in, right this minute.

First, though, he needed to have a talk with Levi about his intentions. Ask his permission to court Shanna. The way Levi had reacted to Nate, Matthew thought it might be best to be up-front about his intentions.

Although he'd probably get a well-deserved warning about how she was essentially Englisch and would return to that world soon. She wouldn't remain in his.

Why did I have to go and kiss her? He stifled a groan. After all his worrying over whether her mamm had told her that first kisses were special and generally reserved for married couples, or at least courting couples, he'd gone and stolen one. And then two, three.... Ach, he had no idea how many kisses they'd shared.

Too many. Yet not enough.

He helped Shanna into the buggy, neither of them saying anything. She'd opened her mouth a time or two but promptly shut it, like a fish when it was brought out of water. That bothered him. What had she been about to say when he'd interrupted her with a kiss? Was she going to reject him? If so, then she'd be even more likely to do so now.

Shanna settled into her corner of the buggy, her gaze fastened on the floor, as he clicked his tongue to prompt the horse forward. His stomach roiled. He missed the physical closeness they'd shared on the drive over to the house. The flirting. The conversation. He glanced over at her a time or two, but she didn't seem to be mad or crying. Had she reacted this way to Nate's kisses? Passionate at first, then deflating like a pierced balloon afterward? He thought about talking to her about it but quickly decided to leave well enough alone.

He needed something else to occupy his mind. Maybe Levi would be free this afternoon to go with him to the ranch and see the barn, the land, and the house; to talk about the possibility of renting it out. Or, maybe—preferably—he'd suggest having a gas line run to the house, instead. Shanna loved the kitchen. Matthew would probably blush like a fool taking her daed into that room.

He looked over at Shanna again. Where had her spark gone? She looked defeated. Sad. He shouldn't have kissed her like a madman. Now, she must be choosing her words to tell him off. He couldn't take her home like this. Something had to be done to fix things. He didn't know what, though. Maybe another apology. Let her yell at him. He'd feel better if she would muster enough emotion to do that.

"Whoa." He pulled the buggy off to the side of the road. When it stopped, he pivoted in the seat to face her.

Creases of confusion lined her forehead. "What—"

"I'm so sorry, Shanna. I didn't mean to hurt you. Please forgive me." He started to reach for her hand then stopped. Best not to touch her right now.

She turned her head in the opposite direction. Away from him. Maybe so that she couldn't see him, not even out of the corner of her eye. She sniffed. "I didn't know kissing me was so awful." She sounded hurt.

"Awful? How could you possibly think that?"

"From the look on your face. Disgust. Abhorrence, even."

"Abhorrence?" That was a word he didn't hear much. "Ach, Shanna. Nein. Kissing you was amazing—the most amazing kiss I've ever had in my life. I definitely didn't abhor it." Not that he had much experience for comparison. He'd kissed only Katie—just once, after they'd started courting. And the sensation had been more platonic than passionate. No fireworks. No trouble breathing.

She glanced at him. "Then, why did you look at me like that?"

"Because I'd overstepped my bounds. Because we haven't made promises, and because I made assumptions. Because you're Englisch, and I'm Amish. Because...." He looked away as heat crept up his neck. Taking a deep swallow, he turned his steady gaze on her. "Because I didn't want to stop."

Her smile appeared like a ray of sunshine bursting out from behind a cloud, warm enough to chase away a chill. "I would have made you stop."

He sucked in a deep breath. "Look, Shanna. I know this isn't the time or the place, but I'm going to be blunt, here, and say it straight. I think I'm falling in love with you. You'll have a ride home from the singing on Sunday nacht, if you'd like." He cupped her chin. "But you need to be Amish. I can't court you if you aren't."

She sighed. "I guess it was fun while it lasted." Immediately, she brightened. "Wait! I'm still in my rumschpringe."

He smiled, released her chin, and fingered the reins. "Let me get you home."

She slid over next to him, apparently wanting to snuggle, since their misunderstanding had been settled. He probably shouldn't have, but he wrapped his arm around her shoulders.

Back at the house, Matthew stopped the buggy by the porch and let Shanna out so that she could help her mamm finish the baking. When she disappeared inside, he flicked the reins again and maneuvered the buggy toward the barn. Levi wasn't anywhere in sight, and Matthew could tell at a glance that the shop was empty.

That left the barn. Or the house.

He'd try the barn first.

Joseph's fishing pole and tackle box were gone. He must have followed through with his plan to go fishing. Matthew didn't see anyone else. He went over to a door leading up to a loft and tried the ancient knob. Locked.

He knocked on the door. "Levi? You up there?"

"Jah?" The voice came from a distance. Thumping sounded behind the door. Seconds later, it opened. "Matthew. Was ist letz?"

For a second, Matthew stood in indecision, staring up at his host. Should he blurt out that he might be falling in love with Shanna? "Um, if now's a gut time, maybe you could kum see the haus and land?"

"Ah, you've already been to see the haus?"

Matthew's face heated. He hoped the dark shadows of the barn kept Levi from noticing. "Jah. We didn't look at the whole haus. All electric. Shanna suggested maybe I could rent it out to Englischers."

Levi shrugged. "I can help you convert it to gas. Won't take much. We could put in some solar panels, too. Heard the Bontragers were installing them. You could check into that." He hesitated, and his eyebrows rose. "Shanna. Did she like the haus?"

Matthew was sure that his glowing face was as obvious to Levi as a neon light in Amish country. He resisted the urge to touch his cheeks to see if they burned as hot as they seemed to. "Uh, she said it was lovely. She could picture canning and baking in the kitchen."

"Hmm. Gut. That's gut. All the more reason to get it changed over to gas, then, ain't so? And the bedrooms? Shanna liked them, too?" Levi hitched one eyebrow higher than the other.

"We didn't go that far. I don't know what she thought."

Levi laughed. "I was teasing with you. Jah, now's a gut time. I can kum."

Teasing. About him and Shanna. Matthew swallowed. "Gut." The Amish tradition was to keep courting secret until it was time to be published, right before marriage. He'd been taught by his daed that it was considered best to approach the girl's father and ask his permission to court her. Mainly because one of his sisters' future husbands had done that. And Daed had liked it.

What would Levi like?

Matthew whipped his straw hat off of his head and ran his fingers through his hair.

Levi knew. He must.

Asking was mandatory, even though all signs said "Go."

"Uh, there's one other thing. I'm considering courting Shanna, if it's okay with you."

"Why are you telling me this?" Levi shut the door behind him. "You think that surprises me?" He pulled the skeleton key out of his pocket and locked the door, then stuck the key back inside his pocket. "I see how you look at her, ain't so?"

Probably the same way he'd noticed her looking at him. No point in analyzing that comment any further. Matthew shrugged. "Jah."

"If you're brave enough to court the girl, then do. Might keep her in the community. Then again, might take you out." Levi's stare speared him.

Matthew somehow kept from squirming. "The real estate agent is waiting. Best get on back."

Shanna peered out the kitchen window and watched the buggy carrying Matthew and Daed travel down the driveway. Back toward the other house. She wished she could have seen the upstairs. Alone. If Matthew bought the property, maybe she would.

He wanted to court her.

A thrill rushed through Shanna, surprising her with its force. Amish were serious about courting, about marriage. This would be more than just a casual date. This would be one-on-one getting to know each other, perhaps with marriage in the future plan.

Possible marriage. To Matthew.

He thought he might be serious about her.

Ach, how she liked him—maybe even loved him. She wanted to get to know him better. But marriage? That would mean giving up all her goals. Her dreams. Her calling.

If only it could be a few-years-down-the-road arrangement. Maybe they could plan to marry after she'd earned her degree, had worked for several years, and was ready to settle down.

Yet, would she ever be ready to settle down in a house with few modern conveniences, drive a slow buggy, and—she shuddered—use a wringer washer? Okay, the slow buggy was pretty romantic, with Matthew by her side. And the soft glow of the gas lamps would give their home a romantic ambiance....

"Daydreaming, Shanna?" Her mother stepped up beside her. "Is Matthew taking Daed to see that property?"

"Jah."

"What did you think of it?" Mamm wrapped an arm around Shanna's waist.

"I love the living room and kitchen. I didn't see the rest of the haus."

If Mamm found that odd, she'd decided to keep it to herself. "Matthew is a nice bu. Glad he decided to be part of the man swap."

"Jah." What else could she say? He was friendly. Thoughtful. Seemed to know his heart. She liked him a lot. But did she like him enough to give up her dreams?

He'd said he thought he might be falling in love with her. This time, the thought landed like a rock in the pit of her stomach.

Shanna twisted out of Mamm's arm. "I need to get those cookies into the oven. Is everything else finished for your sale tomorrow?"

"Jah, mostly. I need a couple more apple pies and some of the cookies when they are finished."

"I quadrupled the recipe." Shanna bent down and opened a cabinet door to retrieve the baking sheets.

"Gut. I planned to work in the garden some this afternoon, too. It needs to be weeded."

This is what her life would be like if she joined the church. Like Mamm's. She'd have a large family, with the first child being born approximately ten months into the marriage, and brothers and sisters following in quick succession. Nonstop housework: cooking, baking, laundry, gardening...the list went on forever, an endless cycle. Somehow, she would need to fit in quilting, butchering, and canning frolics.

Shanna sighed. On the other hand, she could have a rewarding career in nursing and, at the end of the day, come home to nonstop housework: again, cooking, baking, laundry, gardening, and so on.

The difference?

Matthew versus a career. A career versus Matthew.

"Matthew...." she whispered his name, then clamped a hand over her mouth, hoping Mamm hadn't heard.

But she had. The almost-too-smug grin on her face gave it away.

Among the Amish of Lancaster County, Pennsylvania, creamed celery was a traditional part of the wedding feast. In this district, though, the dish had never caught on, maybe because celery didn't grow so well in the rocky, red clay of southern Missouri. If they lived in Lancaster County, though, Shanna could see Mamm daydreaming about the endless rows of celery sprouting up in the garden as an announcement, of sorts, of the upcoming wedding. She could imagine Mamm thinking about all of the preparations that would need to take place, preparations like—

Mamm straightened. "Quilting!"

Shanna blinked at her.

"Ach, sorry. Thinking out loud. But we probably should make a quilt or two while you're home, ain't so?"

Jah, Mamm was transparent. She'd have Matthew and Shanna married by the end of wedding season. This year.

So not happening.

Matthew stepped back as Levi studied the barn. He had already commented that a barn raising would definitely be in order, to build a barn much closer to the house. Perhaps the existing barn could be used to store equipment and tools.

Levi had also quietly spoken his approval of the house and deemed it an easy matter to change it to meet Amish standards. The fancy bookcases and bay window didn't seem to bother him.

Matthew glanced back at the real estate agent. She paced at the entrance to the barn, still chatting on her cell phone. It seemed like she no sooner got off the phone with one person than either the phone rang again or she had to call someone else. He'd hate to be so tied to an electronic device.

Even Shanna didn't use her phone as much as Terri did. In fact, he'd seen her use it only one time.

Ach, Shanna. He restrained a groan. He wished she were there beside him, but he was the one who had decided to take her home. Traded her for Levi. He'd wanted the older man's opinion. After all, Matthew had never bought anything larger than a courting buggy when he'd lived in Pennsylvania. Here, he'd been using Shanna's buggy. She hadn't been home, so Levi had loaned it to him.

This house—Matthew knew it was a potential home. One he wanted to fill with a frau and their kinner. Love and laughter. Those would matter to his future frau, too. But then, he'd already gotten her approval on the house, though he hadn't asked. He knew she loved the kitchen. The land was what mattered to him.

He needed to make a trip to the town library to use the Internet and check for any blueberry farms in the area. If he found even one, he'd know this land would be doable. He'd already asked Levi, but he hadn't seemed to know. If Levi approved, he'd buy the land, regardless, and hope that he would be able to raise blueberries on it. He could always fall back on other crops or livestock, if necessary. The mere possibility of harvesting blueberries would make any piece of land that much more desirable.

But he didn't know how to use the computer. His friend Jacob probably would, since he'd dabbled more in Englisch things than Matthew had dared to during his rumschpringe, mainly due to his former girlfriend, Susie, who'd jumped the fence. Matthew believed Jacob had used a computer a time or two. But if he didn't know how, maybe the librarian could help.

Tomorrow...nein. He'd already made plans with Jacob and his girl, Becky, and Shanna. Maybe even Becky's friend Annie.

Shanna probably knew them. After all, they'd grown up in the same community.

But apparently they hadn't been close. Shanna had said her friends had married and moved to other districts.

Hearing gravel crunch, Matthew turned and saw Levi approaching. "You could keep that barn for equipment, jah. Livestock, not so much. You can make an offer. I'll go with you, if you want. Make it lower than the asking price, so there's room to negotiate. I can walk you through this."

"I appreciate your help, Levi."

Shanna's father nodded, then turned toward the realtor. He scowled. "Ach, talking again."

Terri appeared to have noticed the two of them standing there, staring at her, but she probably didn't understand a word they said. Not too many Englischers knew any Deutsch.

She closed her phone and stretched her painted red mouth into a smile, one that looked as fake as the smile of the bishop's wife whenever she'd had a not-so-private disagreement with her husband. "Well? Did you make a decision?"

Matthew nodded. "Jah. I'd like to make an offer." A wave of excitement washed through him, followed immediately by one of impatience to get the job done so that he could start working on the house, marry Shanna, and move in.

He'd be that much closer to marrying the girl of his dreams.

Chapter 15

"Mamm, can I borrow your buggy?" Shanna used a spatula to transfer the last cookie from the hot baking sheet to the cooling rack. Matthew and Daed had taken her buggy to the house. "I have an errand to run."

She looked up in time to see Mamm's eyes widen. "The buggy?"

She nodded. Driving her car would be so much faster, but for what she needed to do, it would be best not to stand out. A car would be much too Englisch. She'd been thinking about it for days.

"Jah, jah, you can take the buggy." Mamm's smile was huge, and it said more than words ever could. Undoubtedly she was glad to see Shanna reclaiming her Amish roots. *For the summer.*

Shanna returned the grin and began filling an aluminum pie pan with cooled cookies. "I need to borrow some cookies, too."

Mamm raised her eyebrows. "I don't think I'll want them returned. But, speaking of cookies, will you be here to help with the bake sale tomorrow?" She turned away and started washing something in the sink.

"Nein. Sorry, Mamm. I'm scheduled to work in the morning, and I've already made plans for the afternoon."

She was going fishing. With Matthew. That didn't seem like such a good idea anymore. She frowned, fingering the edge of the tin. She didn't want to lead him on—though she already had, to her shame. All afternoon, she'd thought about her dilemma and had decided that she couldn't bear to give up her dream. She had no intentions of sticking around after the summer. Come the middle of August, she'd be gone.

But how could they go back to being just friends after that amazing kiss?

She owed him a major apology for leading him on, for flirting, for indicating that she wanted him to court her.

Well, that hadn't been a ruse. She did want him to court her. So much that it hurt.

But how could she let Matthew pursue her in earnest, with his sights set on marriage, when she knew that she could not yet commit to leaving school and joining the church?

Unless....

Unless he'd consider joining a Mennonite church for her, one that would permit her to pursue her career goals.

Or, unless he'd consider waiting until she finished her schooling. She'd have her registered nurse degree in December. She was already a licensed practical nurse. But what good would a nursing degree do her in an Amish community? None that she could see.

She sighed and pressed her hands to her forehead, rubbing her temples. Wasn't there a nursing home in Seymour? She specialized in obstetrics, not geriatrics, but even so....

If she were to find a nursing job in Springfield, she would make enough money to commute back and forth. Why hadn't she thought to look for a summer job in the medical field? She'd probably had more options available to her than she'd thought.

But it had been nice reconnecting with her family. Rediscovering her roots.

And discovering Matthew.

If only there were a chance she could have it both ways. Matthew and a career.

"Shanna?" Mamm's concerned voice broke into her thoughts.

"Um, jah?" She uncovered her eyes.

"You have a headache, ain't so? Let me get something for it."

"Uh, nein. Danki." She couldn't explain her thoughts to Mamm. She doubted she'd understand. "The fresh air will help." She picked up the pie tin full of cookies and started for the door. "I'll get the buggy ready and go, then, if you don't mind."

Mamm waved her hand. "If you're sure you're all right."

Shanna hurried out to the barn. She put the tin of cookies in the buggy, then approached the stall where the family horse, Penny, was kept. She wished she could use her own horse, Cocoa, but Matthew had taken her. Joseph had told her that Daed had as good as given Cocoa to him.

She hadn't been asked. It didn't matter.

A little bit later, Shanna was on her way. She turned at a fork in the road, headed away from town, until she came to the Kropf farm.

When she stopped the buggy beside the barn, Amos strode out and marched over to her. "Jah? What can I do for you?" He hesitated a moment, then nodded. "Ach, you're the maud the bishop promised to send. I thought he'd kum the first time to introduce you, and I'd give you a run-down of the job. Did you plan to start tonight?"

Maud? She climbed out of the buggy and extended the tin of cookies to him, not sure how to answer his question.

He eyed the cookies curiously before finally taking them, and then he studied her for a long moment. "You look familiar." He tilted his head. "But I don't remember seeing you with the maidels. Who are you?"

Shanna took a deep breath. "Levi Stoltzfus's Shanna."

He took a step backward. "The one who wrecked my buggy," he said flatly.

Her shoulders slumped. "Jah. I'm sorry. That's why I'm here. I want to help. I may not be the maud, but I'll do whatever you need me to do to make it up to you." She shook her head. "I have nein money."

Amos eyed her warily. "You cook? Do dishes? Laundry?"

Of course, she did. She'd been raised Amish. After she'd finished the eighth grade, she'd been trained to be a keeper at home. Staying focused was the problem she'd had then. She was better now. At least she hadn't burned any cookies yet. "Jah. And I'll work for free."

Amos nodded. "Until you earn what the buggy repairs cost. Then, I pay." He gestured toward the house. "No one is home. You'll find the kitchen as soon as you walk in. The washer is in there. I should move it out for you, jah?" With a frown, he turned and led the way to the small stone house.

He hadn't been kidding. The door, with an antique knob and a skeleton keyhole, opened right into

a tiny kitchen full of dirty dishes. They were piled on
the counter, on the table, on every possible surface.
He put the cookies down on top of a wobbly tower of
bowls, grunted, and shoved the washer out the door.
"I'll send my bu Will to fill it for you. Be right gut to
have a home-cooked meal instead of sandwiches or
boxed cereal."

She opened her mouth to say "Danki" but instead shut it without uttering a word. Three laundry
baskets were stacked high with clothes that needed
to be laundered. No wonder he needed a maud!

And she didn't have a clue where to begin.

She stood there for a minute, staring in disgust.
This explained why her brother thought Amos needed
a frau! The woman who agreed to take this on was a
brave woman, indeed.

She glanced up and studied the ceiling. Patched
over, like it had started to collapse. There were two
small holes that had been missed near the wall, and
a brown recluse spider was dangling there, out of her
reach. She eyed it, waiting for it to move. It didn't.
Maybe it was dead.

Shanna stepped over to the sink full of dishes
and saw the faucet. Ach, there was some hope that
this wouldn't be so bad. At least she wouldn't have to
haul and heat water.

Minutes later, with the first load of dishes soaking in sudsy water, Shanna took a peek out the door
leading into the hallway. Two bedrooms. The one di-
rectly across from her had two bunk beds. She wandered down the hall. The other bedroom had two
bunk beds, as well. And there was a full-sized bed in
the living room. There were no chairs, except for two
hard wooden rockers, but there was a small, round
table with a German Bible on it.

Eight people lived in this tiny, spooky house. Unbelievable.

The rest of the rooms were almost spotless. Except for the floors, which needed to be swept, they were kept to the Amish standard of cleanliness.

She went back into the kitchen to look for a rag to wash the dishes, but before she found one, a bu came in. "I'm Will. Daed said to fill the washer for you. It's ready."

"Gut! You kill the spider while I get started." She pointed at the ceiling, then grabbed a bar of lye soap to grate into the hot water.

He glanced up and located the spider, which still hadn't budged. Shrugging, he turned away. "If it's still alive, it'll get away before I can kill it." With that, he walked out the door.

He didn't even try.

Shanna cringed. She'd do what she'd come to do, but the sooner she got out of here, the better.

Matthew glanced toward the barn, hoping Shanna would get back before dinner was over so she could share the meal with them. She'd be very late, but at least she'd be there. Instead, her spot sat empty, like it had when she'd first arrived. Only this time, her absence made for a much bigger hole. She belonged there now.

Deborah passed a pan in his direction. "Have some more apple pie, Matthew. There's plenty."

"Danki." He took a small slice, not wanting more, and hoping to save some for Shanna if she did appear. "Was, uh, Shanna called in to work?"

"Nein." Deborah shook her head. "She took the buggy. I don't know where she went. Maybe to visit friends."

She'd said her friends were all married with families and lived in another district. Matthew frowned.

Levi sat up straighter. "She took the buggy?" He smiled as if this were the best news.

Joseph bowed his head to say a silent after-dinner prayer, then pushed himself away from the table. "May I be excused? There's a frolic at Miriam Shultz's haus. It's her birthday. You're invited, too, Matthew."

"Danki. Sounds fun."

If Shanna came, even more so, but there was still no sign of her.

Matthew swallowed the last bite of pie, bowed his head in prayer for a moment, and then stood. "I'll go put on a clean shirt and get ready." *And pray Shanna shows up before we leave.*

"Ach, Matthew, what happened with the haus you looked at?" Deborah asked as he was about to leave the room.

Matthew shrugged. "I made an offer. Now I wait to see what the owner says." He tried to sound excited, but his enthusiasm had been tempered by the disappointment of Shanna's absence. He wanted—nein, needed—her encouragement.

Levi pushed his chair back. "He'll accept. Cash payment." He peered out the window. "Where'd you say Shanna went? Seems she should be home by now."

Matthew smiled. So, he wasn't the only one missing her.

"I told you, I don't know." Deborah started to gather the dishes. "She'll be back soon, I'm sure."

"Expect so." Levi turned from the window and stroked his beard.

"I'm going to get ready for the frolic." Matthew dashed up the stairs, grabbed a clean set of clothes, and headed for the shower.

When he came down, his heart flooded with relief when he saw Shanna standing in the kitchen. Deborah placed a slice of pie on a plate and filled a cup with coffee. "Shanna, please. Have a little dessert, at least. You have to eat something."

Matthew couldn't stop his grin. He pulled out the chair next to Shanna's empty one and turned to face her. "Where were you?" Ach, he didn't have the right to ask that. His face heated.

She made no move to sit. Instead, she stretched her arms high over her head and glanced at him, her expression drawn. "I got a job as a volunteer maud. Ach, it was so awful. It's like no one's done any work in the kitchen since who knows when. The cupboards were bare. Completely empty. Seriously. Not a single clean dish anywhere."

Deborah poured Matthew a cup of coffee, but he stared at Shanna, slack-jawed. What kind of family would let their house fall into such bad shape?

"So, after I washed some dishes and did some laundry—not all of it, or I would've had nein place to hang it, since the clothesline was full—I looked in the pantry for something to fix for supper, and all I found was one jar of canned corn, and one of beef. I used the last few shriveled potatoes, as well." She sat down and pulled in her chair. "All they have left is one box of cereal, and it's almost empty."

"How awful!" Deborah sat down in the chair on the other side of Shanna. "Which family is this? I'll ask your daed to talk to the bishop so they can have more help."

"It's Amos Kropf, and I'm guessing the bishop knows, since he was supposed to send out a maud." She lowered her arms and bent forward, touching her toes. "I got quite a workout. I'm no longer used to doing so much in one day."

Matthew frowned and sat down. He was familiar with Amos Kropf and his reputation for chasing girls. He didn't want Shanna getting involved in this situation or with this man. But what could he do?

Deborah covered her mouth. "Ach, that poor man. Nein wonder he's been looking for a frau. I'll hold a couple of loaves of bread back from my bake sale to give to the Kropfs. Maybe I can spare a few canned goods, as well. Summer's coming on, and we'll have fresh vegetables soon enough."

"He hasn't even put in a garden yet. Ach, Mamm, I feel so sorry for him. Seven buwe, and they're all stacked in a two-bedroom house with the roof almost falling in. The kitchen ceiling is sloppily patched."

Matthew's frown deepened. "With seven buwe, they should be able to keep the haus up better."

"His last wife died falling through the ceiling to the bottom level." Deborah's gaze bounced from Matthew to Shanna. "The floor had rotted out. Amos found her. Guess that was the patched hole you saw."

"I didn't see any stairs." Shanna straightened and twisted her back from one side to the other.

"There's an entrance to the attic somewhere. A ladder going up. She kept her sewing there."

Shanna's movements intrigued Matthew. He leaned back in his chair and watched the show, though he didn't know where she'd picked up such unusual exercises. Whenever he needed to stretch his back, he usually arched it until it popped. He didn't reach up and down or twist from side to side. But it was fascinating to observe.

Shanna sighed and stopped moving. "I feel so sorry for him," she repeated.

Deborah furrowed her brow. "Well, we'll do what we can to help, for sure, but Amos is known to be hard on women. Some say he's abusive. I've seen nein proof of that, but the truth is, he's buried three wives and two daughters so far."

"It's the haus." Shanna started stretching again. "It's spooky."

"Well, be that as it may...." Deborah stood abruptly. "I know how you feel about strays. We don't need you bringing a stray man and his family home." She patted the table. "Sit. Eat. Joseph mentioned a birthday frolic. Are you going?"

"I am, jah," Matthew answered, though he was sure Deborah had been asking her daughter. A girl who did have a tendency to pick up strays. A woman who might be inclined to marry someone because she felt sorry for him.

His breath caught. He suddenly feared her coming home with Amos Kropf and his buwe. *Ach, Lord. Don't let that be so.*

He studied Shanna and tried to sound nonchalant as he said, "You'll go with me, ain't so?"

Shanna hesitated. She turned and looked at him but didn't quite meet his eyes.

Something about her expression scared him.

"We need to talk," she said.

❦

Shanna stood up and turned to go outside, but Mamm rapped on the tabletop. "I'm going to take the laundry down. You sit and have your talk here. Eat the pie."

"I'd rather go outside. And I'd be happy to take the laundry down. You stay here. And danki for the pie, but nein. Danki."

Shanna opened the front door and took a deep breath of fresh air, then headed for the side yard, where the laundry waited. She wondered if any of the Kropfs would take down their clothes, or if she'd find them still hanging on the line when she stopped by after work tomorrow. The whole situation broke her heart.

Matthew stepped up to the clothesline and reached up to unclip a pair of pants. He folded them. "Was ist letz?"

His voice sounded calm, unconcerned. Nothing like the jumble of nerves she felt.

"I owe you an apology." Shanna turned her back on him and reached for a dress. "I shouldn't have led you on the way I did. I treated you like fancy folk do, and I encouraged you to disobey the Ordnung. Kissing on the lips...." She sighed and pivoted around to face him. "I'm going back to Springfield in the fall, and marriage isn't in my immediate plans. So, I can't allow you to court me. I'm sorry."

Matthew froze. He shut his eyes for a brief moment, then opened them and reached for another pair of pants. "Friends then, jah?"

Even rejection didn't seem to faze him. If only she had the peace he possessed.

"How can we possibly be friends after...? Well, you know."

His lips twitched. "How can we not be?"

Ach, he was infuriating. She wanted him to tell her that he understood, and still wanted to court her, even if she wasn't ready to think about marriage. Instead, he acted as if it didn't matter one iota. She wanted to put a stop to things before they even got started, and he behaved as if it were all "ser gut."

She dropped the dress into the basket, on top of the neatly folded pair of pants. He calmly placed the second pair on top, just as neatly.

"Don't you even care?" She planted her fists on her hips.

Lips pressed together, Matthew glanced at her, then reached for another pair of pants. He shrugged. "Wasn't like we made promises."

"Matthew!" Joseph yelled from the porch. "You coming to the frolic?" He came down the steps and started toward them. "Ach, Shanna. Didn't know you were back. Kum on, there's a birthday frolic."

"I'll be right there." Matthew dropped the third pair of pants into the basket. "Hurry up and finish, Shanna. I'll stall him."

"But...." Shanna stared at him.

"Friends. Just friends." He turned and jogged away.

With her knuckles, she wiped her suddenly burning eyes.

It wasn't fair. He was supposed to feel as miserable about their breakup as she did. Well, it wasn't technically a breakup, since they hadn't been courting. But still.

She reached for another piece of clothing but couldn't see what it was because of the tears that filled her eyes.

He'd been the one to declare that they were going to get married. That the house of his dreams would have her in it. And all those other beautiful words that had led up to *the kiss*.

And now, he was ready to let her walk away without a single "Nein"?

Chapter 16

Matthew hiked over to the buggy, his thoughts whirling. He'd known that the look on Shanna's face meant nothing good. Sure enough, she'd told him she wanted to end their fledgling relationship. Somehow, he'd managed to hold himself together.

Yet thoughts and worries whirled in his head. *Lord, what is Your plan? Will Shanna ever be mine? Is it possible she'll come to love me? I want to be more than just her friend.*

His heart had recognized her from the start. He decided to hold on to the belief that she was meant for him. What else could he do?

"You ready, jah?" Joseph glanced at him from the buggy seat. "Is Shanna coming?"

Matthew shrugged but answered in the affirmative. "Jah. She needs to take the laundry in, and then she'll be here." *I hope.*

Something in his voice or his stance must have alerted Joseph that not all was well, because he narrowed his eyes and hopped down. "Guess I'll go check on her and tell her to hurry."

"Might be best." Matthew leaned against the buggy to wait, but he wondered what Shanna would say. She'd probably insist that everything was fine. And he supposed it was. After all, she wanted to call it quits, he hadn't disagreed, and that was the end of the story.

Except that he didn't want to end the relationship. Their story was just beginning. Where it went from here, he didn't know, but he was willing to wait as patiently as he could to find out.

He looked around and saw the fishing poles leaning against the wall. Would Shanna come fishing with them tomorrow? He could almost feel the tug of a fish on the line. Come to think of it, reeling in a fish took a lot of patience, and, in many cases, it got away.

He hated to compare Shanna to a fish, but somehow that was the analogy that came to mind. He wouldn't give up on her yet. He'd keep playing the line until he landed her, and if friendship was all he could get from her, then that's what he would take.

Joseph came back around the house. "She's taking the laundry inside, and then she'll change clothes and be right here. She says everything is gut, but I could tell she's been crying." He peered at Matthew. "And you look like you ate too many green apples."

Shanna had been crying? Surely, that meant she cared at least a little bit. But she had ended their courtship before it had even begun. Matthew's head throbbed. Too much trouble to figure out how a woman's brain worked. He forced a smile and put his hand on his stomach. "Green apples? Tasty, but the stomachache is a killer."

Joseph chuckled. "Trouble in paradise, jah? My guess is she's the one who caused it."

Matthew shrugged and repressed the urge to tell Joseph it was none of his business. Besides, he wasn't really sure who was more to blame for the problem. He was the one who'd blurted out that she would marry him. He was the one who had kissed her on the lips. Though, why there seemed to be a huge difference between him doing it and Nate doing it, he wasn't sure. She'd said Nate was a casual friend. Matthew wanted to be more.

Maybe that was the issue.

From all appearances, he was the source of the problem.

Still, as amazing as it had been to kiss her, he almost wished he could take it back. He wished he could have waited until their wedding night. The way a first kiss was intended to be.

Shanna came around the corner of the house, and he automatically held out an arm to assist her into the buggy. He doubted she needed his help, but she accepted it, sliding into the middle of the seat. It would be a tight fit, and she'd be as close to him as she'd been when they'd gone to look at the farm for sale. But this time, it wouldn't be because she wanted it that way.

Still, he wouldn't complain.

Ach, his foolish heart. He'd known loving Shanna would mean heartbreak, but he'd succumbed, anyway. Was it possible to fall in love after knowing her not even a week? Most people would probably say nein. But then, how could he help but love her?

He drew a fortifying breath and climbed into the buggy beside her. She drew her skirts close to her side, but she didn't move away. Really, she had no place to go, unless she sat on Joseph's lap, and he doubted she'd do that. Or that Joseph would let her.

"So, Miriam Shultz's birthday?" she said brightly.

Joseph nodded.

"How old is she now?"

"Sixteen."

There was something in his tone. Matthew tilted his head and studied Joseph. He would have bet Joseph was going to ask to take Miriam home from the singing on Sunday night.

Matthew frowned. He'd be going home alone, instead of with Shanna. And Shanna would intrude on her brother's date.

It wasn't right.

He mentally ran through the list of women he'd met since moving to Missouri. There wasn't another girl who interested him the way Shanna did.

Shanna fought to compose herself as the buggy rumbled along the dirt road. An occasional tear escaped one of her eyes and rolled down her cheek, but neither Matthew nor Joseph seemed to notice.

She felt like a world-class fool. Matthew obviously didn't care for her the way she'd thought he did. He must have been teasing with all those remarks about marriage and then taken advantage of the situation by stealing a kiss. Why else would he be so immune to the feelings of hurt and rejection she battled because of his composed reaction? Sure, she was the one who had asked for an end to the relationship, but she hadn't expected him to take it so well.

When they arrived at the Shultzes', she was far from feeling ready to interact with her Amish peers. Buggies and horses already lined the driveway. It reminded her of the college campus when classes were in session, with cars parked in every available space.

Joseph found a spot, engaged the brakes, and hopped out of the buggy. He was long gone by the time Matthew climbed out and turned around to help her. She wasn't sure she wanted his assistance, but he didn't even ask. He grasped her at the waist and lifted her down.

"Are you okay?" He studied her, probably noticing the tracks her tears had taken, or her red eyes
and puffy lids. She should have checked herself in
the mirror before leaving home.

Shanna firmed her shoulders. "I'm fine."

Matthew lifted his hand and rolled his thumb
gently over her cheek. Her breath hitched in her
throat, but he merely caught a tear and wiped it away.
"Jah. I can see that. Look, Shanna, if you want, we
could go somewhere and talk—"

"I'm fine," she repeated.

"A walk, maybe? Will you walk with me, please?"

"Matthew." *Leave me alone.*

He hesitated, his gaze skittering over her face
again. He frowned, and she saw a jaw muscle jump.
Then, he nodded and turned away, as if he'd somehow
heard her unspoken plea.

She shouldn't have come. She shouldn't be here.
She knew Miriam Shultz only as an acquaintance,
but the idea of a frolic had sounded fun.

Of course, it was supposed to be.

She trailed after Matthew, trying to find her
resolve. She would fit in. She would have fun. She
would—

"Matthew!"

Shanna turned and saw a young man she didn't
know coming toward them. He was holding the hand
of a pretty blonde who looked vaguely familiar.

"Jacob, Becky." Matthew stopped walking. "Gut
to see you. This is Shanna." He held out his hand
toward her.

The way his voice softened when he spoke her
name was like a caress coming from his lips. His
friend must have noticed, too, because his gaze shot

from Matthew to her. She tried not to cringe under his perusal. Did he see an Englisch girl hidden in Amish clothing? Or did he think everything was on the up-and-up with her?

It wasn't. She didn't wrap her chest the way Amish women did to hide their assets. She wore the fancy garment, instead. But if he noticed—if anyone did—he was focusing his attentions in the wrong place.

Her breath caught again. Had Matthew noticed her assets during their embrace?

Jacob smiled. "Hi, Shanna. Nice to meet you."

Matthew gently took her arm and drew her nearer before releasing her. "Jacob is my best friend from Pennsylvania. He moved out here before I did. And this is Becky Troyer."

Shanna did remember Becky. Quiet. Shy. A bookworm. And the best cook in the district. Shanna tried to find her smile. It wobbled some.

"They're the ones we're going fishing with tomorrow," Matthew told her. His expression added, "If you still want to kum."

Becky stepped forward, but she still clung to Jacob's hand. "Gut to see you again, Shanna. I heard you were back."

What else had she heard? Shanna didn't know what to say or how to react. She'd been in the fancy world long enough that she was tempted to behave with slight arrogance, maybe say, "All gut, I hope." No Amish girl would be so bold.

Something stayed her. Becky looked kind. Maybe she'd be a friend.

Shanna needed a friend. Especially since she'd gone and ruined her relationship with Matthew.

Somehow she found the strength to move one step closer. "It's nice to see you again, Becky." Becky looked happy. Comfortable. In love.

Shanna glanced at Jacob again. Pennsylvania sure grew some good-looking buwe, and bold ones, too, considering how openly he held Becky's hand. Yet, as shy as Shanna remembered Becky to be, maybe she needed that. Her gaze moved to Matthew. Of course, he was good-looking, too. So cute. Ach, why couldn't she have met him before her rumschpringe?

Matthew grasped Shanna's elbow but released her quickly. "We're just getting here. Are you leaving already?"

Jacob shook his head. "Nein, not leaving. Going for a walk down by the pond."

"I'm going to join the volleyball game, I think, after I say hi to the birthday girl." Matthew gestured to the net set up near the barn, where a game was already in session.

Jacob nodded and took a step, then hesitated. "You want to go with us, maybe? You and Shanna?"

Matthew smiled. "Nein, danki."

Shanna wished he'd said "Jah," but then, why would he? They weren't a couple. He needed to find a woman to marry, and hanging out by the pond with Shanna wouldn't advance that goal.

She was suddenly jealous of this nameless, faceless woman, yet unknown even to Matthew, who might claim his heart.

After Jacob and Becky left, Matthew turned to Shanna. "Do you want to go see Miriam? I can get you some cake and something to drink, if you like."

She tilted her head, studying him. Her eyes still glimmered with unshed tears, but she seemed to be composing herself. He wished she would agree to walk with him so they could sort this out, but she wasn't inclined to do that.

He didn't know how a talk would fix things, though. It seemed pretty cut-and-dried. She wasn't likely to adjust her thinking, and he wouldn't change his.

If a relationship was to develop between them, it would be up to the Lord.

In the meantime, he intended to be a friend to Shanna. Someone she could grow to care for and maybe love. He wouldn't press her, and he definitely wouldn't push her away.

"Jah, we can do that. Wait, do I look okay?"

He let his gaze rove over her face. Devoid of makeup, she was just as lovely as the girl who'd arrived five days ago. Maybe even prettier, since this was natural.

"You're beautiful."

"Seriously. Are my eyes red and puffy or anything?"

He studied her again. "Nein. You're gut."

She huffed as if she didn't believe him. He wished that she could see what he saw—gorgeous golden-brown hair that reminded him of autumn leaves, with just a hint of red mixed in. Brilliant green eyes with long, dark lashes. A slender build, but one that still boasted generous curves in all the right places.

"Ach, Shanna. You are beautiful." *Ich liebe dich.* He swallowed the words. Saying them would only serve to complicate matters more.

"Danki."

"Bitte. Shall we?" He nodded toward the house. "I'm actually not sure who Miriam Shultz is. I'm new, you know."

Shanna shrugged. "She's a few years younger than I am. If Joseph has his way, I'm guessing she'll eventually be a member of our family."

Matthew smiled and resisted the urge to run his fingers over the curve of her cheek. "It seems so." He wanted the same thing for himself, someday.

They walked toward the house. Several people called out a greeting to Matthew, who waved in return. A few said something to Shanna, but to Matthew it seemed that most of them eyed her with distrust, whispering to each other behind their hands. Perhaps they were curious as to why a girl who had jumped the fence would dare to show her face at a frolic.

Shanna grabbed his arm, pulling him to a stop. "I changed my mind. Let's take a walk with your friends."

She must have noticed the looks and whispers, too. Plus, she probably recalled her mamm telling her that she was the latest topic of gossip around here.

Matthew draped his arm over her shoulders, giving her a too-brief hug. "Hold your head up high. Don't let them know that it bothers you."

She looked around, then stopped and stepped out of his embrace. "I ran away from home. Did my parents tell you?" she blurted out. "Daed and I had a huge fight, and that nacht, I went to a frolic like this one, only a little wilder. It was in the Lapps' back field. Some Englisch guys were there, drinking and such. I'd earned my GED and been accepted into college, but I didn't know how I'd get there without attracting attention. So, I climbed in the backseat of a car. When the driver eventually got in and left, I left with him. I don't think he ever knew I was there."

Matthew's jaw dropped. "Seriously, Shanna?" Did she have any idea how dangerous that stunt had been?

"How else would I have left? Do you think Daed would have called a driver for me? The only way I could get out of here was to stow away."

"You must have been pretty desperate." He steered them away from the young people gathered around the barn and a bonfire on the side of the property, then led her out to the fields beyond.

"Jah. Jah, I guess I was."

"Why, Shanna? Why were you so anxious to leave?" He wanted to argue the benefits of being part of the Amish community, but he didn't. He probably shouldn't have bothered asking her why she'd left.

"I wanted to be a nurse," she stated.

Her voice was firm. Unapologetic. Slightly defensive.

Matthew nodded. "You've said that. But why is being a nurse so important to you?" Again, he was tempted to state his case for remaining Amish, but he kept quiet.

"Ach, it's a long story. The short version is that my cousin Rachel was pregnant, and she started having problems. Mamm sent me over to be their maud because the doctor had put Rachel on bed rest. And, well, I probably shouldn't say any more because it'd be inappropriate, but Rachel started having more problems, and they say I saved her life and the boppli's, too. I didn't know what I was doing; I just got lucky. The bishop said I had a gift. I wondered what kind of gift I could have if I actually had some training. Daed told me I didn't need it. He told me that it wasn't luck but God who had saved Rachel and the boppli, and that my desire for schooling stemmed from pride." Shanna shook her head. "I probably shouldn't be telling you all this."

"The bishop said you had a gift...." Matthew studied her profile. "What do you think he was referring to?" He had his suspicions but wondered if she had reached the same conclusion.

Shanna shrugged. "Medicine?"

"Maybe midwifery?" Matthew suggested.

"Ach, that is so funny. I got my training in obstetrics."

Matthew stopped walking. She moved a step or two beyond him, then turned back. "Was ist letz?"

"Shanna, think about it." He reached out and placed his hands on her shoulders, gently pulling her toward him. She didn't resist. He thought she would have stepped into his arms, if he'd let her. "What do nurses trained in obstetrics do?"

"Assist with labor and delivery."

He raised his hand to cup her cheek. "And what do Amish women do best?"

She laughed. "Have boppli?" Then her smile faded. "What are you saying?"

"Kum home, Shanna. Kum home and be a midwife. The only midwife in this entire district is an Englisch woman who lives over an hour away. It would be such a blessing to all the families to have a local Amish midwife, ain't so?"

Her brow furrowed. "Ach."

He waited a beat. Two. Three. She didn't say anything else. That was it? Just "Ach"?

He'd hoped for a more enthusiastic response. Maybe a promise to think about coming home to work as a midwife. A promise to at least consider marrying him someday.

Though that probably would be a bit premature.

He dropped his hands to his sides and stepped back.

He'd dangled the bait. Whether she decided to nibble would be anybody's guess.

Chapter 17

Could she return home as a midwife? Did she even want to? The implications of Matthew's suggestion swirled in her mind like a dust storm. *A midwife.* This needed serious thought.

Shanna turned away from Matthew and strode several yards away across the uneven ground of the field, careful to avoid the fledgling plants growing out of the furrowed earth. If the bishop sanctioned it and the community accepted her, she certainly could come back to be a midwife. At this moment, the thought seemed highly desirable. To be a part of the people. Welcomed. To marry and raise a family and still have the education she'd sacrificed everything for.

Marriage to Matthew might be in the mix, although he'd never actually proposed. Any mention of the possibility had been more in the form of a decree: *"You're going to marry me." "You're going to return to the Amish."* Did he think he was a prophet? Perhaps it was selfish, but she wanted a proposal. Maybe not one like her friend had, with dinner and opera tickets and a carriage ride, but a nice, romantic... something...that she could think back on and catch a thrill over when her marriage settled into the humdrum of normal, everyday life after the honeymoon period ended.

But joining the church would mean returning to so many things that she couldn't wait to be permanently free from. What if she didn't want to return?

Living in the same area as Daed...could she handle that?

Although the Daed she'd lived with for the past week seemed to have softened up some. He had said a couple of nice things about her. He'd allowed her to stay—for the summer. She hadn't really expected that. And he hadn't complained about the kittens she'd brought home.

But he'd called her a stray.

And they continued to get on each other's last nerve.

She and Daed would never get along. Not even with Matthew trying to push them together. Just like he was trying to rearrange the rest of her life. Maybe she'd like to make a few plans for herself instead of falling into his neatly organized blueprint.

"Shanna?" Matthew's whisper broke into her thoughts. "What are you thinking?" His voice held an ache, a hurt, but she didn't know why and didn't want to pursue it. At least, not right now. Maybe later. But it didn't excuse him for trying to take over her life.

"How dare you?" She spun around to face him. He still stood right where she'd left him, pain etching his face. The distance that separated them seemed a tangible thing. "This is my life. Mine. And if I'd wanted to be here, I never would have run away. You have nein right to tell me to kum home."

An expression crossed his face, but it was gone before she could identify what emotion it revealed. A muscle bunched in his neck, and he frowned. "You're right," he said quietly. "I'm sorry."

"You have nein right!"

"Nein, I don't. It won't happen again." Distaste flickered in his eyes, the only indication that he regretted the words, even as he spoke them. Or was it that he found her distasteful?

Why had he acquiesced so quickly? Just as he'd done when she'd ended their relationship. It didn't seem right. But she didn't want to pursue that, either.

"You bet it won't. Just go, Matthew. Leave me alone."

He stood there another minute. Silent. Then, he sighed. "I want to be your friend, Shanna."

"Then, don't interfere in my life."

His frown deepened, and he nodded. "I suppose I need to say something to the birthday girl. Are you coming?"

"Nein. I'll be there later."

"Right. You'll find me playing volleyball, if you care to."

And if she didn't? She didn't say that, though. She'd hurt him enough, judging by the slump of his shoulders as he turned away. Guilt gnawed at her. She should apologize. Should do something to make it right.

She'd probably killed any remnant of love he might have been feeling for her. But that was as it should be. He and she were a combination that never was meant to be. As much as that realization hurt.

Amish and Englisch were not meant to mix.

She wanted to collapse into the dirt and sob.

Instead, she watched through a blur of tears as he disappeared around the barn. Then, she turned and walked off. Alone. Where she was going, she didn't know.

Her life was her own. Matthew knew that. But her choices would affect everything. Especially his heart. He wished she could see how much. Her behavior was selfish—not seeking to serve God and others first. But she had the right to choose what she wanted; he couldn't deny that. And if she wanted her *Englisch* world and not him....

Matthew had stalked off, leaving Shanna alone to think, though he'd wanted to stay and talk. To encourage her to return when she'd completed her schooling, to work and serve the people, to make her home with him. As his frau.

God, do the talking for me. Help her to see.

Activity flooded the barnyard. The big sliding doors stood open, and hay bales were scattered around. Some *buwe* took turns swinging from a rope that hung from a high rafter and jumping into a pile of hay. Matthew had never cared for that activity, not since a childhood friend had missed the hay and fallen to his death.

Matthew moved on and eventually found Miriam Shultz sitting on the porch, surrounded by a group of friends. Joseph wasn't there; he might have joined in a game of volleyball or football. Or maybe he was in the group of *buwe* standing around the campfire, roasting hotdogs on sticks. It was hard to tell in the gathering dusk.

Matthew looked at Miriam. The strings of her white *kapp* dangled behind her head, and her dress was a kind of dusky orange. She wore tennis shoes over her black stockings. "Happy birthday," he said.

She giggled and then nudged the girl seated beside her, who started snickering, too.

He had no use for giggly girls. He turned and opened the cooler on the ground nearby. Rather than taking the time to choose a particular flavor, he grabbed the first can his fingers closed around. When he lifted it out, he saw that it was root beer. Good enough. He'd never had this particular brand, but suddenly he wanted a root beer float. It sounded tasty.

Would Shanna want a soda? He hesitated, then reached back inside the cooler and took another can. Same kind.

Had she had enough time to think? Maybe he should go after her, offer her the drink, and talk her into coming back to roast hotdogs with him.

He walked around the barn and into the fields but saw no sign of her. She'd disappeared.

Perhaps she'd returned to the frolic, and he'd missed her. He hadn't looked for her there, figuring she'd be where he'd left her.

Silly of him.

He returned to the area in back of the house. A few girls played football in the field, but none of them was dressed in the shade of blue that Shanna wore that evening. The volleyball game was in full swing. Matthew stopped to watch for a while. No sign of Shanna there, either.

Sighing, he glanced at the faces of the people standing around the fire.

Still no Shanna.

Disappointment and hurt that she would leave without telling him weighed heavily on his heart. And he felt the nagging fear that she'd accepted a ride from another bu at the frolic. It was possible she'd gone on a walk with someone else. Probably what had happened.

She was beautiful. Buwe would notice her. And, since she wore an Amish dress, no one would know that she'd jumped the fence unless he recognized her. But the Shultz farm was teeming with young people from several different districts, so there were probably plenty of buwe who didn't know her.

That might explain everything. He'd have to be careful not to let his jealousy show. After all, he didn't own her.

His spirits plummeting, he set one can on the ground, opened the other, and took a long swig. Then, he set that down, too, and merged into the volleyball game. He'd told her where he'd be. Maybe she'd come find him.

At the end of the driveway, Shanna stepped out onto the road, then hesitated. Where was she? She looked around and recognized the Kropf farm ahead. The clothes she'd washed still hung on the line, and she didn't see any sign of the family.

She hadn't intended to come out here—at least, not consciously. She glanced back in the direction of the Shultz farm and heard the faint sounds of laughter. She wasn't ready to go back there yet. She wanted to think about what Matthew's suggestion would entail, and whether she could even consider following through with it.

The way her eyes were watering, she probably needed a good cry, too, but she'd rather that happen without anyone to witness her humiliation. She preferred people seeing her happy. Not moping and sad. She shouldn't have agreed to attend the frolic. Not in her current mood, anyway.

Her day was messed up beyond belief. It had started off great, with the flirting, which had actually been wonderful, and then *the kiss*, which had been beyond amazing. But it had gone swiftly downhill from there. She still struggled to find her footing on the uneven road, and, she supposed, in relation to Matthew.

If only someone would make all her decisions for her. She closed her eyes. For a moment, she was tempted to pray, to ask God for His guidance, but she squashed the urge. Back at school, she'd attended church on occasion so she could tell Mamm that, jah, she'd found a good church. But it was extremely liberal compared to her Old Order Amish upbringing. The parishioners lived like the rest of the world; they drove cars, talked on cell phones, used computers, and wore blue jeans. And it wasn't a big deal to them whether you came every Sunday or not. Shanna hadn't told Mamm about any of that, though.

The Lord had turned into the God of her father, and since she didn't get along well with Daed, she had every reason to believe that God was out to beat her down, too. What did He care about her?

The last time she'd prayed? Possibly the day she'd come home. But, nein. She'd merely tried then.

Or maybe it had been this very morning, when Matthew had pressed her head into a bowing position. Had she actually prayed then? Other than to ask God to give her Matthew?

He probably shouldn't have granted that request.

She sighed. *Will the real Shanna Stoltzfus please stand up?*

Life seemed infinitely less confusing in the fancy world. She attended school, worked at her job, studied, and hung out with her friends. There was none of this "You're going to marry me" business. No one telling her, "You're going to return to the Amish." And definitely none of this "Kum home, Shanna, and be a midwife" stuff.

She'd sacrificed everything to follow her dreams. It wasn't fair to expect her to come home before she'd fulfilled them. It wasn't fair to—

A horse whinnied, and she opened her eyes, disoriented. Where was she? She looked around. Ach, at the Kropf farm. Still no sign of anyone. She turned to head back to the frolic, but the clothes on the line caught her attention again. It wouldn't take but a moment to fold them and place the basket by the front door.

As she approached the clothesline, she saw that the wringer washer still sat on the lawn where Amos had set it. She'd hated it, but she'd handled it okay. She fingered a shirt hanging on the line. Dry. She unpinned it, folded it, and dropped it into the plastic basket on the ground.

"You came back." The gravelly voice came from behind her.

Shanna gasped but didn't turn around. She knew it was Amos. "I hate to leave a job unfinished." That was a lie. But what else could she say? That she'd rather fold laundry than attend a frolic?

"Commendable. I'll give you a ride home when you finish, then."

Shanna kept her back to him. "Danki." She heard him walk toward the barn. Ride home with Amos Kropf? Suddenly, she wanted to run away. Maybe back to Matthew and the frolic. She gritted her teeth. She would stay here until the work was done.

When all of the clothes had been folded, she carried the basket inside, then cleared up the supper dishes, making sure the kitchen would be clean for the next day. Would Amos do the grocery shopping? Or did he expect her to, as the maud? She'd have to ask.

She felt a tug on her dress. "Read me a story?" It was the littlest bu. He handed her a worn copy of a book. Overdue to the library, according to the date on the white slip.

She pulled out a kitchen chair, checked the area for spiders, and then sat, cuddling the bu in her lap. "What's your name?"

"Daed calls me the wee one, but my teacher calls me Samuel."

Shanna smiled. "Samuel it is." She opened the book. "Once upon a time...."

It was well past dark when Amos finally stopped the buggy at the end of Daed's drive, a courting tradition Shanna was glad he'd chosen to observe, because Matthew wouldn't see who had brought her home. If he was still awake. He'd probably gone to bed hours ago. She glanced at the house and didn't see any lamps glowing. She'd planned to sit with the family for devotions tonight, as she had when she'd still been at home, but that hadn't happened. Instead, she'd had devotions with the Kropfs and waited while most of the buwe had been tucked in before Amos had hitched up the buggy to take her home.

He came around to her side and helped her out, his thumb grazing the top of her hand as he did. She resisted the urge to yank her arm away. "Danki, Shanna. Appreciate your help. You'll be a gut fr—maud."

Had he started to say "frau"? As in, his frau? Shanna shuddered. *Frau. Right.* She then remembered what she'd wanted to ask him. "You're out of groceries. Were you going to do the shopping, or would you like me to?"

He hesitated a second. "I hired Janna Kauffman to do all the shopping. She is an Amish woman for hire for the infirm and widowers in the community. Lives down the road, and," he chuckled, "loves to shop. Her buggy is always loaded full. She should be by the haus tomorrow with my order."

Shanna stepped away. "Do you want me to kum back tomorrow? I have to work second shift at the restaurant, but I could kum to your haus afterward." On second thought, she'd promised Matthew she'd go fishing with him and his friends.

Amos eyed her clothes. "I thought you'd returned."

She raised her eyebrows but didn't respond.

Finally, he shook his head. "Monday will be gut. Whenever you have the time."

Shanna nodded, turned, and hurried through the darkness down the drive toward the barn.

When she slipped inside, a form moved out of the shadows near her apartment door. She froze.

Her heartbeat escalated when she saw that the door to her apartment loft was open.

A scream started to materialize, but a hand slid over her mouth, muffling the sound.

Chapter 18

Matthew tightened his grip on Shanna's mouth. He didn't want her to scream. It would scare the livestock and possibly wake the other members of the family, if they were even asleep. They'd been pretty concerned when they'd found out that Shanna had gone missing during the frolic. Deborah had made a brief reference to the time she'd run away, and she'd looked extremely worried, but Levi had assured her that Shanna was probably fine.

Now, Shanna twisted violently in his arms. She hit him hard in the stomach with something—maybe her elbow—and stomped down on his bare toes with a tennis-shoe-clad foot. When her palm slammed into his nose, mercifully not head-on, Matthew clamped his lips together to keep from howling in pain. He released her quickly, his hands flying to his nose to stanch the inevitable flow of blood. "What was that for, Shanna?" Pressing his nostrils shut with one hand, he reached with the other inside his pocket and whipped out his handkerchief.

"Matthew?"

"Who'd you think I was?" He brought the handkerchief to his nose, hoping she'd heard the peevishness in his voice.

"What are you doing skulking around out here in the dark? You could have gotten hurt."

Could have? He supposed a blow to the stomach and a bloody nose didn't count. He pressed the handkerchief more firmly against his nostrils. Thankfully, the bleeding was not excessive. Good thing her aim had been slightly off. Though he might end up with a black eye or a bruised cheek. "I was worried when you disappeared. Your family was concerned, too."

"I needed space to think." He sensed rather than saw her shrug.

"Jah, but it's still not safe for a woman to roam around alone after dark. Even if you do seem more than capable of protecting yourself." He certainly hadn't been prepared for her counterattack.

"I took a series of self-defense classes when I moved away. Bad part of town, you know." She fell silent, and he heard her hand patting the wall. A moment later, she flicked the lights on. Matthew shut his eyes to block out the sudden brightness.

"Why was my apartment door open, anyway?" Shanna frowned at him, then glanced up the stairs. "Joseph?"

"You're blinding me." Her brother had his hands over his eyes. "We were checking to see if you'd snuck in. When you started beating Matthew, I decided to stay up here."

"Wimp. He's lucky I didn't SING."

Matthew frowned. "Sing? Why would you sing?"

Joseph frowned. "Right. Your singing is pretty awful." He scooted past them. "I'd best be getting back to the haus. Gut nacht."

"SING: stomach, instep, nose, groin—"

"I get the picture." Matthew winced. "You need more practice. Your aim was off on two out of the three. But don't practice on me anymore, okay? Gut nacht."

Shanna laughed. "Gut nacht." She touched his hand. "Danki for being concerned about me. You're so sweet."

That wasn't the sort of statement he'd been fishing for. He shook his head. "Glad you're back. Did you have a gut walk?"

She sighed. "Nein. I went across the fields, and I didn't know where I was. Then, I saw Amos Kropf's haus across the way, and the laundry was still on the line, flapping in the breeze. So, I went over there to fold the clothes and clean the supper dishes, and—"

"Shanna." It wasn't his place to tell her to stay away from Amos Kropf. He needed to choose his words carefully. "You aren't his maud."

"I am, just until I've worked enough to pay off the damage I did to his buggy. Then, I'll owe you for paying the driver who came to haul him and his horse and buggy back home. How much did that cost, anyway?"

Matthew shook his head. "Never mind. Doesn't matter."

"But it does. I want to pay my debts. Before the summer's over, so I can leave with a clear conscience."

The pain in his heart stung worse than his nose. "Jah, I can see why that's important." He paused. "But I still wish you'd stay."

She leaned against the open door. "Speaking of which, I owe you an apology. I like you, Matthew. Maybe too much. That scares me. I don't know whether to run away or to stay and see where this goes. And that makes me uncomfortable, because I walked out of the Amish lifestyle, and I was ready to throw it away forever." She waved a hand at the surroundings. "I embraced the Englisch life. So, it's difficult for me to imagine giving up my dreams for something I hated."

"Hated?" He tried to keep his voice sounding noncommittal, to disguise the pain her word caused him.

"Okay, maybe 'hated' is a bit strong. But...." She hesitated and licked her lips, drawing his attention to them. He forced his gaze away. "I guess it isn't as bad as I remembered. I've actually enjoyed being home, helping Mamm in the kitchen and the garden, even doing the laundry. Not to mention, riding in buggies again is...kind of romantic, with the right person." She grinned, but her smile quickly faded. "Still, I'm not sure."

Matthew raised his eyebrows. "I guess my job is clear, then: convince you that I'm worth returning for." He fought the hopeful sensation that swelled within him. No point in getting his heart trampled on if he scared her off again.

Shanna looked thoughtful for a moment. "It's the rules, I think. I don't want to be forced to obey the Ordnung, and some of those rules vary, depending on the local bishop. I mean, in one district, you're allowed only a woodstove and a water pump in the haus. The women have to heat water to do dishes. Can you imagine how hot those kitchens would get in the summer? Intolerable. Plus, whenever you wanted to take a bath, you'd have to heat the water and fill a metal tub. And what if we get a new bishop who wants to change things?" She shook her head. "And being told I have to fix my hair a certain way, only to wear it covered under my kapp? One district requires the women to twist their hair over their ears. It's like everyone has to wear a uniform, to be cookie-cutter copies of each other. Maybe that's what I hate the most."

"Those rules serve a purpose, though," Matthew reminded her. "If you wore fancier clothes or fixed your hair in a showy manner, you might be tempted by pride. But I do agree that some bishops are more progressive than others. Back in Pennsylvania, I was allowed to ride a bike or use a scooter to get around. Here, it's against the Ordnung." He did miss his bike.

"Exactly."

A smile tickled the corners of his mouth. "Well then, Shanna Stoltzfus, I'm going to take myself off to bed. You still want to go fishing tomorrow?"

"Jah, I might like to."

Matthew chuckled. "Then, I might take you." He reached up and trailed a fingertip along her soft cheek. Somehow, he resisted the urge to kiss it. "Gut nacht, Shanna."

The next morning, Shanna put in four hours of work at McDonald's. When she came home, several cars were parked in front of the house, and a sign hung on the front door that read, in Mamm's handwriting, "Kum in." Shanna hurried toward the barn to get out of her work uniform and shower before anyone saw her. A coworker had dumped a container of hot grease into the sink, and she'd been within splattering distance. Her arms were speckled with minute yet painful burn marks.

When she was clean and dressed in an Amish dress, she exited the bathroom and heard noises coming from the barn below. She peeked out the loft door, looking for Matthew, but found only Judah, cleaning out one of the horse stalls.

The shop would be closed unless Daed had a special order come in, so she headed to the house. Four or five Englisch couples stood in front of the kitchen table, which Mamm had shoved against the wall and filled with a display of jams, jellies, breads, pies, and cookies. Daed leaned against the hutch, silently looking on, while Mamm sat at the head of the table with her money box and answered the occasional question from one of the Englischers.

Desperate to escape the customers' prying eyes, Shanna scooted around the corner into the living room. Funny how different it felt to be scrutinized in one's own home versus in town. Matthew sat in a straight-back chair, a fishing pole in his hand and a reel of line beside him.

He looked up with a smile. "Hey, Shanna. I'm getting this rod ready for you."

Shanna frowned. She'd never been fishing before; Daed had taken only her brothers. She didn't have the slightest idea how to handle a reel. But fishing was something Matthew obviously enjoyed. He'd probably show her what to do. "Danki."

"Your mamm already said we'll plan on fish for supper."

"That assumes we'll actually catch some."

"We will. Your daed keeps the pond well stocked."

He sounded confident. She wasn't so sure.

"I've never been fishing before, you know."

Matthew shrugged. "It's not that hard. I'll teach you." He glanced at the battery-operated clock on the end table. "I'll be finished soon, and then we can go."

"Okay. Just let me know." Shanna wandered over to the end table and picked up a library book that someone in the family must have been reading. She turned it over and read the back cover. An Amish mystery. Sounded interesting. She sat down in the chair next to Matthew and opened the book to the first page.

She'd read barely five pages when Matthew stood. "Are you ready? We'll walk down."

The pond wasn't all that far from the house, but Shanna had envisioned another romantic buggy ride with Matthew. In reality, though, walking made the most sense. In the time it would take to hitch Cocoa to the buggy, they'd be there, or almost there, depending on their pace.

Shanna glanced at the top of the page to memorize the number, then set the book back where she'd found it. After slipping into her flip-flops, she followed Matthew through the kitchen, thankfully free of Englischers at the moment.

"Ach, wait. Do I need to pack us a picnic lunch?" Shanna hesitated, eyeing a plate of chocolate chip cookies that hadn't been bought yet. Matthew's favorite.

"Nein. We'll be back for supper. Besides, I'm sure Becky will bring something. She usually does."

A surge of jealousy raged through Shanna. Matthew would rather eat Becky's cooking? But he hadn't said that, exactly; only that she usually brought something.

"A couple of Cokes, then?" Shanna headed for the refrigerator.

Matthew didn't respond, so Shanna spun around and said, "Let me guess. Becky brings that, too?"

He smiled. "Jah. Or, if Jacob takes her to McDonald's, she brings cappuccinos. But they're usually cold by the time she delivers them to us at the pond."

Shanna wrinkled her nose and turned to Mamm, who counted out the money she'd made so far. "Bye, Mamm. Matthew says we're bringing supper home."

Mamm looked up with a smile. "Have fun. I already planned on coleslaw and hush puppies to go with the fish. Just as long as he cleans them first."

"Shanna will have to clean her own." Matthew winked at her, then opened the door just in time for Shanna to see a minivan pull to a stop outside. He headed for the far end of the porch and vaulted off, leaving her to walk down the steps and past the vehicle full of staring Englischers. She shuddered.

"Clean my own?" she called after him. "Wait just a second there, Matthew Yoder." She hurried after him to the barn. "Didn't I tell you that I don't know anything about fishing?"

He grabbed his pole, which had been leaning against the wall, and picked up his tackle box. A grin split his face. "Just teasing. I might clean your catch." He brushed past her. "If you ask nice enough."

"Ach, so you won't do it for me simply because I'm a girl? I have to ask 'nice enough'?"

"My sisters could always fillet fish with the best of them."

"Ach. Well, I'm not your sister."

Matthew turned and studied her. His slow perusal made her blood heat. "Jah. I'm aware of that."

His dimples flashed, which caused her to shiver.

Then, he spun around and set off in the direction of the pond.

She followed, daydreaming of kisses—lots of kisses—once they were out of view of the house.

Yet, after they'd rounded the corner of the barn and reached the top of the hill that led down to the pond, she saw Jacob's buggy, already waiting down by the water, with the horse tethered and left to graze. So much for enjoying a moment of privacy. She assumed that Becky had spread a blanket under a grove of trees and placed the picnic basket on top of it, though she wouldn't have packed a whole meal.

Sure enough, as they got closer to the pond, her prediction held true. Becky was seated on a blanket, reading a book. Jacob already had his line in the water.

As they came closer, Becky looked up and straightened her posture. "Hullo, Matthew. Hi, Shanna. Annie is here, too. She went into the woods to see if she could find any wild strawberries."

"Strawberry jam sounds gut." Shanna dropped down beside her.

Matthew stood there for a moment, holding the two rods and his fishing equipment, and frowned. "You're going to fish, ain't so?"

Shanna leaned forward and whispered something to Becky, and then they both laughed. She smiled up at him. "If I don't catch any fish, I won't have to clean any."

"There is that." He stared down at her. "But you'll miss all the fun."

His stomach rumbled, and he glanced at the picnic basket. Was it too early for a snack? From past experience, Matthew knew Becky had probably packed fresh fruit, some individual fruit pies, and maybe some cookies, plus a big thermos of something to drink, along with cups, or soda cans. Unless she'd brought coffee. He looked around but didn't see any of the brown cups from McDonald's. He breathed a sigh of relief. The fancy cappuccinos were much too sweet, and Becky never seemed to remember to get him a plain old coffee.

Giving in to temptation, he leaned over and opened the basket lid. Sure enough, there was a tin filled with cookies. He grabbed two and shut the lid. Becky grinned at him. "It's a new recipe. Cappuccino chocolate chip."

"Sounds gut. Danki." Matthew turned away and grimaced. He should have known she'd find some way to sneak her fancy coffee into the cookies.

"Let me know if you like them," she called after him.

He waved his hand in acknowledgment and headed toward the water's edge, where Jacob worked at landing a fish. A good-sized one, too. He hoped Shanna would decide to fish with him and not spend the whole time sitting with Becky.

He glanced back at Shanna. Then again, maybe she did need a girlfriend. To his knowledge, since she'd been home, she hadn't spent any time with friends, except for the night when Nate had come to take her out.

That still bothered him.

Trying to change the direction his thoughts were going in, he dropped the extra rod and his tackle box between him and Jacob, hooked on a lure, and flipped the pole back to cast out. As he went to flick it out into the water, something white fluttered over his head. A prayer kapp?

Shanna opened her eyes. She'd closed them when she'd seen the hook coming at her. Bad idea to try sneaking up on Matthew. She was immediately surrounded by a sea of faces, awash with shock and concern: Matthew, Becky, Jacob, the fish dangling from his line, and a dark-haired girl who looked a little familiar.

"The hook didn't scratch you, ain't so?" Matthew stepped closer and inspected her scalp.

She waved away his concern. "I have a hard head. And you aren't supposed to see me uncovered."

Matthew stared at her. "A little late to be worrying about that now. You had your hair down when you came home, and it's uncovered when you go to work every day."

"McDonald's." Jacob snapped his fingers. "That's where I know you from."

Becky grinned, then turned to the dark-haired girl, who held a small pail filled with wild strawberries. "Annie, you remember Shanna Stoltzfus, ain't so?"

"Jah." Annie smiled at Shanna, a little too sweetly. "You said you were leaving and never coming back. What are you doing here?"

The remark stung like a slap in the face. No way would she explain herself to Annie, though. She wouldn't tell her how her peers had gone to Mexico on a mission trip, but she hadn't saved enough money, and she'd come home as a last resort. And she definitely wouldn't admit that she didn't want to leave because Matthew was here. She bit her lip to keep from saying anything. Instead, she tilted her head and touched her hair, making sure it was secure.

"Young kinner often say things they don't mean," Becky said, smiling kindly. "We are glad she came back, whatever the reason."

"Jah. It doesn't matter. What does matter is that she's here." Matthew reeled in her prayer kapp, wrung it out, and handed it to her. "You have a little rip on it. Sorry. I didn't know you were right behind me."

"I thought I'd go ahead and let you teach me to fish." She shrugged. "I think I might enjoy it."

Matthew grinned. "Right. Rule number one: Never walk closely behind someone while he's casting. You might get hurt."

She laughed and fingered her wet kapp. "Lesson learned." She walked back to the quilt, hooked the kapp on a low branch of a tree to dry, and hurried back to Matthew.

He held out his arm. "Kum, and I'll teach you." When they reached the water's edge, he moved behind her and brought his rod around front, placing it in her hands and showing her how to hold it. Wanting to be closer to him, Shanna leaned back so that her shoulders touched his chest. She felt Matthew hesitate, and then he wrapped his arm around her, his muscles moving against her, and guided her through casting. Thankfully, fishing required minimal concentration, for Shanna could think of little else than how wonderful it felt to be this near to Matthew. After several minutes, she felt a tug on the line, and he guided her again through reeling in her catch.

She wasn't sure what kind of fish it was, but it didn't look too happy to be dangling there from the hook. She frowned at the fish. It seemed to frown at her. "Are we going to throw it back?"

"What would we do that for?" Matthew left the rod in her hands and came around in front of her. "You caught a gut-sized trout. Go ahead and take it off the hook."

"You want me to touch it?" Shanna shuddered. "But it's looking at me!"

"I thought nurses weren't squeamish."

"I'm not squeamish with humans. Fish that frown and stare are a different matter."

Laughing, Matthew took the pole from her and deftly removed the fish, tossing it into a cooler that Jacob must have brought. "Want to try again?"

Shanna waved her hand. "As fun as that was... well, maybe." She grinned at him.

"On your own this time. Last time, you held the pole, but I did all the work."

She blinked. "Ach, I'm not sure I'm ready for that. If I could hold the rod and watch once more...." *And have your arms around me again....* She didn't dare say that old loud. Much too bold, for one thing. And, considering their audience—she glanced in Annie's direction—she needed to guard her tongue. Why had Annie come, anyway? She wasn't fishing. She'd just collected strawberries, and now she sat beside Becky on the quilt.

Perhaps she was interested in Matthew.

Yet Matthew had made it more than clear he didn't have reciprocal feelings by inviting Shanna.

On second thought, had she invited herself? She tried to remember the conversation with Matthew but couldn't recall all the details.

Maybe she was the one intruding on a date. Maybe this was supposed to be a double date, and she was the third wheel.

She shook her head. She had no reason to expect Matthew to focus his attention exclusively on her. He was the one who'd stated that Shanna would marry him. Nein, Matthew wasn't interested in Annie.

Shanna smiled and allowed herself to relax against Matthew's chest as he again walked her through the steps of fishing.

"Matthew Yoder."

Shanna's spine stiffened at the sound of the deep voice, and she moved away from Matthew, though she was certain a fish was on the line.

Matthew glanced over his shoulder. "Hello, Bishop Sol." An interesting shade of red crept up his neck. He met Shanna's gaze briefly, then turned his attention to the line and whatever dangled at the end.

The bishop frowned and looked at Shanna. When his gaze fell on her uncovered head, his eyes widened.

Shanna's face heated. "My kapp got torn. And wet. And—"

The bishop waved his hand, cutting her off, as if her explanation didn't matter in the least.

"Dishonesty is a sin, Shanna Stoltzfus."

She drew back, shocked at the implication she was being untruthful. But it was probably better to be accused of lying than of purposefully inciting lust.

The bishop turned away and gestured with his arm. A young girl stepped into view. "Matthew, do you know my granddaughter, Ruth? We were driving by and saw you out here. Ruth loves to fish. Mind if she joins you?"

Ruth giggled.

Shanna studied her, trying to estimate her age. Sixteen, maybe. Kind of immature. Homely, really, but she knew that outward appearances weren't truly important. She fought a surge of jealousy. The bishop obviously didn't approve of her and had decided to push his granddaughter at Matthew. Ruth might be young, but Matthew would—should—act wisely and agree.

Matthew turned tortured eyes on Shanna, then glanced over at Jacob, who watched with an amused smirk on his face.

It was Annie who answered. "Jah, the more the merrier. Ain't so, Shanna?"

Had she imagined the censure in Annie's voice? And was there something going on between the still-giggling Ruth and tomato-red Matthew that she was clueless about?

Chapter 19

Matthew had managed to ignore Ruth's cow eyes and giggles the past several months. Yet, now that she'd chased Shanna away, off into the woods with Annie and Becky, he struggled to forgive her. Thankfully, Jacob's presence meant that they weren't totally alone.

At least Ruth knew how to fish. She used the pole he'd prepared for Shanna and never asked him to show her how to use it, though she still giggled too often. As in, every time she glanced at him, which was every other second.

Obviously, Ruth had a schoolgirl crush on him. It made him uncomfortable. She couldn't be more than sixteen. Much too young for him.

He eyed the strands of strawberry blonde hair that had escaped her kapp, and the small, square glasses that framed her brown eyes. He supposed she might be cute, in a girl-next-door sort of way.

Yet she was nowhere near as appealing as Shanna.

Jacob leaned close. "She likes you."

As if he didn't know. Matthew glared at Jacob, who chuckled.

At least Jacob didn't start teasing him about it. Or about Shanna. Matthew was pretty sure his affections for her were crystal clear. In fact, he knew they were. Levi and Joseph had realized his interest almost immediately, and Jacob knew him even better than they did.

Would it be acceptable for him to leave Ruth to her fishing and follow Shanna and the other girls into the woods to look for strawberries? He liked the fruit, and Shanna had said something about making jam if they gathered enough.

The thought of homemade jam made his mouth water and his stomach rumble again. He set his fishing pole down and headed for the picnic basket.

Then, he heard footsteps behind him. Ruth. "I'll be at the singing tomorrow nacht, Matthew."

Ignoring her, he knelt down on the blanket and opened the lid of the picnic basket.

"Will you be there?" She tilted her head and batted her eyelashes.

He pulled out a couple of Cokes. "Want one?"

"Jah. Danki." She took it from him. "Will you be there?" she asked again.

He reached back inside the basket to find whatever goodies Becky had brought besides the cookies. Individual fried pies. Apple, probably. He held one up to offer it to Ruth, but she smiled and shook her head.

He shrugged. "I'm not sure yet."

He'd asked Shanna to ride home with him if she decided to go. She'd accepted, but that had been before their "breakup." She'd apologized, though, and the way she'd encouraged him today, welcoming his closeness as he taught her to fish, he was pretty sure that conflict was far behind them. He didn't want to ask her about it, though, for fear of triggering an adverse reaction.

He settled down on the blanket and unwrapped the clear plastic wrap from around the pie.

Ruth sat down next to him and popped open her Coke can. "I'll be at the singing."

As if he hadn't heard her the first time. "I'm glad. Maybe someone will offer to take you home." He tried to let her down gently. Could she really be that clueless?

She giggled.

His heart sank. She probably hoped he was hinting at himself. But he couldn't take her home; not when he had his eyes on someone else. He couldn't tell her who, though. That would be completely unacceptable.

"Ruth, I—"

Shanna came out of the woods, followed by Becky and Annie. He was ashamed to realize that he hoped she'd feel a little jealous.

Forgive me, Lord. Keep my thoughts in line.

He did want Shanna for his frau, but that would be up to the Lord. As much as he disliked the possibility, God might have someone else in mind for him.

Ach, Shanna.

As if she could read his thoughts, she met his gaze and winked. Ever so bold. Beside him, Ruth gasped. She'd noticed it, too. And she would probably report it to her grossdaedi, the bishop. He hated the idea of Shanna getting into even more trouble than she would when word of their not-so-private cuddling while fishing and the absence of her head covering made it back to Levi.

What would he have to say about it? Shanna was still in her rumschpringe, so the kapp might not even rank as an important topic. But a public display of affection?

Jah, that would be discussed, with him and Shanna alike.

Ruth had seen it, too, and yet she persisted in making her interest known to him. Maybe their actions hadn't been as obviously affectionate as he'd thought. Either that, or Ruth was as dull as a fence post.

After another moment of deliberation, Matthew caught Shanna's attention and winked back. There. The damage was done. Anybody who was watching would know that he cared for Shanna Stoltzfus.

Shanna approached the blanket with a mischievous smile, which faded immediately when a strange musical sound broke the silence. She pulled her cell phone out of her apron pocket. Time seemed to freeze as she glanced at it, then abruptly pivoted and headed in the opposite direction, pressing the phone to her ear.

Memories of the last time Matthew had seen her answer her cell phone surfaced. *Nate.*

Ruth touched his hand ever so lightly, but it was enough to draw his attention away from Shanna. She looked up at him, her eyes wide and filled with expectation. Had she said something while he'd been lost in his thoughts?

He furrowed his brow. "Uh, jah?"

He'd meant it as a question. But, judging by the way her plain face brightened, she'd taken it as an answer.

What had he gotten himself into?

Shanna trudged up the hill as she listened to Nate ramble on.

"I'm so sorry, Shanna. Really. Let me make it up to you. If you're free tonight, I could take you to dinner and a movie."

Translation: Another movie he didn't want to see by himself was playing. If she agreed to accompany him to a film that would either bore or scare her, she'd be rewarded with dinner, a big bucket of buttery popcorn, and an icy-cold Coke.

"I'll even let you pick out the movie."

Wow. She hadn't expected that. "I have no idea what's playing, Nate, and tomorrow is a church Sunday."

He was quiet a moment. "Church Sunday? Well, you can sleep in if you get in too late. Not a big deal, right? You missed church a lot last semester."

Shanna winced. He was right. She'd have to do better.

Nate cleared his throat. "I have some ideas. The downtown theater has a movie playing I want to see, and it's only there through tonight. Tomorrow, they have something new starting, and...."

Miss church? While living under her daed's roof? Ach, he'd have plenty to say about that. And besides, she'd kind of looked forward to walking in with the other maidels and seeing the young men gathered by the doors, watching them.

Matthew would be among them.

Would his eyes be on her?

She shivered with anticipation.

"Shanna? Are you listening, or what? Will you go out with me?"

She should say no. A super-firm, I-mean-it "No" that he wouldn't dare question. Especially after his shenanigans the other night. Had he actually messed with his car on purpose so it would break down, as Daed had so vehemently insisted he had?

Maybe she shouldn't take Daed's word for it. Shouldn't Nate be allowed to speak for himself? Maybe it had been an accident. Maybe all of it had been. And Matthew had no claim on her. He was free to court whomever he pleased. Even Ruth. She glanced back at them, sitting there on the blanket, talking and looking so cozy. She and Matthew had made no promises to each other.

"You're going to marry me."

Ach! She had to quit thinking about that. It would drive her insane. Degree or not, she wanted Matthew to whisk her off to the bishop and be published. But that would never happen unless she joined the church.

And that could never happen if she was away at school.

"It's all pride."

Daed's statement from the night of their big argument pricked her memory. Maybe it was pride that had kept her going during the first semester of nursing school, as she'd striven to prove she had what it took to be accepted into the LPN program. Failing hadn't been an option. Maybe it was pride that had driven her during eleven months of nonstop classes and then the requisite on-the-job training. Pride that had earned her a spot in RN school. Now she had only a semester to go to earn her RN designation, followed by a semester of clinicals. She couldn't quit now.

You're too proud. The condemning words whispered into her thoughts again, sounding exactly like Daed.

Shanna dipped her head. As much as she liked Matthew, she had to explore her own options, and let him explore his.

"Shanna?" Nate was beginning to sound impatient. "I'll pick you up in an hour."

"Wait—"

But he'd already hung up. She tried calling him back, but she was directed straight to his voice mail. She didn't leave a message.

It didn't matter. Shanna straightened her spine. She'd go out with Nate and give him the opportunity to explain what had happened the other night.

If he would be there in an hour, she needed to head back to the house and start getting ready. Maybe Matthew would still be fishing when Nate arrived, so he wouldn't see her leave with him. He might think she'd been called to come in to work. She could take the car and meet Nate somewhere.

Dishonesty.

Pain knifed her conscience. *Ach, Lord.* She wasn't worthy to wipe the dust off of the sandals of the Almighty. Not to mention waste His time with her prayers.

"All our righteousnesses are as filthy rags."

Did He hear the prayers of people like her? Ach, but she wished He did. She had so much to repent of.

A kneeling confession…she couldn't think of that now.

Shanna turned and hurried down the hill to the tree where her kapp hung. She snatched it off the branch. It was dry and stiff. She dangled it in one hand and, with the other, reached to pull the bobby pins from her hair. Too bad she didn't have time to wash it. A good brushing would have to do. "I have to go," she said to Matthew. "I got a call…."

She didn't say who had called, but it didn't seem to matter. Matthew's eyes widened as her hair tumbled loosely around her shoulders—after she'd said it was improper for him to see it uncovered! Too bad she'd strayed so far from the church, and for so long, that she'd forgotten. Ruth clasped a hand over her mouth, probably in shock at seeing Shanna release her hair in front of an unmarried man. Two of them, in fact. She felt a pang of regret for making things harder for Matthew. News of her impropriety would surely reach the bishop.

It all would reach him. Everything she'd done today would be brought up and scrutinized. And that would open the door to a discussion about her past. Her disobedience, her every transgression, would be made public. She'd be the subject of local gossip once again, and not just because she'd come home for the summer.

It was a blessing that no one else but Matthew knew about *the kiss*. Ach, she'd be raked over the coals for that.

So bold. So blatant. So...beautiful.

Shanna didn't glance at the others in their fishing party. She turned and ran up the hill, her steps faltering when Becky called after her, "We'll be going in to McDonald's later for koffee. We'll see you there, ain't so?"

Matthew jumped up and started to follow Shanna, but Jacob's hand on his arm stayed him. "Let her go. We'll see her later when we go into town."

"She must have been called in to work. I hate that they take advantage of her like that. She worked this morning. It isn't right."

Ruth drained her soda can. "Let's get back to fishing so you can have that fish you said you promised the Stoltzfuses for dinner tonight. We have only three so far, ain't so?"

Jacob shook his head. "Six now, but it's not enough for three different families. Let's give it another hour, then I'll take Bex into town. Matthew, too, and anyone else who wants to go." His gaze fell on Annie and Ruth.

Matthew didn't answer. He picked up his pole, memories of Shanna coloring his every movement. He probably shouldn't have held her like he had. They'd be in trouble, for sure. Not only that, but he doubted he'd ever fish again without remembering the feel of her in his arms.

And they were going into town for coffee? He'd put his foot down and order a plain, simple drink, not one of those fancy ones that Becky liked, full of fake sweetener and topped with whipped cream and elaborate drizzles. Not as the good Lord intended. Maybe if Shanna filled their orders, she would remember his preference.

Still, he hated that she'd left them for work. Couldn't she have said nein, she had plans? After all, they'd been on a date, of sorts.

Leaving a date to go to work. Who did that?

Should he be concerned about the message that sent him about her priorities?

About an hour later, Matthew delivered the cleaned, filleted fish to Deborah, then went upstairs to shower and change before meeting Jacob and Becky for the ride into town. Annie had said she'd go along, but Ruth needed to check with her grandparents. They'd probably agree, which meant Matthew would be stuck in the narrow backseat with a maidel on either side of him. And neither one the girl of his dreams.

Before leaving the house, he stopped in the kitchen and found Deborah. "I'll be home after a while, but it might be a little late. Save me some dinner, please."

"Jah. Where'd Shanna take off to?" She studied him.

Matthew shrugged. "Work. She said she had to go."

"Work, you say?" Her eyes narrowed. "She went running down the lane in tight blue jeans and a white shirt. Not her work clothes. Someone picked her up out by the mailbox."

Shanna hadn't ditched him to work but to go out with another man. Matthew's heart sank as he mentally went over the list of possibilities. It was a short one. In fact, Matthew was almost certain there was only one name on that list.

An Englischer.

Nate.

He felt as if his heart had cracked right down the middle. He didn't want to decipher the nonverbal message Shanna had just sent him. It'd be too painful. Even more so than going into town with absolutely no hope that she'd be there.

But it didn't matter. If she'd had more than a whisper of feelings for him, she would have remained with him at the pond. Apparently, he was no more than a plaything. Someone to amuse her when no one else was around.

He'd hoped for so much more.

Seeing Jacob's buggy coming around the bend, Matthew forced a smile. No point in letting everyone know about this latest heartbreak. He'd go and have fun with his friends.

He was done being Shanna's toy. He wouldn't make the same mistake again.

Never again.

Chapter 20

When the house lights turned on at the end of the movie, Shanna handed the empty popcorn bucket back to Nate and looked around the ancient theater. Not too many people were there; just a handful, really. They'd seen the film Nate had been interested in. She wished she'd insisted on something else. Some of the images...her face heated. She picked up her Coke, stood up, and followed Nate down the row of seats toward the aisle, passing another couple that remained seated, watching the credits. As they made their way up the aisle, he turned to her. "Do you want to stop at Starbucks on the way home?"

"No. Thanks, anyway. I'm tired, and I want to go to church with my family tomorrow." Besides, she probably needed to apologize to Matthew. Again. If he'd gone into town with Jacob and the others for coffee, he would have realized she wasn't working.

She didn't want to imagine what his thoughts must be. She was a world-class fool.

He probably would have checked behind the barn when he got home from fishing to see if her car was there. And he would have found it, undisturbed.

She remained deep in thought as they walked to the car. She'd ditched her outing with Matthew, and for what? Weak excuses from Nate. A movie she'd hated. Seriously. It was worse than the first one. And dinner had been disappointing, as well: intolerably spicy dishes at a Chinese buffet. Maybe she should have insisted on the food court. At least there would have been a variety of options to choose from.

Maybe she was a high-maintenance drama queen, as a former college roommate had once called her. She tried to focus on the positive. She'd managed to find a few items on the buffet that she'd moderately enjoyed, and several scenes in the movie had been good.

Okay. Time to stop being dishonest, even with herself. She wanted to be with Matthew. She loved him. And an unpalatable buffet dinner and a terrible movie would have been so much better in his company.

She would never see a movie with Matthew, though. He'd already joined the church. Made the kneeling confession. Not that giving up movies would be a big loss. She'd never been really into them, anyway, always preferring to spend her free time curled up with a good book. It was much easier on her budget, too, and much more pleasant to be entertained by the written word.

Ach, she hoped he'd forgive her for running off on him to be with Nate.

Nate started the car. Seconds later, he pointed at his dash. "I need to stop at home. My oil light is on." He looked at Shanna. "Want to come in for a bit? I'll make some hot chocolate." He flipped on his turn signal, then merged into the left lane.

Shanna's heartbeat doubled with dread. Was this a repeat of the attempt he'd made the last time she'd been at his house? She wouldn't fall for the same trick twice. "Uh, no, thanks. I'll wait in the car. Um, actually, why don't you stop at the gas station and pick up some oil?"

"I already have a bottle, but it's at home. Won't take long."

She watched the traffic as they drove through the city. Soon, they turned onto the street where Nate lived with his roommates. It was dark, with no street-lights. Not too far from their college. He'd thought it'd be cheaper to commute than to pay room and board. It probably was, but she'd been more comfortable with the communal living in the dorms. Maybe because of her upbringing in a close, cloistered community.

Nate turned the car into his driveway. "You sure you don't want to come in?"

She hunkered down in her seat. "No. I'm staying right here."

He shrugged. "Suit yourself. I'll be out in a few." He got out of the car, shut his door, and headed for the house. When he opened the back door, a shaft of light flickered across the driveway for a moment, then disappeared when he shut the door.

A few minutes later, the outside light came on, and Nate sauntered back out, holding a couple of plastic bottles. He set them down in front of the car, then opened the driver door and reached under the dash to pop open the hood. "Be done in a jiffy." He slammed the door and went back around front, but she couldn't see what he was doing under the hood.

A few minutes later, the hood slammed shut. The whole car shook with the force. Shanna watched Nate carry the plastic bottles across the driveway and dump them in a trash barrel next to the back door.

"Done!" he said as he slid back into the driver seat. "We'll be on our way in no time." He grinned at her. "Sure you don't want to stop for coffee?"

She hesitated. At work, she was permitted to drink all the coffee she wanted, but it had been a

while since she'd tasted some of Starbucks' special-
ty drinks. "Maybe an iced latte. That sounds good.
Thanks."

"No problem." He inserted the key in the ignition
and turned it. A weird sort of scratching sound came
from the engine.

"Hmm. That doesn't sound good. My battery must
be dead again, but my roommate isn't here to give it a
jump. I probably need a new one. Too bad. Come on in,
Shanna, while we wait for Tom to get back."

Shanna scooted closer to the passenger door
and tried to think. She wished there was someone
she could call to come and pick her up. Daed might
be willing to call a driver to pick her up, but he didn't
carry a cell phone. Matthew carried a phone, but
she didn't have his number. None of her close friends
would be in town. The medical mission trip in Mexico
was supposed to last most of the summer.

She should be with them. But she wasn't close
enough to the Lord to serve as a missionary, anyway.
The Almighty must have recognized that. She should
have known better than to expect to go. He'd closed
that door, good and hard. Slammed it, really.

Lord, help me think.

Shanna pulled her cell phone out of her pocket
and fingered it. Joseph had one. She'd almost forgotten. And she'd entered his number months ago. She
found his entry on her contact list, pressed "send,"
and held the phone to her ear.

"Aw, Shanna, you don't need to call anyone. I'm
sure Tom will be here in no time. Come on in. We can
watch TV, and I'll make some hot chocolate. He'll be
back before you know it."

She ignored him. Four rings. Finally, her brother's voice came on the line. "Joe speaking."

Joe? Shanna had never heard her brother go by a nickname. "Hey. It's Shanna. Can you ask Daed to call a driver for me?"

There was a long pause. "Shanna. I'm, uh, not at home. Why don't you call Daed?"

"He doesn't have a phone!"

Joseph chuckled. "Ach, Shanna. So much you don't know. Daed carries one. Business related. Let me text you the number."

She ended the call. Seconds later, her phone made a sound to alert her that a text message had arrived. She hated having to call Daed and ask for his help after he'd warned her and she hadn't listened. She'd gotten herself into this scrape, but she'd need his help to get out of it. No choice but to call and ask him to rescue her.

"Don't come crying to me...."

His words thundered through her mind.

Maybe it wouldn't be so bad to go inside with Nate and wait. Drinking hot chocolate beat having to eat humble pie, for sure.

"When do you expect Tom to get back?" She looked up at Nate.

He leaned back, a satisfied expression settling on his face. "Oh, hard to say. An hour, give or take." He shrugged.

Something about his smirk bothered her enough that she opened her phone again. And dialed Daed's number.

Matthew had just settled into a chair in the living room with the family for evening devotions when a strange ring broke the silence. Levi stood and reached into one of his pockets, his face flushing. Phone calls were certainly a rare occurrence at the Stoltzfus house.

"Usually leave this thing in the office," Levi muttered. "Don't recognize the number." He frowned, studied the phone for a moment, then pressed a button. "Levi Stoltzfus." He fell silent, presumably listening to the caller, and then nodded. "If you feel uncomfortable, you did right to call. I'll see if Tony is free. You stay put." He listened for a second more before snapping the phone shut and glancing at Deborah. Seconds later, his gaze moved to Matthew. "That was Shanna. I need to call a driver. She went into the city with Nate, and he's having car trouble again. Honestly, that girl." He shook his head and stormed out to the kitchen.

Matthew's heart lurched, and he jumped to his feet, adrenaline pumping through his body. Nate was really trying the same trick again? This Englisch boyfriend of Shanna's was enough to make Matthew forget that he was a pacifist, and then he'd have to make a kneeling confession before the bishop. It was good Nate wasn't in the room right now. He wouldn't be left standing. And, judging by the anger radiating from Levi, he might have done something to require a kneeling confession of his own.

Levi turned around in the doorway and faced Matthew. "He'll be here in about ten minutes. Matthew, do you want to go?"

He hesitated, deliberating over his decision. She'd dumped him for Nate, but now, she was in trouble. If he truly cared for her, there was no choice to be made, really. Even though he'd vowed never to be used by her again.

He drew in a deep, shuddering breath. "I'll go." The words left a lump in his throat. He didn't feel at all at peace with his decision, but he needed to have a talk with her. Clarify where they stood with each other. And make it clear that if she wanted to be with him, then Nate would be ancient history.

Levi gave him a concerned look, as if he was worried Shanna might have pushed Matthew too far. And she had. The Bible story of Hosea going to rescue his prostitute wife from the auction block crossed Matthew's mind.

"We'll have time for devotions before Tony gets here." Levi slid his phone back into his pocket, then returned to his seat beside the table where the big family Bible lay. He sat down, opened the Book, and started to read the German text. From the book of Hosea. Levi must have been struck by the parallels, too.

When he finished reading, he shut the Bible, and they all closed their eyes for a silent prayer. Matthew's bolted open again when a bright light lit the room. Headlights shone through the window.

He shot a glance at Levi, whose eyelids fluttered open. The older man nodded subtly before closing his eyes again. Matthew got up and left the room quietly. As he slipped into his shoes, he breathed a silent prayer that God would go with him to guard his words and his actions—and his heart.

"Oh, come on, Shanna. You know I won't hurt you. Call your dad back and tell him to forget it. You can wait until Tom gets back and jump-starts my car. Church is no big deal. You hardly ever go when you're at school." Nate put his left arm on the steering wheel in a relaxed stance. "Come on inside. I don't know why you have to be such a prude."

"I can't help it, Nate. I guess a prude is what I am. And Daed's already called for a driver." She couldn't believe he'd done so without taking the time to lecture her about her poor choices. Of course, that discussion would probably happen when they got home. She'd hear another version of the "Why don't you listen to me?" talk Daed was so good at giving. Like he was the be-all and end-all of knowledge. Well, come right down to it, he was usually right. Why couldn't she listen to him?

She sighed. It probably boiled down to pride, just as Daed had told her.

Nate tried a few more times to convince her to come inside. When she steadfastly refused, he called her a few choice words, further opening her eyes to his character, before jumping out of the car, slamming the door behind him, and disappearing inside the house once more.

Shanna sat in the darkness with nothing but her thoughts and the shadows to keep her company. She mulled over what Daed had accused Nate of the last time. After a few minutes, she leaned over and popped the hood open. Then, she got out of the car and lifted the hood, propping it on its support. Nate had left the outside light on, and she was able to make out the battery. It had been disconnected. Evidence seen with her own eyes. Why hadn't she believed Daed in the first place?

Fury, fast and hot, overtook her, and she started for the house, prepared to give Nate a piece of her mind. She'd barely taken two steps when her foot touched something, and she stumbled. She shrieked before looking down. A cat. A silly cat. She picked it up, cuddling it in her arms. Just then, the door burst open, and Nate strode out.

"You okay? Thought I heard a scream."

"The cat scared me." Scared the anger right out of her. She tried to find the remnants of it. "And I just checked under your hood. Your battery was disconnected! I can't believe you did that. Everything my daed said about you was true." To her dismay, tears burned her eyes. She refused to cry now.

"Aw, Shanna. You're so lovely. I want you, but you seem happy just being friends. How else am I supposed to make you see me as more than just a friend?"

"Definitely not by lying to me or tricking me. Wrong move, Nate."

He stepped forward and took the cat out of her arms, dropping it on the ground. It landed on all fours with a hiss and a swish of its tail. Ignoring the animal, Nate grasped Shanna by her upper arms, yanking her to him. His mouth searched for hers and landed with a hard kiss.

Shanna jerked away, resisting the urge to slap him. "Leave me alone, Nate! I don't want to see you again. Ever." She stomped down the driveway, hesitated a moment, and set off down the sidewalk toward a gas station.

Nate shouted a few uncomplimentary names after her, but he didn't follow her, thankfully.

Shanna fought down mounting fear as she walked toward the gas station. Gangs roamed these streets, and the news often reported murders and rapes and other bad things happening in this area.

She kept imagining she heard footsteps, but whenever she checked behind her, she saw no one.

Still, Shanna was almost running by the time she reached the relative safety of the convenience store, praying that it wouldn't be robbed by an armed gunman while she was there. That would be the last straw. It was a good thing she didn't have any money to be relieved of.

A bunch of young men stood under a burned-out streetlight at the edge of the parking lot, and some teens were smoking, laughing, and pushing each other in front of the door. They parted down the middle for her to dart through.

"Where's the fire?" one of them asked. The others snickered.

Inside the store, Shanna skidded to a stop in front of the desk and pressed her palms against the counter as she gasped for breath. The clerk stared at her for a moment, then looked over her shoulder. "Are you being followed?"

Shanna turned around and saw a creepy-looking man whose arms were covered in tattoos enter the store. He strolled past her to the cooler in the corner, pulled out a quart of milk, and carried it to the counter, where he set it down while Shanna backed away. "Just need some milk for the kid." He slapped some cash down and looked at Shanna. "Haven't seen you in here before."

She shook her head.

The man shrugged, took his change and the milk, and walked out.

"It's going down tonight," said one of the guys gathered outside the open doors.

Shanna turned and met the clerk's eyes. "You're not being robbed, are you?"

Chapter 21

Matthew took in their surroundings as Tony pulled the minivan into a driveway. The headlights flashed on the faded numbers hanging from the beat-up black mailbox, then on Nate's old blue Chevy. But Matthew didn't see any sign of Shanna inside. He was glad Levi had decided to come along.

When Tony stopped the van, Matthew and Levi scrambled out the door and up the driveway. Matthew was first to reach the faded brown front door. He raised his hand and gave it a sharp rap.

Moths and other ugly-looking insects flew around the dim light. With his other hand, he swatted them away from his face. Finally, after what seemed like forever, the door opened to reveal Nate, his brown hair tousled, his shirt untucked and unbuttoned. Matthew hated the idea of Shanna sitting in his house with him in this state. What could it mean? He didn't want to think about it.

Nate smirked as he studied him and Levi. "May I help you?"

"We've come for Shanna."

"Yeah, so? What makes you think she's here?"

"Where is she?" Matthew growled.

Nate shrugged. "You expect me to know?"

Levi stepped forward. "She gave me this address, and I told her to stay put."

Nate chuckled mockingly. "When have you ever known her to listen?"

Sorely tempted to grab Nate by his shirt collar and jerk him around, Matthew glanced at Levi. Violence was not their way. He sucked in a breath and forced himself to calm down. "Listen, we came for Shanna, and we aren't leaving without her."

"You the boyfriend? The one she dumped for me?" Nate sneered. "Not just a boarder, huh? I don't know where she is, okay?"

"Do you need some help jogging your memory?" Matthew balled his fist. Ach, the temptation.

Lord, please let him tell us what he knows.

Nate's shoulders slumped, and his head dipped. Maybe it was because of the two Amish men standing there motionless, the implied threat, or the Lord's hand; or a combination of the three, but he finally yielded. "Okay, okay! I don't know where she is. My battery wouldn't turn over and she got all drama queen on me and took off. I don't know what her problem is."

"Which way did she go?" Matthew resisted the urge to shake him.

Nate raised a trembling hand. "Um. That way. Probably went to the convenience store."

"Right." Matthew stepped away. "She'd better be there."

"Hey, she's not my responsibility." Nate backed up and grasped the doorknob. "If she isn't there, don't go blaming me." He slammed the door shut.

After what seemed like hours, a white minivan pulled into the parking lot. Shanna hesitated a moment to make sure she knew the driver. It was Tony, so she hurried outside. She'd been so distracted by the possibility of witnessing a robbery right before her eyes, she'd forgotten to call Daed to tell him that she'd left Nate's. Fortunately, there hadn't been a robbery, but her nerves were still overworked.

The front passenger door opened, and Daed got out. He looked completely haggard. "I'm trusting this won't happen again, daughter."

She shook her head. "I'm never talking to Nate again. It was awful. Daed, you were so right. I should have listened to you." It almost hurt her throat to confess that. She wished she could throw herself into her father's arms for a hug, as she used to when she was little. She could imagine his reaction, though. They hadn't embraced in years.

Daed's frown deepened. "You made a foolish mistake. You weren't hurt, were you?" Concern flashed across his face. "He didn't—" He blushed.

"Nein." Shanna sucked in a sharp breath. She'd been hurt, but not in the way he meant. Emotionally rather than physically. This was betrayal, the deepest sort of hurt.

She pulled the sliding door open and hesitated. Matthew sat there, hunched forward, his hands clasped between his knees. He met her gaze, his eyes full of pain, and then he frowned and looked away. Shanna's heart collapsed. Perhaps he and Daed did have a sense of what she was going through. She slid into the middle passenger seat and finally found her voice again. "Danki for coming for me."

She wished she could curl up against Matthew's side and soak up some strength. Hers seemed all but depleted after this evening. If the convenience store had been robbed while she'd been there, she probably would have been curled up on the floor in a fetal position, whimpering and not moving. Or maybe she would have taken on the robber single-handedly. She'd surprised herself by standing up to Nate as she had.

She glanced at the silent man sitting beside her. Rock solid. Dependable. Strong. Dedicated to the Lord. Jah, she loved him. Wanted a life with him—someday. She shifted a tiny bit closer to him, but he moved the same distance in the opposite direction. She sighed. She'd hoped Matthew would be willing to go on a long walk down the lane after they got home so they could talk. She needed to be with him. To explain. Beg his forgiveness. She'd grovel, if need be.

The van door slid shut, and Daed climbed back into the front seat next to Tony. Moments later, they merged onto the highway.

Tears slid down Shanna's cheeks. At least the darkness would prevent anyone from witnessing her humiliation. Except for the man sitting beside her. The one ignoring her. She decided that her tears could wait. A good meltdown would be beneficial, but not until she was alone. Would Daed allow Tony to stop for some ice cream? A pint of chocolate would go a long way toward making her feel better.

She leaned forward. "Tony? Do you mind stopping by a grocery store? I *need* ice cream."

Daed chuckled.

She jolted her head back in surprise. Daed was laughing?

Tony glanced at her in the rearview mirror. "Would the one in Seymour do? Or do you need it right now?"

"Seymour will be fine." Now would be better, but she leaned back, content to wait. "Danki."

"Ice cream?" Matthew whispered. His eyebrows rose.

"Comfort food."

"And a spoon, jah?"

Was he really joking with her? Perhaps all wasn't lost with him. She grinned. "Maybe two."

He didn't answer.

Fifty minutes later, after a quick trip to the store, the van pulled into the circular drive outside the house and stopped. Daed handed Tony some cash and said something to him. Shanna glanced outside and saw that all the windows were dark. Everyone must have gone to bed. Matthew slid his door open and climbed out of the van, then came around to her side to help her out.

She searched his face, but it still seemed as if it were set in granite. A muscle flickered in his jaw. Shanna lowered her eyes, grasped the plastic bag that held her ice cream, and hopped out. She started for the barn but stopped when she felt a touch on her elbow.

Daed stared down at her, silent, as Tony drove off. His eyes glistened. A moment later, he pulled her against him. His face was damp with moisture when he pressed his cheek against hers. But he quickly released her and turned away without a word.

"Daed?" Shanna blinked at the tears burning her eyes. "Ich liebe dich."

He glanced over his shoulder. "Ich liebe dich, too, Shanna." His voice was gentle. "Gut nacht."

Matthew stood and watched Levi head inside. He wished he dared to tell Shanna everything that was on his mind. Wished he dared to embrace her like Levi had. If he pulled her into his arms, though, he might never let her go.

There was too much to resolve before that could happen.

By his going inside, it seemed that Levi had left the lecture to Matthew. Not something he looked forward to. He took a few deep breaths. "We need to talk."

She looked up at him, crinkling the plastic grocery bag in her hands. "I'm sorry, Matthew. And, jah, we need to talk. Let me put this ice cream in the freezer so it doesn't melt. Unless you would rather sit at the table and eat it while we talk...?" Her voice brightened.

"If we talk in the kitchen, we're sure to be overheard." Matthew preferred privacy. "The ice cream can wait."

"I could grab a couple of spoons and take it back to my apartment."

That kind of privacy he didn't need. Too much temptation. Matthew shook his head. "Let's walk."

He waited on the porch while she hurried inside, then returned moments later without the bag. They descended the porch steps and started toward the road. "You can go first," he suggested. If she had second thoughts about him, he needed to know right away. And, if she told him she did, she'd get to her ice cream a lot faster, because they'd have nothing left to discuss.

She sucked in a breath. "Nate called and asked me if I wanted to see a movie. I didn't want to, I don't care about them at all, but I did want to find out whether Daed's suspicions that he'd rigged his car to break down were valid. I wanted to ask him."

She'd abandoned him to ask Nate a question? "You couldn't ask over the phone?"

"I needed to be able to see his facial expression to know whether I could believe him. He was my friend." Shanna's voice cracked. "Past tense. I don't know if I can call him a friend now, and that bothers me more than anything. And to think I hurt you for this...I'm so sorry."

"You ran out on our date for another man." Even he could hear the hurt in his voice.

She raised her head, and, in the light of the moon, he saw surprise flitter across her face. "A date? I didn't know it was a date. It was an uneven pairing and...and I couldn't remember if I'd invited myself, or if you'd invited me. I thought maybe I was interrupting your date with Annie Beiler."

Maybe he hadn't been as clear as he'd thought. He shuddered. "With Annie? Nein. She invited herself along when Becky mentioned it to her. She's nice enough, I guess, but she's sort of scary. Not for me. And, before you ask, neither is Ruth."

"Who is for you?" Her tone said she was teasing, with a hint of laughter, but there was an undercurrent of uncertainty.

He frowned. He couldn't answer her, not until they'd finished the rest of their discussion. "If I'm courting someone, I expect it to be exclusive—as in, all other previous relationships are history. And stay that way."

"Jah."

He heard disappointment. Did she think he was ending the relationship? Or was it that she couldn't promise exclusivity? She fell silent.

"Care to commit, Shanna Stoltzfus?" he asked after a long stretch of quiet.

She kicked something in the road. He heard it clatter against the ground. A soda can, maybe. "I still have some reservations."

Reservations? His heart felt as battered as the pop can.

"Not about you."

They'd already discussed that. Matthew frowned. "The Ordnung."

"Nein, my nursing degree. It might be about pride, but I do want to earn it. If I came back here as a midwife, I'd want to have all the training I could get to do the job right. I'm also not sure the bishop will permit me to return. You saw how he looked at me. He accused me of lying without even bothering to verify whether I'd told the truth, which I had."

He sympathized with her. After all, it seemed he had some explaining of his own to do. The bishop had seen him cuddling with Shanna in public, not to mention driving her car.

"Would you return if he let you?" A hard question, but he needed to know. If she said nein, he'd need to decide if he was willing to leave the Amish for her.

"Would you leave if he didn't?" She kicked the can again.

Matthew closed his eyes and considered it. Since he'd already joined the church, if he left, he'd be shunned. But he doubted that would harm his relationship with his family. Daed's sister had been shunned, and Daed still welcomed her into their home whenever she visited. He'd be afforded the same grace. But could Matthew abandon his beliefs? His current relationship with God? He knew that some

Englischers professed belief in the Lord, but this faith was all he knew, and he didn't want to lose his Savior.

"Never mind. That wasn't fair of me to ask." The can clattered in the road again. "Ich liebe dich, Matthew, and I want to come home to this community. After I get my degree, though."

His heart lightened. She loved him? He couldn't control his grin. "Which will be when?"

"December. But I'll graduate in May. Next year."

He reached for her hand, curling his fingers around hers. He didn't want to wait that long for her, but he would if he had to. If only they could work it out so that she could have the best of both worlds. He had to try. "I'll talk to the bishop."

"About what?"

"About what it'll take to get you home. Sooner, rather than later." He stopped and pulled her against him in a hug. "I'm so glad you weren't hurt, Shanna. Please, don't ever do this again."

"I won't." She wrapped her arms around his neck. "But really, you shouldn't waste your time talking to the bishop. I'm not ready to kneel and confess. I want my degree, and that's still frowned upon." She snuggled closer as her eyes drifted to his mouth and lingered there. The air between them sizzled.

Matthew caught his breath, and his gaze dropped to her lips. He immediately forced his eyes up to meet hers. "I'm not going to kiss you again, so don't look at me like that." He didn't dare. Not now.

"But you want to."

"But I won't."

She leaned in a centimeter closer.

He released her and backed away. "I can't wait till we get married."

"But you haven't asked me to marry you, Matthew Yoder. You just assume I will. What if I won't?"

Matthew smiled. "You will. Might as well get that into your head right now, Shanna Stoltzfus."

"Are you sure?" she teased him.

"Jah, I'm sure. You wait and see." He touched her nose. "I'd best be getting you back so you can eat that ice cream."

"You sure you don't want to make out first?"

Ach, he wanted to. "Nein."

"Why not?"

"Because it'd be about me being an ice cream substitute."

"I can't think of a better one."

He laughed and elbowed her playfully in the side. "Kum on. Let's go." He grasped her hand in his, and they began retracing their steps. They'd barely reached the turnoff to the driveway when they heard the clip-clop of horse hooves and the crunch of buggy wheels over gravel.

Matthew glanced over his shoulder and lifted a hand to wave to whoever was driving by.

The bishop.

Chapter 22

When the Sunday preaching service ended, Shanna trailed out of the barn after the rest of the women and went to help set up the cold meal on the tables. She tingled as she remembered the awareness of Matthew's gaze on her when she'd walked into the church service with the other maidels. She hadn't dared to look at him, knowing she'd blush. Instead, she'd shyly dipped her head and focused her gaze on the ground.

Throughout the service, she'd struggled to keep her attention on the messages by the different preachers. It'd been so long since she'd listened to High German that her mind wouldn't cooperate. Instead, her thoughts had wandered over to the opposite side of the barn, where Matthew sat with the other unmarried men, next to his friend Jacob. Matthew had caught her eye once and winked at her, and she'd daydreamed the rest of the time, imagining what their future together might be like.

Now, she yanked her mind back to the present, just in time to keep the platter of sliced ham from slipping off of the table and onto the floor.

"Want to help me with the desserts?" Becky came up beside her, carrying her boppli. "There is this luscious-looking chocolate cream pie that I dream about after every church Sunday, and yet I've never had a piece. It's always all gone by the time I go through the line, since I have to feed Emma first. I've often considered taking that pie before the meal and eating it all by myself." She laughed.

Shanna shook her head to help clear her thoughts. *Concentrate.* "I'll help you. I love chocolate cream pie. I ate a whole pint of chocolate ice cream last nacht, single-handedly. And I want more."

"A woman after my heart." Becky looked around and lowered her voice. "I attempted to duplicate that recipe and brought a couple along. They're in my picnic basket, along with some fried chicken, potato salad, and bean salad. I learned my lesson about going through the line. There's hardly anything left by the time I feed Emma and get out there, so I've started fixing a plate before church and hiding it in my basket. Want to share one of the pies?"

"I'm with you." Shanna resisted the urge to giggle. "Just don't tell my former nutrition professor."

"Your secret is safe with me. That pie is ours, then. I'll go put my basket aside someplace where no one else will get into it. Ach, my stomach is rumbling already." Becky took a step, then turned and looked at Shanna. "We'll talk about what made you eat a whole pint of ice cream when we're alone. Hopefully, it isn't too serious."

Shanna waved her hand in dismissal. "Not worth talking about. Just the death of a friendship."

Becky's brow wrinkled. "Not with Matthew?"

Shanna's face heated. "Nein." Should she even be talking about that relationship?

Becky smiled. "We'll talk." She bounced her boppli a little higher on her hip and hurried off.

Shanna quickened her pace and followed her into the kitchen. Becky deposited the boppli in a playpen in the corner and then headed for the dessert table. She handed an apple pie to Annie, who'd come up behind them, and then picked up the chocolate cream pie. "This is the one that Sara Shultz made. Doesn't it look wonderful? Oh, there's my basket. I'd better grab that before someone checks it and takes my pies." She followed Annie out of the kitchen.

Shanna eyed the desserts. She was glad Becky wasn't actually planning to take someone else's pie and had brought her own. Shanna picked up two pans of brownies, one iced and the other topped with walnuts, and followed several other women outside to the long line of tables, where she put down the pans next to the chocolate pie Becky had carried out. It did look yummy.

"Not there." Annie picked up the pans of brownies and moved them. "Brownies down here. I'm trying to keep this organized."

Shanna studied the table briefly and then shook her head. "Nein. You have an apple pie over there, and then the brownies, and then cherry pie and chocolate pie. The peach pie is way down there."

"Alphabetical." Annie turned and flounced off toward the house.

Alphabetical? Was she kidding? Who did that? Shanna studied the table a bit more, then picked up the apple pie and moved it down next to the cherry one. Then, she retrieved the peach pie and set it down with the others. Was that mean of her? Probably. She looked up to make sure Annie hadn't noticed.

As she glanced around, she noticed Becky hurrying back up the hill from a grove of pine trees near the pond, where Shanna could see her basket sitting on a quilt she must have spread out. "There," Becky said, brushing her hands on her apron. "Our spot is saved."

The men had been released from whatever business they'd been discussing after the service, and they started lining up for their food. Shanna hurried back to the house for a few more desserts—cakes this time. At least they had already been sliced.

After all of the desserts were on the table, Shanna moved into line behind the men, though she wasn't sure she wanted to eat anything besides chocolate cream pie. But that would count as gluttony, the last thing she wanted to be guilty of. Especially after last night's ice cream binge.

She filled her plate with some sliced turkey breast, a roll, a scoop of cottage cheese, and some salad, then started down the hill toward the spot Becky had saved. Matthew and Jacob were already waiting there. Shanna suddenly felt awkward. Becky hadn't said anything about the men joining them. Surely, she didn't expect Shanna to talk about private issues in front of them. So not happening.

When Matthew saw her, he waved his hand, motioning for her to come and sit near him. After a moment's hesitation, she carried her plate the rest of the way down the hill and lowered herself next to him on the blanket.

She balanced her plate on her lap, set her tumbler of unsweetened iced tea beside her, and bowed her head in silent prayer.

When she finished, she looked up and caught Matthew eyeing her plate. "You're eating light. Is that all you want?"

Shanna glanced at his dinner plate, piled high with an array of foods, and then his additional plate, which held a single slice of apple pie. She laughed sheepishly. "Becky promised to give me half of her chocolate cream pie. I'm saving room."

Matthew shook his head. "A whole pint of ice cream last night and a chocolate pie today? One would think your world was collapsing."

"Just a lot of stress."

He suddenly frowned, then leaned in closer. "I'm contributing to it, ain't so?" he whispered.

She wanted to say nein, but that would be a lie. Still, she didn't want to make him feel bad. "Ach, maybe a little. Decisions, decisions, you know. I need to hire someone to make them for me. Then, I'll just do what I'm told."

Matthew's lips quirked. "You don't have a very gut record of doing what you're told. But that's part of your charm."

She blinked at him. "What do you mean, I don't do what I'm told? I do."

He shrugged. "Well, I tell you to return home to the Amish, and you tell me nein. And that's just one example."

"Are there more?" Becky looked up from where she sat next to Jacob. "Ach, I'm so hungry." She opened up her basket and took out the plate she'd filled earlier.

"Jah, there's more. Lots more." Matthew balanced his plate on his knee and reached over to tug Shanna closer to his side. "I tell her she's going to marry me, and she says she needs to finish nursing school." He winked at her. "It'd be so much easier if you'd just agree."

Shanna's cheeks heated, and she shrugged his arm off.

Becky laughed. "I don't know what it is about these Pennsylvania buwe. They seem to make up their minds quick. Jacob had to convince me, too."

Jacob gave her a tender smile, then turned to Matthew. "Speaking of which, I heard that the rest of the men in the swap are supposed to be arriving soon. Josh Esh told me in a letter that he's packed and ready."

Matthew nodded and looked at Shanna. "He's the other man in our trio. Jacob, Josh, and I are best friends. So, you'll probably get to know him well." He turned back to Jacob. "I'm considering parceling up some of that land I'm buying. Maybe Josh will want some. I won't need all that acreage."

"I'd take you up on it, but Daniel has already offered me land on his farm," Jacob said. "With only girls in the family, he's glad to have me marrying Bex and willing to stay and work in his blacksmith shop. We've started preparations for building a haus. Want to come out and help sometime?"

Matthew shrugged. "Jah. I can find some time in the evenings, maybe."

"Bring Shanna. We can spend more time together." Becky picked up a chicken leg and waved it in the air. "And, Shanna, your mamm said something this morning about having a quilt frolic at your haus next week. She mentioned getting a late start on your hope chest."

Shanna could feel her cheeks heating. "She didn't say anything to me." But apparently Mamm had her sights firmly set on Shanna getting married soon. "Besides, who said I'm getting married?"

"Other than me, you mean?" Matthew grinned at her.

Becky put a hand on Shanna's. "Most Amish girls start their hope chests early. You know that."

"Is there room for me, or will I be in the way?" Annie stood above them, holding a plate of food. She smiled at Shanna, but it looked like a sugary-sweet smile. How much of their conversation had she overheard? The way Annie looked at her, sitting so close to Matthew, she suddenly became aware of how it must appear. Less than six inches separated them. If anyone looked down the hill and saw them....

He'd been the one to tug her closer. Truthfully, she didn't want to move away. But there was their reputation to consider, and she already treaded on dangerous ground. She didn't want to drag him down by association.

Annie's smile remained intact. "If you sit any closer, you'll be in his lap."

Matthew picked up his glass and took a long swig of iced tea.

Now, there's an idea. Shanna bit her tongue to keep from saying it out loud. She could imagine how that'd go over.

She looked up at Annie, then over at Matthew. She hoped no one saw the tears of hurt that stung her eyes at being chastised for breaking the rules again, at being judged unfairly again. The pain of Annie's judgment burned through her, and she quickly tried to cover it with humor. She shrugged. "Ach, I considered it, but I didn't want to muss my dress by sitting on his dinner. Maybe later." When Annie's eyebrows shot up, Shanna took the bait and moved away, putting a good foot between her and Matthew. She missed his closeness immediately.

"Please, join us," Jacob finally said, then went back to teasing Emma with a mashed-up piece of potato from his salad. The boppli opened her mouth every time the fork came near. Finally, he slid the food into her mouth.

Annie sat down opposite Matthew. She put her plate on her lap, then looked at him head-on. "So, Matthew. I heard you put a bid on a property. Care to tell us about it?"

Shanna raised her eyebrows. Matthew had never told her that he'd made an offer. It seemed as if he would have.

He lifted a shoulder. "Ach, there's nothing to tell. Levi guided me through making an offer, and now, we wait. We should hear something soon, I think."

Annie fluttered her eyelashes. "Well, I'm sure you made a gut choice. I can't wait to see it."

He gave her a small, noncommittal smile but then turned his attention back to his plate, making no promises.

When Shanna finished her meal, she set the plate aside, ready for dessert. Yet she'd feel uncomfortable digging into Becky's picnic basket to get the chocolate cream pie. Though she had said she'd share it.

Becky seemed to read her thoughts. She handed her empty plate to Shanna, then reached inside the basket, lifted out the pie, and set it in the middle of the quilt. "This is for us to share. I attempted to duplicate Sara Shultz's recipe. You'll have to tell me how I did." She closed the lid. "I have another one for Shanna and me to share."

So, they'd have the pie, but private conversation would be out.

"I'd kum over tonight, but we have the singing. Are you going?" Becky pushed the basket off of the quilt and leaned back.

Shanna nodded. "I plan to."

"Gut. Maybe we can talk then. If not, I can kum over tomorrow nacht. Will you be home?"

"Jah. But I'm sleeping in the barn."

"Matthew told me you're staying in an apartment out there. I'd be curious to see it," Becky said.

"I wish you would have told me you brought dessert for just us." Matthew eyed the chocolate cream pie. "It looks wunderbaar, but I already have a slice of apple pie."

Becky glanced at his plate. "You can make room for a small slice. That one isn't very large."

"Maybe later." Matthew consumed the slice of apple pie in several bites, then set his empty plate on the ground and stood.

He needed to escape. Annie had been eyeing him like he was her favorite candy bar. And wearing a fake-looking smile that seemed to indicate to Matthew that she was upset with someone, but for what? Shanna, for being the one he was interested in? Probably. After all, Jacob had tried to fix Matthew up with Annie soon after he'd arrived. He hadn't been at all interested in her, though. And Annie hadn't seemed impressed with him, either. At least, not until he'd made an offer on that property and gotten involved with Shanna, for lack of a better way to put it.

"Want to go for a walk?" He extended a hand to Shanna.

She met his eyes, then put her hand in his and rose to her feet.

Matthew didn't let go but still held her hand as they walked downhill toward the lake. When they stepped into a copse of trees, he moved his hand to her waist and turned her to face him. "Are you better today?"

She frowned. "Better?"

"Over whatever happened between you and— that Englischer. The thing that made you inhale ice cream like you did." At least he'd assumed she'd inhaled it. His sisters always did whenever they had a pity party. Their kitchen turned into what his daed called "junk food central" when one of his older sisters cut off a steady courtship.

"Jah. Pretty much," Shanna said. "Being with you and your friends helped."

"They want to be your friends, too." He pulled her close and rested his chin on her head.

She wrapped her arms around his waist, hugging him tight. "I need friends. I like Becky."

He hugged her a few more seconds, then slowly pulled away and raised his hand to cup her cheek. She closed her eyes, and he trailed his finger down to her neck, where he felt her pulse pounding.

"You'll come to the singing tonight, ain't so?"

"Jah. Joseph will take me."

"I'll take you home, if it's okay, Shanna. I know I've sounded presumptuous with some of the things I've said, so I'll ask you now: Will you be my steady girl?"

"Jah." Her eyes shone with excitement.

His mouth hurt from smiling, so relieved was he that she'd agreed to making their relationship official. He felt like celebrating, and his gaze drifted to her lips. If he kissed her, would he see fireworks, as he had the first time? They'd reminded him of the ones he and Jacob used to set off in the back field.

Until one of them had misfired and burned down a barn.

That had ended that pastime. He'd gotten into huge trouble. His usually mild-mannered daed had yelled at him and made him go to confess to both the barn owner and the district preachers. And Jacob and he had helped with the barn raising.

He knew he shouldn't kiss her. It would only be asking for trouble. Still, his hand slid around the back of her neck, and he slowly lowered his head. She met him halfway, her arms wrapping more tightly around him. "Matthew," she whispered, seconds before his lips met hers.

It did seem that fireworks were going off, but at least he wouldn't have to confess over this type.

He pulled her closer, deepening the kiss.

There was the sound of a twig snapping on the ground, and then an "Ahem."

Matthew dropped his arms and stepped back. Shanna staggered backward, and he fought the urge to shelter her with his body to conceal her identity. Instead, he sucked in a breath and turned around to face the person who'd dared to interrupt this private moment.

It was one of the younger preachers. A new one, whose name had been drawn in the past three months. Not the bishop, thankfully, but this was bad enough. Especially after being caught out with Shanna by Bishop Sol last night, when she was dressed in form-fitting Englisch clothes.

The man gave Shanna a cursory glance, then shifted his attention to Matthew. "The bishop and the preachers would like a word with you. Could you kum to my farm tomorrow after the noon meal?"

His stomach churned, but somehow he managed to nod. "Jah, I'll be there."

The preacher gave him directions and turned away, but the moment was ruined.

Shanna gave him an apologetic look. "I'm sorry, Matthew. I suppose it's all on account of me."

It was, partly. But he'd been complicit, too. He'd initiated their public displays of affection, and he'd offered to drive her car after the buggy accident.

And this discussion with the preachers might be related to that incident, since Bishop Sol had yet to speak to him about it. He'd have to confess to driving a car, which wasn't permitted for anyone who had joined the church, but that should be the extent of the repercussions.

He grinned at Shanna. "You're causing all kinds of mischief. Don't worry, though. Everything I did was my choice. Besides, it's probably not a big deal. It's not as if they're going to send me back to Pennsylvania." They couldn't do that, could they?

"If they do, I'll miss you. I might even kum visit. I'd love to see Lancaster County."

"They won't," he said firmly, checking to make sure his hat was on straight. "But I'll take you there on our honeymoon so you can meet my family." He winked at her. "Kum on. We should get back to our friends before we find ourselves in even more trouble."

After Joseph had parked the buggy at the farm where the singing was to be held, Shanna walked up to the barn with him, scanning the yard for Matthew. He'd left the house a bit earlier, taking her horse and buggy. She finally found him, playing volleyball with a large group. She watched him serve the ball, and then some other bu, a young one she didn't know, hit it back over the net.

She went inside the barn and found Becky seated on a bench along one side of the row of tables. The other side was reserved for the buwe. The chaperones, the parents who owned the farm, had a daughter, Lindy Zook, who was about Shanna's age. Shanna had been sure Lindy Zook would have married by now. She'd had a steady bu soon after she'd turned sixteen. But it was now three years later, and she still hadn't wed. Shanna wondered what had happened. Lindy Zook wore a kind of pinched, unhappy expression. She was probably upset that the singing was at her house, with her parents as chaperones.

Shanna understood. She'd been uncomfortable whenever her parents had hosted a singing. It always seemed that Daed had his eye on her the entire night. None of the buwe had ever asked her to take a ride with him. Though, even then, she'd had a reputation for being somewhat of a troublemaker, hanging out with the wild buwe, going to parties, and such. No wonder none of the good Amish buwe had asked her out.

She was surprised Matthew had. Maybe he hadn't heard the whole story about her yet. If that was the case, it would surely be rectified tomorrow when he met with the bishop and the preachers. Would he change his mind about her when he found out how much trouble she used to get herself into? He probably ought to. Or maybe Daed had already told him, and he'd concluded that she must have outgrown her mischievous ways.

After all, she hadn't raced a buggy horse bareback across the fields with the neighbor bu once this summer—of course, she hadn't even seen him. She hadn't gone down to the back road where the wild buwe used to race their buggies. And she certainly hadn't attended any parties, aside from the respectable event of Miriam Shultz's birthday frolic. She'd never tried alcohol or drugs, but she'd been friends with the Amish kids who did. And the preachers probably believed she'd acted the same, or still did.

Daed had definitely been of that mind-set. He'd always assumed that if she hung out with a certain type, then she would be just like them. Simple as that. He'd quoted the same proverb over and over: "*He that walketh with wise men shall be wise: but a companion of fools shall be destroyed.*"

She was certain Daed had classified her as a companion of fools.

Maybe she had been.

Her life would have certainly been different if she'd been a good Amish girl right from the start. Going to singings instead of parties.

Becky touched her hand, startling her out of her daze. "Shanna? Was ist letz? You seem like you're in a trance or something."

She shook her head and forced a smile. "I'm okay. Just woolgathering, I guess. Did you say something?"

Becky smiled. "Ach, I've been chattering on about nothing."

"I'm sorry. I guess I'm naerfich. I haven't been to one of these in...well, not since I ran away from home." Before that, really.

"I'm glad you could kum tonight. You'll have fun."

Shanna shrugged. "A preacher found Matthew and me when we were...." Her face heated. "I mean, after lunch. He told Matthew that the bishop and the preachers want to talk to him tomorrow."

Becky's eyes widened. "Why? Jacob told me that Matthew never gets into trouble."

"I don't know. Matthew says it's probably nothing. But I can't help worrying that it's about me."

"Not everything is about you." Annie plopped down on the other side of Becky.

Becky patted Shanna's hand and cast Annie a look of censure. "What has gotten into you? You've been acting so sugary-sweet today."

Annie sighed. "I'm sorry. This morning, right after church, I got snapped at by a couple of parents who don't think I'm doing a gut enough job at the school. They don't like my style of teaching, and they've threatened to go to the bishop and have me removed. Plus, a board member has talked with me about further complaints. I either had to cry or smile, so I've been smiling." She glanced at Shanna. "I'm sure it's nothing, like Matthew said."

But Becky and Annie hadn't seen the bishop talking with Daed after the service today. Nor had they seen the look Daed had given her when they'd gotten home. In her mind, it had totally erased the tender words he'd said the night before.

She'd scurried off to the barn to take a nap and avoid her family for the afternoon. She hadn't wanted to be the target of any more of Daed's silent glares, which he could give her in abundance since he wouldn't yell at her on the Lord's Day.

The barn suddenly seemed to come alive as the youths who'd been playing or talking outside all came in. The girls took seats along the benches on the same side of the table where Shanna, Becky, and Annie sat, while the buwe jostled for positions on the other side of the table. Jacob sat across from Becky, and, a few minutes later, Matthew filled the space next to him, across from Shanna.

He grinned at her and nudged her foot with his own under the table.

She smiled back, forgetting all about Annie and the bishop and her worries. At least she had tonight to enjoy.

Silence prevailed for a while as everyone waited for some brave person to start the singing. Finally, a bu did. Shanna didn't remember this particular song extremely well, and she wished for a copy of the Ausbund so she could follow along. Matthew seemed to know the song, though she couldn't distinguish his voice from the others that had quickly joined in.

Shanna scanned the length of the table, trying to locate Joseph. She found him seated almost at the end, but she couldn't see the girl across the table from him. No big deal, though. He hadn't necessarily sat across from Miriam, the girl she believed he was interested in. Many buwe didn't. And others openly paired up with their girls, disregarding traditional discretion. Like Matthew and Jacob, who'd boldly staked their claims.

When the singing ended, Matthew waited by the door. Ruth hovered by his side, all talkative and giggly, obviously hoping he would offer her a ride home. When Shanna approached the door, Matthew said good-bye and fell into step beside her. Ruth's countenance fell, and she gave Shanna a look that could have curdled milk instantly.

Still, Shanna's emotions were mixed. She felt privileged and proud that Matthew had chosen her over the other maidels, yet hurt by the mean looks and spiteful words of those who had been passed over.

She shrugged it off as they went out to his buggy. Her buggy, actually. Well, it didn't matter. The buggy. If she returned to the Amish, though, Matthew should consider getting his own. She'd need hers if she worked as a midwife.

That reality was doubtful, though. The bishop probably wouldn't remember telling her she had a gift, as focused as he seemed to be on her failings. And she did have many shortcomings. She wasn't Amish, but she wasn't Englisch, either. She tried to fit in as best as she could. In both worlds.

Matthew helped her into the buggy, then jogged around to the other side and climbed in. "Jacob will probably take Becky into town for a fancy koffee. You can live without that, ain't so?"

"Jah. I get enough of those at work."

"Gut. I figured we could ride around, maybe stop and look at the stars or something. Is that okay?"

"Jah." She scooted closer to him. Anything sounded good, as long as they were together.

Matthew wrapped one arm around her shoulders. With the other, he flicked the reins, and they were on their way.

"There's a blanket under the seat, if you're cold," he said.

Shanna reached down to retrieve the folded cloth, shook it out, and spread it over their legs. "Danki. It's a little chilly, but not too bad."

"Nein, not bad at all," Matthew agreed as she settled back into his embrace.

Snuggling against him, Shanna remembered her curiosity at something he'd said earlier. "Tell me

about when you were a young bu. What did you do?
Jacob and Josh were your best friends, you said. Are
they your cousins, too?"

Maybe if Annie and Ruth found their own buwe,
they would leave Matthew and her alone. What about
this Josh? Perhaps he could take one of them. Then
again, she might not want to wish either of them on
Matthew's good friend, for that would entail spending lots of time together. And if Josh was a relative,
it would mean seeing Annie or Ruth at future family
gatherings. Though maybe Annie could be excused
for her behavior. Hearing multiple criticisms from
the parents of her students and from a school board
member couldn't be helping her attitude any.

"Josh is my cousin on Mamm's side. Jacob, nein;
he lived on the farm next to ours. We were together almost all the time, Jacob and I, from getting up to going
to bed. We helped each other with the chores and sat
next to each other in school. The only thing we didn't
do together was court. Until now." He smiled. "I got my
learner's permit when he did because he didn't want to
go into the testing center alone. He had a motorcycle,
but he's written to Josh and asked him to sell it."

"Did you drive the motorcycle?"

Matthew shook his head. "Nein. But I wasn't all
that impressed with it when I rode on it with Jacob. I
learned to drive another friend's truck. He was Mennonite, so it was allowed."

"I learned to drive before I left home, too. Daed
wasn't very happy when he found out."

"Mine wasn't, either, but what could he say? I
was in my rumschpringe."

Matthew had kept the horse at a walk, but they
managed to get back to the farm far earlier than

Shanna wanted to. She could have ridden with him all night.

He parked the buggy and then came around to help her out. "I had a gut time tonight."

"I did, too. Danki." It seemed strange to be saying "Gut nacht" when they both were going to the same place.

Matthew smiled and walked with her the few steps to the barn. Outside the door to her loft, he waited while she fumbled with her key. "You'll go out with me again soon, ain't so?" He touched her cheek lightly, then leaned forward and kissed it.

"Jah." As soon as she could.

"Maybe a walk tomorrow nacht?"

Shanna shuddered, realizing that, by then, he would have met with the bishop and the preachers. And he would want to share it with her. Ach, this couldn't be anything good.

Chapter 23

At the designated time the next day, Matthew trudged up the front porch steps of the home of Preacher Philip Miller, his stomach churning. As he raised his arm to knock on the door, he noticed that his hands were trembling. Not good. He didn't want his fear to be obvious.

Lord, I don't know what's going to happen here, but You do. Go before me.

The door opened before he could touch it, and he looked into the kind eyes of Nancy Miller. "Matthew. Kum in. Do you want a pretzel? I made soft pretzels today for the first time, and I think they turned out well. Here, let me get you one. Have a seat. Philip will be right in, I'm sure. The preachers and Bishop Sol are out in the barn, looking at a lame horse."

Matthew hesitated. "Maybe I should go out there, then."

"Nein, he told me to make you comfortable. They'll be right in. Lemonade?" She bustled over to a cabinet and took out a glass.

Seconds later, a pretzel and a glass of lemonade appeared in front of him. He didn't think he'd be able to partake of either one.

She poured herself a glass and sat down across from him. "So, how do you like Missouri, Matthew?"

He shrugged. "I haven't been here long."

"Just four months, ain't so? But what are your impressions so far?"

"So far, I like it. I might miss the snow kum winter, though."

"It snows here sometimes." Nancy shuddered. "Snow, ice...I can live without them. I'd be happy if the temperature stayed in the seventies year-round."

He'd liked having four seasons to enjoy in Pennsylvania. But he didn't answer, because the door opened, and five men walked in. Nancy jumped up and filled five more glasses with lemonade, then set a plate piled with salty pretzels on the table.

"Matthew. Gut of you to join us." The bishop sat down at the head of the table and surveyed him.

There seemed to be a kindly glint in his eyes, but Matthew wasn't sure. He nodded.

"We checked references of all the buwe who signed up for the swap. Contacted your family, too. Heard nothing but gut things about you." He picked up his glass and swirled the pale yellow liquid around before taking a sip.

Nancy picked up something and walked out of the room.

"Jah." Matthew had expected his parents would have been contacted. He straightened his posture. "If this is about driving that car, I know I was wrong, and I'm willing to kneel and confess."

"Were you trying to impress a pretty girl that day, Matthew?" One of the other preachers leaned forward.

Matthew considered the question, then shook his head. "Nein. Her driving, it scared me. I am much more cautious, and I wanted to get back alive, if I had any control over it. I've refused to get into a vehicle with her behind the wheel ever since. That is my only excuse."

The bishop chuckled and shook his head. "She did run into Amos Kropf's buggy, and it was parked in the drive-through lane. Though he tells me that she's been trying to make restitution by working as his maud for no charge. He considered it a fair trade, but he's keeping track of her hours so he'll know when she's made it up."

Jah. Matthew knew this. But he still didn't like it.

The bishop took a sip of lemonade and then studied Matthew again. "I've heard tales about her driving. She drives too fast, going airborne over some of the bumps in the road. She'll ruin her car at that rate. I can understand your fear. Don't think I'd care to ride with her, either."

Matthew didn't answer. Bishop Sol acted a lot friendlier than he'd expected him to. More human, more caring. But if this meeting wasn't about his punishment for driving a car, he couldn't imagine what other thing concerned them enough to call him here today.

"How is she at handling a horse?" Philip Miller asked, his mouth full of pretzel.

"I don't know. I haven't let her try. But she did borrow Levi's once with no mishaps."

"She used to race buggies with the buwe when she was younger." The bishop shook his head again, as if trying to imagine a girl doing such a thing. "She is ser gut with a horse. Unfortunately, she used to ride bareback, too."

Some bishops didn't like buggy horses being ridden. Matthew lifted his glass to take a sip, but he noticed that the condensation had left a wet ring on the table. He quickly rubbed it off with his sleeve, hoping it wouldn't leave a mark on the wood.

"We were just going to address the issue of your driving." The bishop studied him a long moment. "Not her. We understand buwe and pretty maidels. We were young once, too. A long time ago." He chuckled. "But there was some touching when you went fishing the other day. I've prayed long and hard about these public displays of affection. Knowing my granddaughter likes you, I'll admit I did some gentle nudging, asked her to invite you to dinner. She did, said you'd accepted. But she also says you aren't interested. That you are courting Shanna. So, I felt I needed to step in."

Dinner? That must have been what he'd unknowingly agreed to that day at the pond. Matthew opened his mouth to decline politely, but the bishop held up his hand, silencing him.

"As your bishop, I must remind you that you're playing with fire. A friend of the world is an enemy of God." .

So, that was the real point of this meeting. Shanna. Matthew settled back in his seat, hoping to appear relaxed, nonconfrontational.

"She's joined the Englisch, Matthew," Bishop Sol went on. "She jumped the fence. You know girls who experience modern conveniences rarely return. You are too smart, too grounded, to get involved with someone like Shanna Stoltzfus. There are too many nice Amish girls around here who would welkum your attention."

Some of the other preachers nodded, and Matthew recalled Shanna's concerns about the bishop and his rules. Had she been right to worry? Any bishop who meddled this much in an individual courtship had to be a control freak. Or, was he involved only because he wanted to play matchmaker for his granddaughter?

The bishop picked up a pretzel and waved it at Matthew. "But you need to choose God and let Him guide your relationship, let Him choose your potential frau. You shouldn't allow your head or your heart to be swayed by the Stoltzfus girl, though I admit she's lovely."

"Very," one of the preachers acknowledged. "Yet, *'Favour is deceitful, and beauty is vain: but a woman that feareth the Lord, she shall be praised.'*"

Matthew recognized the verse from Proverbs. He nodded, an automatic response to fill in the heavy silence in the room. Then, he took a deep breath and turned his attention to Bishop Sol again.

"She left because of you." Ach, he hadn't intended to blurt that out. Not in that way, at least. A little more tact was in order.

The gray-haired man raised his eyebrows. "Excuse me?"

"She said that you told her she had a gift...the gift of healing. That her presence of mind in the midst of a crisis was a rare thing that ought to be developed. She wanted to get professional training so that she could kum back and serve the community." He stumbled over the words in his rush to get them out before the bishop could interrupt him. "But education is forbidden by the Ordnung, and she didn't know how else to go about getting the schooling she needed. She studied obstetrics. It's the branch of medicine that deals with childbirth and the treatment of women before and after labor. That's what she said. She intends to return."

Thoughtful expressions appeared on the men's faces. One had a furrowed brow.

The bishop nodded slowly. "I did say that Shanna had a gift. And she has always been smart. Top of her class all the way through school. I'd thought the Englisch midwife would train her. I even approached her about it, the day Shanna left. She'd always been the type who would want the education. And the Englisch midwife was rather noncommittal about training her. But why didn't she say anything?"

"Levi told her it was all pride." Matthew took another drink.

The bishop closed his eyes briefly. "Jah. But I think the other preachers would agree that if she wanted to do this for the gut of the community, we would have supported her, we would have found someone to teach her. As I said, I tried to find training for her before she ran off."

Matthew's eyes widened. If only Shanna had known this bit of information.

"We need her here," the bishop went on. "Too many times, our women give birth without proper assistance because the midwife doesn't make it in time."

The other preachers nodded. "My Nellie had to do it alone; I wasn't home," one said. "A local midwife would be beneficial."

Matthew glanced at the man who spoke. His beard was short, indicating he'd been married only a brief time. A year, perhaps. He had reddish hair that curled around his ears.

Matthew sucked in a deep breath. "She has a half year of school left. But she's willing to kum home now, if she's allowed." She hadn't exactly said that. She'd said she wasn't ready to return, but that was only because her schooling wasn't complete, he was certain. "And I want to marry her, kum December, after she's through, except for graduating."

The bishop's eyes widened. "Promises have been made?"

Sort of. He hadn't officially proposed. But he had talked about them marrying. Multiple times. He looked down. "We have an understanding."

"You have given us much to consider and pray about, Matthew Yoder, before we can make a decision." The bishop leaned back. "You will kneel and confess on church Sunday for your driving transgression."

Matthew nodded. That he could do.

"God go with you."

"And you. Danki for listening to me." He stood, hoping that his shaking knees would support him. His stomach still churned. Their decision would be regarding Shanna. Would they tell him whether he was permitted to continue courting her, or whether she was permitted to continue her education? He couldn't see the latter happening. And Shanna would never yield to a demand to quit school.

Nancy Miller hurried back into the room, carrying a plate. "Here," she said, holding it out to him. "Take this to the Stoltzfus family. I'm sure they'll enjoy some pretzels." She smiled encouragingly and patted his hand. Then, she turned and picked up his plate, which held his untouched snack. "And take this one with you. You can eat it on the way."

"Danki," Matthew said again, though he still wasn't hungry. He started for the door.

"Matthew," the bishop said. "We will contact you within the week."

Shanna had decided to go to Amos Kropf's house after her morning shift at McDonald's to fill the time Matthew spent meeting with Bishop Sol and the preachers. She washed the last of the week's dishes, dipping them in the rinse water that filled the other sink basin, then setting them in a drain pan to dry. Next, she used the dishrag to wipe down the counters and tabletop, then wrung out the cloth and hung it over the sink to dry. As she picked up another towel to dry the dishes, she heard footfalls behind her. She glanced over her shoulder.

Amos took off his hat and turned it in his hands. "You're doing a gut job here, Shanna. Haven't seen this haus so clean since before...." He clamped his mouth shut and hugged his hat to his chest.

Since his wife died. Tears welled in Shanna's eyes, but she couldn't think of an appropriate way to comfort him. She turned back to the sink to give him some privacy.

He cleared his throat. "Well. I think you've worked enough time to pay back what it cost to repair the buggy. If you want to continue working for me, I'd be obliged, and I'd pay you the going rate."

She wanted to make sure the debt had been paid in full. Her eyes still burned with tears, but she set the towel down and spun around. "I know I caused a greater inconvenience than simply breaking your wheel. You had to rely on others for rides, and—"

"Just the one, from McDonald's back home that day. And Matthew Yoder paid for that, though I told him he didn't need to. He said you'd reimburse him."

Jah, she fully intended to. But he still hadn't told her what it had cost. Would Amos tell her? She didn't know how to ask. Probably best to just say it. "How much was that, anyway? Matthew wouldn't say."

Amos eyed her. Then, with a grimace, he tugged his hat back on his head. "Not my place, then." He strode out the door, then stuck his head back inside. "Will you want a ride home when you finish?"

"Nein, danki. I can walk."

"Have you considered returning home for gut? Maybe marrying?" Amos cocked his head and took a step back inside. "Seems you'd make a gut frau. Gut with the kinner."

Shanna's eyes widened. What was he saying? Men didn't talk about marriage, unless.... Her brother had said that Amos needed a frau.

"Ach, nein. I'm thinking...I don't know. I'm going to school. Not likely to be coming home soon. Can't be thinking about marriage." *Except to Matthew.* "I'm not getting married," she added, firmly.

He grunted. "We'll see." He frowned, studying her. "You're seeing someone. Promised, maybe. Ain't so?" Then, he disappeared again.

Shanna finished drying the dishes and then checked the pantry. It was full. Whomever he'd said did his shopping must have been here recently. The shelves were overflowing with baskets of apples, boxes of cereal, canned goods, and even bags of junk food—potato chips and the snack cakes that have a shelf life of forever.

She turned and checked the refrigerator, then took out a package of chicken legs and thighs. She would start some chicken baking in the oven with a few potatoes, but then she'd need to head home, especially with Becky coming over with that chocolate cream pie. Her mouth watered just thinking about it.

An hour later, Shanna had the chicken and potatoes in the oven and a pot of sliced carrots simmering on the back of the stove. She told Amos about the food so it wouldn't burn, then took off.

When she arrived at home, an Englischer's pickup truck waited in the driveway. Shanna didn't recognize the vehicle. She hurried over to the barn, hoping not to run into anyone. Except maybe Matthew. She glanced around, hoping to catch a glance of him. Was he still meeting with the bishop? Not seeing him, she quickened her pace. She wanted to get cleaned up before Becky arrived.

As Shanna slipped into the barn, she noticed that the door on the other side of the big buggy room stood open. *Daed's special room.* A light shone down the steps into the area, leaving a block of brightness. It appeared too bright to be from a lantern. *Daed has electric on that side of the barn?* She hurried over that direction, hoping to catch a glimpse up the forbidden stairs, but the sound of men's voices stopped her. She turned and hurried back to her apartment. *What's going on up there?*

When Matthew returned from the Millers' house, Levi sent him out to the back field to spread manure among the growing stalks of corn. Not a pleasant job, but the manure made for good fertilizer. After a little while, his stomach rumbled. He wished he'd actually eaten the pretzel, but he hadn't been hungry. He paused to wipe some sweat off his forehead. It seemed unseasonably warm for June, with temperatures in the nineties, according to some of the preachers he'd overheard earlier.

Definitely hotter than Pennsylvania would be at this time of year. For a few moments, a wave of home-sickness washed through him. He'd sure enjoy a cold glass of Mamm's lemonade about now, sitting around the table with Daed and his brothers, seeing Mamm and his sisters bustle around the kitchen, keeping them supplied with refills of the freshly squeezed lemonade or delivering bowls of newly churned ice cream. That was a rare treat, though, and they usually ate the entire batch in one day.

He was supposed to call home tonight. It'd be nice to talk to everyone. He'd forgotten about that when he'd asked Shanna to go for a walk with him. But maybe she wouldn't mind if he talked with his family for a little while. She might even say hi, since she'd be marrying into the family. Hopefully. Though she might be uncomfortable talking on the phone to strangers.

Matthew wiped his forehead again, then pulled his watch out of his pocket to check the time. Dinner might be ready soon. He should head back and get washed up.

He started walking toward the barn to take care of his equipment and the horse.

"Matthew!"

He looked up and saw Shanna running across the field toward him.

She slowed to a stop when she reached him. "I earned back what I owed Amos Kropf. He told me he'd been keeping track of my hours."

"Gut. So, you won't be working for him any-more?"

Her brow furrowed. "Well, he didn't fire me. He said that I'd be paid for any additional hours I worked. I figure this is gut. Besides, I owe you for his transportation after the accident, remember? How much was that, again?"

Matthew glanced at his filthy hands and resisted the urge to run a finger down her cheek. She was clean; he could smell a flowery scent. His touches wouldn't be appreciated at this point.

"Ach, Shanna. I thought I told you not to worry about that. I don't want your money."

"But you're buying a farm. And you'll need a horse and buggy of your own. You're not so independently wealthy that you can afford to throw away, what, twenty dollars?"

"I didn't throw it away, Shanna. Let it go. Besides, your daed already reimbursed me. He said that he was responsible, since you are his daughter. So, if you pay anyone, it'll have to be your daed."

"Maybe I could pay you back, and you could give the money to him?" She wrinkled her nose.

Matthew smiled. "Ask him yourself. He's not a scary ogre."

She sighed. "Maybe you're right. He's different from the daed I ran away from. I think you've been gut for him."

His grin widened. "I think having you home is gut for him. But, since you brought it up, I need to call home tonight. Would you want to say hello to my parents?"

She backed up, her eyes wide. "Your parents? Whatever for?"

Ach, he wished he could draw her near. Punctuate his every word with a kiss. If only he weren't so filthy. He took a deep breath. "Because you're my future frau. They'll want to get to know you."

She laughed. "You haven't proposed. I haven't accepted."

Matthew shook his head. "You agreed to be my steady girl. You know the direction we're going."

She sobered. "Jah, I know. But maybe your family would be better off not talking to me right now. I haven't joined the church yet, nor do I plan to this year."

He opened his mouth, then shut it, figuring it best to keep his discussion with Bishop Sol and the preachers quiet until they'd reached a decision.

But she looked him straight in the eyes. "Speaking of which, how did your meeting go? Are you in trouble?"

Matthew shook his head. "Nein. Next church Sunday, I'll kneel and confess for driving your car. Then, it will be over. Forgiven and forgotten."

She reached out and touched his hand, seeming to pay no attention to the dirt. "Ach, Matthew. I'm so sorry. I should have said nein."

"I shouldn't have asked." He shrugged. "I knew better."

"I suppose we should get back to the haus. Mamm was finishing up dinner. I helped her set the table and told her I'd call you and my brothers in. But I'm not sure where Joseph is, and Daed is still visiting with whoever owns the truck parked outside the shop."

"Joseph mentioned something about being invited to dinner somewhere."

"I still can't believe my brother is courting someone." Shanna shook her head. "But he's seventeen. He'll probably be married next year."

Matthew shrugged. "Maybe so." He took a couple of steps toward the barn, his thoughts straying to his hopes and dreams...Shanna, the farm, and blueberries. He still needed to go into town to research the prospects of growing the fruit. "I heard from the realtor this afternoon. The owners are prepared to accept the offer I made."

Shanna squealed. "That's great! Are you going to move in soon, then?"

"Well, there's other stuff. Inspections that are required by law, the renovations...you know. Maybe we'll be in by wedding season." Oops. That had come out without thought. Hopefully, she wasn't listening too closely.

Her gaze held his for a moment, and then she looked away. "Ach, Matthew," she whispered.

"I...I meant...hopefully, I would be in by the end of autumn."

Her smile appeared and disappeared so fast, like a drawing on an Etch-a-Sketch that was shaken away. But she let his comment go and simply nodded toward the house. "Dinner's ready." She took off at a trot.

Right. And maybe he was coming on too strong. If he kept this up, he would probably drive her away rather than wear down her resistance. Maybe he should ask his brothers for courting advice.

Or maybe he should concentrate on friendship. She'd made it clear that she wasn't ready, even though she'd agreed to be his steady girl. Yet she knew what that meant. Why did he have to keep pushing it?

"Gut things kum to those that wait," he muttered as he watched her hightail it toward to the house. Depending on the bishop's decision, he might have to wait a lot longer. *Lord, help me to be patient*, he prayed.

Chapter 24

As everybody filed into the kitchen, Shanna filled their bowls with beef stew. She'd made it by herself, with no instruction or supervision whatsoever from Mamm. She snuck a glance at Matthew as she put his bowl in front of him, praying he'd like it. She wanted to be a good cook for him someday. He'd want a frau who would prepare a satisfying meal for him after every hard day of work. Mamm had helped her with the corn bread, talking her through the steps, but Shanna had done all the work. She was proud that it hadn't burned.

After they'd bowed their heads in silent prayer, Daed talked about the big order he'd gotten that day, to be shipped to someplace in Branson. "I'll need both you and Joseph to help," he said, looking at Matthew.

Matthew nodded as he slathered a slab of freshly churned butter on a thick slice of corn bread. "I'll be glad to help."

"And I heard about a blueberry farm up closer to Springfield. Thought you'd be glad to know there're some around here."

"Jah. Gut to know. Danki." Matthew took a bite of the corn bread, then looked at Mamm. "This is ser gut."

Mamm smiled. "Shanna prepared the meal."

His gaze slid to her, and he smiled even more broadly.

She grinned back, dipping her head.

After the meal, Shanna helped Mamm pour coffee and set out a plate of peanut butter cookies. She'd made those, too. They were left over from the bake sale.

Daed waved the cookies away. It was the first time Shanna had seen him turn down dessert. "Sorry, Shanna. I have a touch of indigestion." He rubbed his chest. "Something about the stew must have disagreed with me. Did you do something different?"

Shanna shrugged. "I thought I did it the usual way. I don't know. Did it taste bad to you, Matthew?" He'd said it was "ser gut," right? Nein; he'd said that about the corn bread. Her stomach churned.

"It was gut." Matthew wiped his chin with a napkin and smiled.

"I didn't say it tasted bad," Daed clarified. "I said it's disagreeing with me." He pushed away from the table. "Deborah, can Joy and Joanna help you with cleanup? I need to talk to Shanna for a bit."

Shanna's stomach cramped. This was it, then. Daed would yell at her for whatever it was that she'd done this time. She glanced at Matthew, and he shrugged, but his gaze was sympathetic. Apparently, Daed hadn't talked to him first about this issue. She almost wished he had.

"Step outside a moment, Shanna." Daed headed for the door, still rubbing his chest. "Let's take a walk."

She decided to cut to the chase. "Did I do something wrong?" No point in wasting time on small talk. On the evening of Matthew's talk with Bishop Sol and the preachers, this couldn't spell anything good.

Maybe it was all about her, and they were going to oust her from the community. Send her back to the Englisch. Would she be able to find a job as a nurse?

He shrugged, then rubbed his left arm.

"Are you okay?" She eyed him with concern. Beads of sweat had appeared on his forehead. He had feelings of indigestion, and, from the looks of it, arm pains. "Daed?"

"Hmm. I must have pulled a muscle or something. But never mind me. I'm fine." He leveled a glance at her. "Not sure what you did. Perhaps you can tell me. I've heard rumblings about you acting inappropriately around some of the young men."

Shanna's eyebrows shot up. "Inappropriately?"

"Letting your hair down in front of them. Going without your kapp."

Shanna blinked back tears. "That—"

Daed shook his head. "Plus, you've been running around in tight jeans and T-shirts that show too much skin."

Too much skin? Jah, she supposed so, according to Amish standards. In the world's eyes, though, her clothes would be considered modest.

"Not sure how much I should say. You're still considered to be in your rumschpringe, but the complaints I've heard make it sound as if you weren't. Besides, you've been dressing mostly Amish while you've been home. Appreciate that. Danki."

"Ach. Well, the incident with the kapp and my uncovered head was an accident. Matthew caught my kapp with his fishing hook, and it landed in the pond. And I forgot about not letting my hair down until I saw the shocked looks on the faces of him and Becky and Jacob."

Daed waved his hand. "I wasn't condemning. Just saying that maybe you should be a bit more careful for the remainder of the summer. Try to abide by the rules more closely."

When had Daed mellowed? Shanna couldn't remember any of his lectures being delivered so calmly and quietly. He hadn't raised his voice at all. If only she could keep herself from sounding defensive.

Daed pulled in a breath and frowned. "I promised I'd speak to you about it. Also, I was supposed to mention the public displays of affection. You and Matthew were caught kissing after church yesterday. Not that I mind so much. Matthew's a gut man. But the bishop saw him with his arms around you at the pond Saturday. Said you were openly cuddling." He sighed. "I imagine he spoke to Matthew about that."

Her face heated. Private matters were supposed to be taboo as topics of discussion. But then, since they'd been seen, it'd hardly been private. She sighed. "Probably so." She kicked a rock. "Becky is supposed to come over in a while, and...." She looked at Daed. His complexion appeared ashen. "Are you sure you're all right, Daed? You don't look so gut."

"Never mind. Supposed to mention your driving, too. Scaring...horses." Daed gripped his chest again. "This heartburn is...really bad. Feels like...elephants. What...did you do...to the stew?" More beads of sweat covered his forehead.

Shanna stopped walking and stepped in front of him, knowing by now he was far from fine. "Daed?"

"Just not...feeling...up to par." He gasped, then collapsed to his knees.

"Daed!" Shanna reached out to keep him from falling face-first in the dirt. Then, supporting him with one arm, she reached with the other hand inside her pocket and fished for her cell phone. All the while she tried to find her professional side, to distance herself emotionally. It wasn't working so well. This was her daed. She lowered him to the ground, helped him roll over on his back, then dialed the number for emergency help. "Hello? I think my daed's having a heart attack. He complained of shoulder pains and arm pains and what he thought was indigestion. We need an ambulance." Her eyes took in Daed's worsening condition as she rattled off the address.

"There is an ambulance relatively close by," the dispatcher told her. "It's en route."

Shanna clicked the phone shut and dropped down beside Daed. "Help is on the way." She looked around for something to elevate his head. Seeing nothing potentially useful, she untied her black apron, yanked it off, and folded it to make a sort of pillow, which she tucked beneath Daed's head.

He stared up at her, his green eyes filled with tears. He reached out with his right hand and grasped hers. "Ich liebe dich."

She held his hand and, with the other, felt for his pulse. She wasn't wearing a watch, so she counted silently. Her estimate was in the thirties—dangerously low, but still high enough to keep the oxygen flowing to his brain. She released his wrist and scooted behind him. "Ich liebe dich, too, Daed. I'm going to sit you up a little and let you rest your head in my lap. Hang in there. The paramedics will be here soon." She was glad Daed was conscious and breathing.

Lord, send an aspirin. Now.

She never should have come home. Her being here had put too much stress on Daed.

Matthew came outside to finish the chores he'd started before dinner. He did a double take when he saw Shanna sitting in the driveway, with Levi half sitting, half lying there, holding her hand. Matthew started running toward them. "Shanna? Levi?"

"We need an aspirin," Shanna said, her tone authoritative. "Adult. Break it in half. Hurry!"

Matthew spun around and sprinted back to the house and rushed to his room, where he retrieved a bottle of aspirin from his toiletries. He ran back outside, working on the lid. Stopping beside Shanna, he dumped a pill into his palm, broke it in half, and handed it to her.

Shanna put the two pieces into Levi's open mouth. "Chew, Daed. They'll get into your system faster."

A siren wail pierced the silence. Moments later, a fire truck pulled into the driveway, followed by an ambulance, lights flashing.

Deborah came flying out of the house. "What's going on? Levi? Oh, nein."

Shanna stood up. "He'll be okay, Mamm. They'll take him to the hospital, and he'll be fine."

"You'll need to step back." One of the emergency medical technicians approached, carrying an oversized medic kit, while several other EMTs hoisted a stretcher out of the back of the vehicle. "We'll need the room to work."

The EMT knelt next to Levi and slipped an oxygen mask over his face. "Sir, I'm going to hook you up to a monitor and take your blood pressure, and then we'll get you to the emergency room."

The EMT standing near Deborah asked her, "Does he have any allergies?"

"Nein."

"Any history of heart problems?"

"Nein." She wrung her hands. "I want to ride with him."

The EMT shook his head. "It'd be better if you found a ride."

Shanna looked on intently. She whispered something to another EMT, probably giving him information regarding Levi's condition. Then, she stepped aside to make room for the stretcher.

Deborah cried as the EMTs worked and talked quietly among themselves. Matthew put his hand on her arm. He wished he could comfort Shanna, as well.

"I'll drive you, Mamm." Shanna stepped toward her. "If you want."

"Jah. You shouldn't have been fighting with him." Deborah glared at her.

Matthew swallowed, wanting to defend Shanna. He clenched his fists but quickly released them. Shanna and her daed were prone to arguing. And maybe they had been. He didn't know, since he'd arrived on the scene too late to see whatever had triggered Levi's heart attack.

Shanna opened her mouth for a moment, then shut it and nodded.

"Matthew, will you keep an eye on the children?" Deborah looked at him. Her eyes were red, the skin around them puffy. "When Joseph gets home, send him to the bishop, so the word can get out to the community."

"I will. Don't worry." He nodded, watching as the EMTs loaded Levi onto the stretcher, then slid him into the ambulance. He wished he could go along to support Shanna, but she certainly seemed to be holding up well, in spite of the tension. "I'll be praying, too."

"Danki." Deborah squeezed his hand briefly. "I'd best get ready to go."

"I'll bring the car around." Shanna glanced at Deborah, then caught Matthew's gaze. There was a wildness in her eyes that he'd never seen before. Maybe she wasn't as calm as she seemed.

An expression akin to regret passed across her face, and she looked away. "Danki for taking care of my siblings, Matthew. We'll keep you updated." She glanced at the ambulance, siren wailing as it turned onto the road. "Okay, time to get the car. Keys. I need the keys." She turned toward the barn.

"Shanna." He waited until she looked at him. "It'll be okay." He probably shouldn't have stated that assurance; he didn't know how it'd end. He sucked in a breath. "If you need me, or just want me to come, call my cell. I'll be there."

She nodded. "Danki, Matthew." She backed away. "I need to go." The same strange, wild look was back again.

"I'm praying."

She didn't respond.

Shanna hurried to her apartment and quickly changed into a pair of jeans and a T-shirt. She didn't want the hospital staff treating her like an idiot because she was dressed differently. It would be bad enough to see them treating Mamm that way.

However, she wasn't sure Mamm wanted her there. After all, she blamed her for Daed's heart attack.

Tears burned Shanna's eyes as she realized it probably had been her fault. She'd argued with Daed enough in the past that Mamm had good reason to believe she'd done it this time. And Daed had been obligated to discuss her recent behavior with her. That couldn't have been easy for him, knowing her tendency to react defensively. *Lord, forgive me*, she prayed.

Coming home had been a bad idea from the beginning. In addition to prompting Daed's heart attack and the ensuing pain for her family, she'd gotten Matthew, a good Amish man, in trouble. Dragged him into the mud with her. Messed with his heart.

And torn hers wide open in the process.

He deserved a good Amish girl. Not her. Never her.

A tear escaped the corner of her eye.

Shanna wiped it away and swallowed the lump in her throat. Then, she grabbed a duffle bag and stuffed it full of clothes. After shoving her driver's license in one pocket and a wad of cash in the other, she picked up her cell phone, swung the duffle bag over one shoulder, and grabbed her keys.

She'd leave the rest here, until she'd found a place to stay. Then, she would sneak back here on a church Sunday and retrieve her things while the family was at services.

This time.... This time, she wouldn't write. No one would beg her to come home, because no one would know where she'd gone.

It was best that way.

Chapter 25

Matthew checked his pocket watch. It seemed like hours had passed since Shanna and Deborah had left for the hospital. In actuality, less than an hour had elapsed since then.

The news concerning Levi had spread fast. Within ten minutes after Shanna and Deborah's departure, one of their neighbors stood at the door with a shoofly pie, curious about all the activity. Soon, casseroles and other dishes showed up in the arms of other concerned folk, all of them wondering if he'd heard any updates on Levi.

With all the visitors' questions, Matthew barely had time to check on the younger children.

Thankfully, an older woman who had started a pot of coffee on the stove had offered to read a story to the little girls and get them ready for bed. It was early for sleeping, but this mammi was convinced that a bath and a story would calm them down after all the activity. Sounded wise to Matthew. A bath and a story might go a long way toward calming him down, too. Instead, he paced the floor and whispered prayers for Levi and Shanna.

Some of the men had gone out to the barn to do the evening chores. Everything was getting done, but Matthew felt misplaced, with nothing to do. Nothing but pray and pace. *The most important things.*

Matthew was pouring himself a cup of coffee when yet another knock sounded on the door. One of the neighbor ladies opened it, and there stood Bishop Sol, his wife, Bertha King, and their granddaughter, Ruth.

"Any news yet?" The bishop cut straight to the point while Bertha set a casserole on the table.

"Nein." Matthew eyed the food, wondering where it would go. The refrigerator was completely filled with meals others had brought, and they'd already eaten supper.

The bishop tugged at his beard. "I called a driver to take us into Springfield to sit with Deborah in the hospital. He'll come here to pick us up. Would you like to go, Matthew? Ruth can sit with the kinner until Joseph gets back, which should be anytime now. One of the wives has offered to stay overnight in case something is needed."

He'd already had several offers and had politely turned them down. "Jah, I'd be grateful," Matthew told the bishop, remembering Shanna's wild expression. "I'd like to be there." He didn't mention the women and men who still filled the house and barn. Only a few had gone home. This community was more generous than he'd realized.

"Ser gut."

Ruth walked over to the table. "Have the kinner eaten?"

"Jah. Shanna made stew." Matthew looked at the bishop. "I would appreciate you taking me into Springfield with you. Danki."

The bishop nodded.

The door flung open, and Joseph burst in. "What happened to Daed? People are saying he had a heart attack. Was he arguing with Shanna again?"

Ach, Matthew hated hearing her be accused. Declared guilty without representation. And yet, he kind of blamed her, too. He went to the door to retrieve his shoes. "I don't know. He was having a talk with her when it happened, so it's likely." That might explain the wild look he'd seen in her eyes. He bent to tie his shoes, hoping he'd be able to take Shanna in his arms and comfort her the way he'd longed to. She needed him. That look....

"We're going into Springfield to sit with your mamm," the bishop said. "You're welkum to join us. Leah Troyer will be spending the nacht here."

"Jah, I'll kum." Joseph nodded. "Let me take care of the buggy and horse."

"The driver should be here any minute." The bishop walked over to the window and glanced out. "Jah, I see his van coming."

"I'll hurry." Joseph ran out the door.

Matthew blinked the tears out of his eyes. He was thankful the bishop had arrived and taken charge. He might not be able to hold Shanna, not with the bishop watching, but he could be there to support and comfort her. He might help calm her some. And he'd be there to hear any updates firsthand.

The hospital bustled with activity, yet the waiting room remained eerily quiet. Doors whooshed open and closed as nurses and technicians dressed in scrubs entered and exited. But there'd been no word on Daed since a nurse had whisked him away, leaving Mamm with a clipboard of forms to fill out. Shanna sat two seats away from Mamm, wishing she'd dared to sit closer. Wishing she could throw herself into her arms and weep. Tell her that she hadn't meant to kill Daed, if she had actually done so. They didn't know yet.

A television played in the corner, the station set to a cartoon show, and several children sat around a table in the play area nearby. The other adults seated in the room talked on their cell phones or thumbed through magazines.

Shanna didn't know how they could concentrate. It was all she could do to keep from crying and demanding admittance to wherever they'd taken Daed. She'd been in this hospital before for a clinical rotation and was certain she could find her way around.

Mamm was crying. And, seeing her head bowed, Shanna knew she was saying prayers, as well.

Ach, if only she weren't to blame for this. If only she could comfort Mamm and be able to reassure her. But they'd sat in silence the whole drive into Springfield, neither one saying a word. Mamm hadn't even sat in the passenger seat next to her. She'd crawled into the back. As far away from her as she could get, like Shanna was her chauffer and not her daughter.

Jah, it had hurt.

Just when she'd begun healing the relationship with Daed, Mamm had practically accused her of murder. So many times before, Mamm had been her defender and her comforter. And now, it seemed she wanted nothing to do with Shanna.

She wiped another tear away. *Lord, please spare Daed.* She shouldn't try to strike a deal with God— she'd been taught not to—but it was still tempting to promise Him she'd be the best Christian ever if He allowed Daed to live. He shouldn't have to die because of her mistakes. *Forgive me, Lord. Forgive me for all my sins.*

She squirmed in her seat and glanced at Mamm. If she couldn't offer her emotional comfort, perhaps she could at least help with a physical need.

"Do you want some koffee, Mamm?" Shanna asked, getting to her feet. "Or hot tea?"

"Hot tea would be gut. Danki." Her voice shook.

"I'll be right back." Shanna walked to the small room beside the nurses' station, where there was a coffeemaker with one coffeepot half full of thick, dark liquid, the other filled with steaming water for tea. A basket filled with packets of hot chocolate mix, various herbal teas, sweeteners, and creamers sat nearby. She thumbed through it and picked out a chamomile tea bag for Mamm. She could use something like that to calm her nerves.

Shanna needed something with caffeine, because she needed to think. Where would she go?

No worries about her family. They'd be glad to see her go. Her, and all the havoc she'd brought with her.

She sighed.

"Shanna? Girl, is that you?"

Shanna set down the cup she held and raised her eyes to the pretty, lilac-print scrubs and then to the dark-skinned face of Dionne Relefourd, an LPN who had supervised one of her clinical rotations.

"Are you crying? What's wrong?" Dionne grabbed Shanna's hands and pulled her away from the coffee service, through a door, and into a private conference area with couches and end tables topped with boxes of Kleenex.

Shanna wiped her eyes again. "I'm okay." But her voice cracked. Right now, she appreciated Dionne's solicitous ways and her habit of taking charge. Her chatter had always made the nursing clinics fun.

"Right. Then, let's start with why you aren't here as a nurse. Girl, you were one of the best students in the class. You could have had a job immediately! Where'd you go? Did you get to go on that mission trip, after all?"

"No, I went home. I didn't think things through very well." She straightened her shoulders. "But I could use a job now."

"Obstetrics, right?" Dionne took a pen and scribbled something on a note sheet she ripped off a chart. "Talk to her when your crisis here is over," she said, handing the paper to Shanna. "You probably don't want to go with bloodshot eyes."

She felt a stab of regret. Why hadn't she thought of pursuing this kind of opportunity instead of going home, working at McDonald's, and causing health problems for Daed? A lump formed in her throat. *Matthew.*

This would be a career confirmation, of sorts. A second chance to do it right, maybe.

"Dank—thank you." Shanna sucked in a breath. "My daed—dad had a heart attack. My mom is blaming me for it."

"You know better. Those things happen."

"Stress can trigger them, though. And my dad and I...we don't always get along." She wiped her eyes with a tissue. "I need a place to stay, too. I can't go home again."

"Well, that problem's solved. You can stay with me. My roommate's away on vacation with her family for two weeks. When she gets back, you might have to sleep on the couch, but it turns into a bed. You'd be fine for a while."

"Thanks, Dionne. You're a life saver."

"And don't you forget it, honey. But you'd better get back to your mom. I'll go check on your dad for you. What's his name?"

"Levi Stoltzfus."

"I'll send someone right out to talk to you." Dionne reached out and wrapped Shanna in a hug. "It'll be okay, honey. The doctors know what they're doing. You know that. Have faith, sugar." She walked to the door, then glanced over her shoulder. "Will you be coming home with me tonight, then? I get off work at ten."

Shanna squared her shoulders. "Jah. I mean, yes."

At the hospital, Matthew followed Joseph, Bishop Sol, and Bertha King into the waiting room to which they'd been directed. He spied Deborah sitting by herself, gripping a Styrofoam cup with both hands, as if trying to warm herself. He glanced around the room, his eyes skimming over the other people seated in chairs, but didn't see any sign of Shanna.

Bertha walked over to Deborah, wrapped her in a hug, and whispered something in her ear. Bishop Sol, Joseph, and Matthew all sat down near the two women, Matthew perching on the edge of his chair. The bishop bowed his head in prayer. After a moment, Matthew did the same. *Lord, heal Levi, if it's Your will. Be with Shanna.*

"Mamm? Any word?" Joseph clasped his hands in front of him.

Deborah shook her head. "Shanna knows someone, a nurse. She said she'd go see. She's waiting over there." She pointed to a nurses' station. Beyond it, Matthew saw Shanna pacing in front of the double doors. She wore jeans and a blue T-shirt that covered her waist, but the V-shaped neck dipped rather low in front, providing a tantalizing glimpse of.... He averted his gaze, mentally chastising himself for looking. A nurse dressed in black pants and a purple shirt stood near her, talking quietly.

After a minute or two, Matthew jumped to his feet and walked briskly over to her. Not paying any mind to the others waiting, he came up behind her and stopped her pacing by wrapping an arm around her shoulders in a hug.

She stiffened before turning to look at him. Recognition flashed in her eyes, and she sagged against him. "Ach, Matthew." A sob caught in her throat.

He pulled her nearer. "Shh. Any word?" He directed the question to the nurse.

"He's conscious and stable. They took him back for an EKG. He'll need to stay in the hospital for a few days, maybe longer, depending on the results of the tests they run."

Right. He didn't understand much of that. An EKG—that stood for what? He didn't ask, not wanting to appear dumb in front of Shanna.

"Is there anything else we can do for you?" the nurse asked. Her gaze flittered over him, his Amish clothes, to the others in their group, then returned to rest on Shanna.

Matthew glanced at her name tag. "Dionne, thank you for your help. How soon will we be able to see him?"

"The doctors are still evaluating him, but as soon as he's taken back to a room, someone will come out and talk to the family."

"Thanks again."

Dionne nodded and winked at Shanna, then disappeared through the double doors.

Matthew wrapped his other arm around Shanna. "Are you doing okay?" He brushed a kiss over the loose hairs that swept across her forehead.

She straightened, pulling away from him. "I'm fine."

That strange, wild look was still in her eyes. It made him nervous. He wondered what was going on in her head. "Shanna. Let's talk—"

"I need to tell Mamm what Dionne said. She needs to know."

"And then you'll walk with me? We won't go far, in case they come out with news. I saw a koffee kiosk when I came in. Would you care for one of those fancy koffees? I'll get one for you." He was babbling. He slammed his mouth shut.

Her head rose. The hardness in her gaze startled him. "There's nothing to say, except I'm sorry. It won't happen again."

Chapter 26

I gnoring Matthew's frown of confusion, Shanna walked over to the group of people waiting and quietly explained what she had learned concerning Daed. Matthew stood silently behind her, a source of strength, one she wished she could lean on. But she didn't.

The bishop's eyes surveyed her Englisch clothes, and he frowned, then looked at Matthew and raised an eyebrow. Shanna didn't have a clue what that meant. Probably a nonverbal communication regarding her attire. She didn't look at Matthew to see his response. Really, what did it matter? This situation with Daed spelled the end of her Amish life. Who would care how she dressed?

She went back to pacing, certain she'd wear a hole in the linoleum before someone came out with another update about Daed. Maybe she wouldn't be a very good nurse, after all. She couldn't handle being on the other end. Then again, maybe this would make her more empathetic, more compassionate.

"I'm going to get you a koffee, not that you need the caffeine." Matthew stopped her at the far end of her pacing route. "Maybe a decaf?"

"A latte, please. Iced. Hazelnut, if they have it."

A small grin flickered on his face. "Right. Maybe I'd better write that down."

"Maybe so." She didn't smile. Her heart hurt, knowing she was about to break his. "They aren't going to know what to think if you order a fancy koffee." Ouch. That had sounded harsh. She should probably apologize.

His smile died. The light went out of his eyes. "Nein, I suppose they won't. Iced hazelnut latte, if they have it. I shouldn't have trouble remembering." He walked off, shoulders firmed, back straight, and head up. He didn't turn around. She blinked back some tears.

Fifteen minutes later, the double doors opened again and a doctor came out. He glanced down at a file. "Stoltzfus family?"

Mamm, Joseph, the bishop, and Bertha all stood. The doctor led them off to the side a little ways. Shanna trailed behind them.

"Mr. Stoltzfus is currently stable, but we'll know more after all the tests come back in the next forty-eight hours. In the meantime, he's been admitted for observation. We'll be monitoring the cardiac enzymes in his blood over the next twenty-four to forty-eight hours, but I anticipate that he'll be released in a few days."

"Can I see him?" Mamm blurted out, her hands twisting her black apron.

"As soon as we get him settled upstairs, we'll allow family members to see him, one at a time."

Shanna's eyes brimmed with tears. She fought to keep them under control, but they escaped and ran down her cheeks, anyway. Daed would be fine. She hadn't killed him. As far as she knew, "admitted for observation" was doctor speak for "Nothing's wrong, but we just want to make sure." *Danki, Lord.*

Even though the doctor was still talking, she slipped away from her family and the bishop and headed toward the double doors separating the ER from the rest of the hospital. She wished she could order some flowers, but they wouldn't be allowed in an intensive care room. And that was probably where they'd take him. Nein, the time had come for her to exit his life. Their lives.

They probably wouldn't even miss her.

Matthew carried two iced hazelnut lattes toward the ER waiting room. He'd mentally repeated the name of what Shanna wanted several times so he wouldn't forget before he got to the kiosk, or while he waited in the long line.

As he came around the corner leading to the waiting room, one of the double doors opened. Shanna stepped through, tears streaming down her cheeks.

His heart stuttered. "Nein. Ach, nein."

She blanched. "Ach. Daed's fine. Really. I'm, uh...." She glanced around. "I'm going to look around the florist shop."

"I'm so glad. Want some company?" He studied her in concern as he handed her the coffee and a napkin. "Your iced hazelnut latte."

Her smile wobbled. "You remembered." She wiped her eyes with the napkin.

"Jah. I haven't forgotten anything I've learned about you."

She lowered her eyes. "Maybe you should." She started walking down the hall in the direction of the florist, and he followed her. "What kind of flowers do you think a man would like?" she asked.

"He'll love anything from you."

"Maybe carnations? They're supposed to symbolize health and energy."

"Really? I've never heard that."

Shanna waved her hand. "Flowers have different meanings, based on the type and color. I read about it once in a magazine. Thought it was interesting."

"Ah. So, which flower stands for 'Ich liebe dich'?" The scent of the blossoms was overpowering. Matthew resisted the urge to hold his breath.

"A red rose." Shanna studied the display of flower arrangements wrapped in cellophane.

"Then, out front by the porch of our haus, I'm going to plant a red rose bush."

She picked up a vase full of red carnations and baby's breath. "This is pretty. Daed might like this." Then, she hesitated and turned around, her eyes widening. "What? What did you say?" She ducked her head and blushed.

He hoped the blush was a positive sign.

"You don't give up, do you?"

"Nein reason to."

"I don't understand why you want me." She put the vase back on the shelf. "I can't order any." Her voice cracked.

"Why not?" Matthew tilted his head.

"He's in intensive care. Flowers aren't allowed." Shanna stepped away from the displays. "But they are pretty."

"You could send a card."

Shanna walked over to the rack of cards and studied them. Matthew reached around her and picked up a plain one with gold trim. "Your daed would like this one. Nothing fancy."

"Danki. What should I say?"

He shrugged. "Say what's on your heart. I heard you tell him that you loved him. That might be a gut place to start."

Shanna paid for the card, then borrowed the pen at the checkout counter and wrote something on the inside of the card, slid it into the envelope, and sealed it. Next, she wrote "Levi Stoltzfus" on the outside and handed it to the clerk. "Thanks for your help." She turned to Matthew. "And danki for the koffee. You'll need to get back so you can catch a ride home with the bishop."

"Nein, I'll ride home with you." And pray the whole way home that they'd survive. He walked out of the shop and breathed in the unscented air.

Shanna touched his arm. "Nein. I'm...I'm not going back."

"You're running away again? You can't mean that." His heart ached. He hesitated a moment, praying for guidance. He'd rather be Englisch with Shanna than Amish without her. He could still serve the Lord. But maybe she'd realize where she truly belonged, and they could stay Amish together. *Ach, Lord, let that be so.* "Then, I will leave with you, Shanna."

"I can't ask you to do that." She shook her head. Fresh tears started streaming down her cheeks.

"I'm offering, Shanna. Ich liebe dich. And nothing will change that."

"But you're Amish. You'll always be Amish. And I don't fit."

"Ach, Shanna." Tears burned his eyes. He reached out and cupped her face in his palms. "You do fit. But that doesn't matter. Ich liebe dich, and I always will, even if we're Englisch."

The double doors opened again.

Shanna stepped to the side, and Matthew dropped his arms, moving closer to her, his hand reaching for hers. Then, he looked over her shoulder and saw the bishop.

Shanna grasped Matthew's hand, trying to draw from his strength. "Ich liebe dich, too, Matthew, but I can't let you do that. You'd regret leaving for me. You are Amish to the core."

"Shanna Stoltzfus," the bishop boomed. "I need to talk to you."

Shanna jerked to attention, horrified to think the bishop had heard her. But at least he would have heard her trying to talk Matthew out of leaving the Amish. Surely, he couldn't condemn her for that.

Matthew squeezed her hand, then released it and stepped away. "I'll wait...." He looked around.

"Nein," the bishop said. "This concerns you, too. You can kum." He headed toward the lobby. "Where is the chapel? That would be a quiet place to talk, if no one else is in there."

"It's that way." Shanna nodded toward some doors on the far side of the lobby. "But, really, it's okay. I understand that I'm breaking the rules. Daed already spoke to me about it."

"You're in your rumschprine. I want to talk to you about your future. Matthew says that you want to come back as a midwife after you get your degree."

Shanna glanced at Matthew. He had suggested that. But she'd gotten upset with him and didn't remember agreeing. Or maybe she had, nonverbally, when she'd agreed to let him court her. She knew the natural order of things.

"And he says that with our approval, he'd like to marry you in December."

Shanna's steps faltered. Matthew had already talked to the bishop about her? She stopped walking. The two men did, as well. Matthew studied the carpet and avoided her gaze.

"I've prayed about this, and I discussed it with the preachers this afternoon after we met with Matthew, yet we didn't reach a decision. But, now, I have. The doctor we spoke with said that Levi's life was saved because of your quick actions. That he likely would have died if you hadn't been there to help."

"I saved Daed's life?" Shanna couldn't believe it. "But they're blaming me for causing the heart attack."

"Nein. They know now that you didn't provoke the attack, and they know you saved him. They all do. Your mamm cried when the doctor said that. She said something about running you off." He took a deep breath. "But let me finish. I think this training you're getting is a gut thing. And we will—quietly— finance the rest of your training, if you agree to kum home and use it for the gut of the people."

Shanna blinked. "Really? You'd pay for me to get an *education*?"

"I tried to find training for you before you ran away the first time."

She shook her head and opened her mouth, but she couldn't find words to say.

"God has His hand in this," Bishop Sol went on. "His ways are not our ways. Gut for us all to remember, ain't so?" He rubbed his chin. "I'll agree to your going through instruction, joining the church, and marrying Matthew this winter."

Shanna's heart thudded. Joy swept over her. She'd be able to marry Matthew and have her education. Then, reality crashed in. "But...but...but I'll have to wear scrubs at school and for on-the-job training. And—"

"Jah, I understand. But you will give up your car and get a ride into Springfield for your classes. You'll stop wearing these...." He waved at her jeans and T-shirt. "And you will obey the Ordnung at all times, with the exception of your school uniform."

"You're not going to make me leave?"

He shook his head. "You have a gift, Shanna. The people need you. And God is providing your training. I'm not going to question how He moves."

"Danki!" Shanna flung her arms around the bishop's neck and hugged him, forgetting the iced latte she held until she smashed it against his back. "Oops. Danki so much." Then, she released him and turned to hug Matthew, being more careful with her drink. "Danki."

The bishop pulled on his beard. "But this impulsiveness of yours...." He grinned. "Maybe it has its place."

Chapter 27

"Y ou still haven't asked me to marry you. And we're approved to marry in December?" Shanna planted her fists on her hips. "What's wrong with this picture?"

Matthew gave her what he hoped was a cheeky grin and didn't answer. Instead, he pushed through the double doors into the waiting room.

Joseph met them on the other side. "Mamm told me to stay here until you returned. They took Daed to a room in intensive care." He led the way to an elevator and pushed a button. "They showed me the way to the room, or I wouldn't ever be able to do this."

"I could have gotten us there," Shanna said quietly. Matthew didn't hear a smidgen of pride in her voice. Just a statement of fact.

"Danki for saving Daed, Shanna." Joseph pulled her close in a hug. "Sorry I blamed you."

She shrugged. "You're not the only one. I know my reputation. It's okay."

A few minutes later, Shanna and Matthew followed Joseph into the ICU unit. Bertha stood alone outside the door.

"I'll go back and wait for the bishop." Joseph took off down the hall.

Bertha looked at Shanna. "Your mamm is inside the room with him." She reached out and patted her hand. "I understand there was some quick thinking on your part. How did you know he was having a heart attack?"

Shanna's face flushed. "They taught me to recognize the signs and symptoms." She sounded almost shy.

Matthew reached for Shanna's hand, feeling a bit of sinful pride. Then, Deborah came out of the room. "Ach, gut. You're here, Matthew. He's wanting to see you. And Shanna." She embraced her daughter. "But you need to go in one at a time, and they limit how long." She glared in the direction of the nurses' station. "Don't they realize we worry and want to be with him?"

Matthew squeezed Shanna's hand, then went into the room. Levi looked frail and sick, lying in the bed. This was not the robust, healthy farmer he was used to seeing. "You gave us quite a scare, there, Levi."

The older man nodded. "They tell me I'm lucky to be alive. That it was due to my daughter." His voice caught. "Tell me she didn't run away again."

"She's right outside the room. Do you want to see her?"

Relief washed over Levi's face. "I was so afraid she would leave. So afraid. I want to see her, jah, but first, I need you. Upstairs, in my room in the barn loft, there are two things. One, the more important thing, is a box. It's for Shanna. Her name is on the outside of it. Give it to her."

Matthew nodded. "I'll be glad to. And the second?"

Levi glanced around, even though they were alone in the room, and lowered his voice. "My furniture, it is shipped all over the United States and Canada. I have permission to have a Web site. A computer.

It is up there. I'll need you to check my e-mail and respond to any order requests. You and Joseph can handle it for a while, until I kum home. I have my computer set up so that my e-mail account opens automatically when it's turned on. If you don't know how to use a computer, get Shanna to help you."

"A computer?" Matthew raised his eyebrows.

"Shh. It's a secret. Business related. I agreed to keep it locked up and out of sight, secret from even my family. Since the barn was already wired for electric for my brother...."

Matthew swallowed, overwhelmed at the task Levi asked of him. "I'll need Shanna to help. I have no experience with computers."

Levi nodded. "Shanna will know how. I trust you to keep it secret. I want Shanna now."

Shanna passed Matthew and entered the dimly lit room. Daed still looked pale, and unhealthy, especially with all those wires connecting him to the monitor. She glanced at the numbers, but they didn't register. She stumbled up to Daed's bed, blinded by her tears as she mentally replayed parts of their last conversation. She searched his face. "I'm so sorry, Daed. It's all my fault that you got so upset."

Daed made a hushing sound. "It's okay, Shanna." He opened his arms a bit, and she threw herself into them.

He held on like he'd never let go. "Don't leave... can live in the apartment."

Shanna leaned back and gazed into his eyes. "Don't worry about me. I'm not going far. I'm going to join the church."

"Gut." His hands tightened around hers. "Ich liebe dich."

"Ich liebe dich," she whispered.

Shanna stayed in Daed's room until the nurse came in and told her to go home. She promised to call her on her cell phone if anything changed. It was past midnight, but Shanna was sure she was too keyed up to sleep.

When they arrived at home, Mamm went inside and collapsed into a chair. Joseph hitched up the bishop's horse and buggy, as he had offered to take Mrs. Troyer and Ruth home. The bishop and his wife had been taken home from the hospital by the hired driver.

Shanna prowled around the kitchen. She'd been so sure she'd never be in this house again. She opened the refrigerator and saw a chocolate cream pie. Becky must have brought it over, after all. She set it on the table and cut herself a slice. After the suspense about Daed and her excitement over the bishop's decision, she figured she had an excuse to indulge. Coping mechanism. She grabbed a fork and dived in, savoring every bite, overwhelmed at the outpouring of love the entire community had showed.

Joseph came inside about forty-five minutes later. "That girl giggles nonstop. Don't know how anyone can stand it." He shook his head and staggered toward the stairs, maybe hoping to catch a few hours of sleep before the morning chores.

Matthew came into the kitchen next, carrying a flashlight. "I need to do one more thing before going to bed," he told Shanna. She watched him take a key off the hook by the door. The skeleton key to Daed's special room.

"What are you doing?"

"Your daed told me to go up to the loft and get something for you. He wants you to have it right away."

Shanna set her empty plate in the sink and followed him out the door. "What is it?"

Matthew shook his head. "He didn't say."

They hurried over to the barn. Matthew flicked on the flashlight to dispel the gloomy darkness inside, and then Shanna followed him over to the forbidden door. He handed her the flashlight to hold and then inserted the key into the keyhole. A few seconds later, the door creaked open. Matthew took the flashlight from her and started up the stairs.

"I've never been up here before," Shanna whispered as she crept upward after Matthew, feeling a mixture of fear and excitement. She was glad for Matthew's presence. When they reached the loft, Shanna pulled on the string that dangled from a bare lightbulb. Her gaze fell on an old desktop computer in the center of a wooden table. Ledgers were spread out beside it, and a cell phone charger stood nearby. "Ach, look at this!" She stepped over to the machine. "A computer! Matthew, did you know about this?" She shook her head. "I kind of suspected Daed had something like this. I never could figure out how else he'd get all his business orders from other states."

"I'll need you to teach me to use it. But show me tomorrow. Right now...." Matthew looked around. "He wanted you to have this." He lifted a box, similar to those Mamm received books in when she ordered them from a catalog. "Shanna" was scrawled on the outside.

He picked up the box and carried it down the stairs. Shanna turned off the light and followed behind.

"Where do you want this? The haus or your apartment?" At the bottom of the stairs, he handed her the box and relocked the door, then pocketed the key.

"Ach, this feels like Christmas. Let's take it to the apartment." She quivered with excitement as she opened the door and flipped the light on. "I probably shouldn't use the electric, since I'm joining the church, but...." She set the box on the coffee table in front of the couch.

"It's okay," Matthew said. "I'll leave you alone."

"Nein. Stay." She sat down on the couch, and Matthew came to sit beside her.

Taking a deep breath, she opened the top flaps of the box and peeked inside. "Letters?" The box was full of envelopes, and, as she began shuffling through them, she realized they had all been addressed to her.

She lifted one out, opened it, and carefully removed the letter inside. When she unfolded it, she glanced at the date. It had been written two months ago.

Dear Shanna,

Not a day goes by when I don't miss you. I want you to kum home. I'm sorry for what I did to drive you away. You're my daughter, and ich liebe dich. Maybe someday I'll have the courage to mail these letters. All of them ask the same thing....

Her eyes filled with tears.

"Daed loves me. All this time, he's loved me." She remembered his words, whispered at the hospital. "All this time...." Tears filled her eyes.

Matthew scooted closer and wrapped his arms around her, pulling her to his side. "And ich liebe dich."

Shanna's heart pounded as his finger traced over her lips. But he didn't lean in for a kiss.

Instead, he swallowed, his Adam's apple bobbing. "Shanna, I've loved you since the day I met you—the strange, fascinating, beautiful woman who talked about going to Mexico. I want to spend the rest of my life getting to know you, if you'll have me. Will you marry me in December? Please?"

"You're supposed to be on your knees." Shanna choked back a sob, but when he started to release her, she held him tighter. "Never mind that. Ich liebe dich, Matthew. Jah, I'll marry you."

His fingers moved to tangle in her hair, and he leaned in, his lips meeting hers.

Shanna sighed. Home—at last.

A Preview of

Promised to Another

Book Three in The Amish of Seymour Series

by Laura V. Hilton
Coming Soon

Chapter 1

"May I take you home from the singing?"

Annie Beiler's breath hitched, and her gaze shot from the dusty toes of her powder-blue tennis shoes to the drop-dead gorgeous man standing not three feet in front of her. Unfortunately, his tentative smile wasn't aimed in her direction.

Nein, Joshua Esh's hazel eyes were locked on Rachel Lapp. Annie had to admit Rachel was cute, with her strawberry blonde hair and green dress that perfectly matched her eyes.

Joshua was what her Englisch friends called a "player," for sure. Everyone talked about how he never took the same girl home from singings twice. And Annie couldn't help hoping that he would eventually make his way to her.

Rachel's face lit up. "Danki, Joshua. I'd love a ride."

Annie scowled. If and when he got around to asking her, she'd reject him. Someone should have the willpower to say nein. Just that evening, Rachel had been talking with Annie and some other girls about Joshua's flirtatious ways. It appeared that she'd merely been jealous since he hadn't asked to take her home.

Okay, to be honest, Annie did feel a bit envious, too. Make that more than a bit. And it wasn't just because of Joshua, although he had played a big part in it. The truth was, none of the buwe who'd come from Pennsylvania in the man swap had ever offered to give her a ride. Not a single one.

She didn't consider herself that unfortunate-looking.

Annie brushed past Joshua and Rachel and left the barn. Immediately, she regretted having gone outside, because she did need to find a way home—unless she rode along with another couple. But she didn't think she could stand there alone by the barn doors, hopeful, when all the buwe she noticed didn't seem to know she was alive.

Like Joshua Esh.

Especially Joshua Esh.

Annie kicked a rock and winced when it didn't budge.

"Annie? Is that you?" A familiar male came sounded from out of the darkness ahead of her.

She jumped. She hadn't expected to hear that voice. Not in a month of singings. She frowned. "Luke?"

"Jah." He moved into the circle of light from the lanterns hanging around the barn.

Annie planted her fists on her hips. She wouldn't make the mistake of falling for Luke Schwartz twice—not that she'd really fallen for him the first time. It was just that he'd asked. And a bird in the hand is worth two in the bush, right? Okay, she'd realized he wasn't what she wanted—he wouldn't make her top-ten list of the dreamiest Amish men—but he was better than nothing. She pulled in a deep breath, steeling herself. "What are you doing here?"

"Ach, that's a wonderful way to welcome me. I've come home."

She stilled, her hope building, despite her internal warnings. "For how long?" She didn't want to spend her life alone. Didn't want to rely on the kindness of other couples for rides. Didn't want to be the only girl left unattached, unaccepted, unwanted.

Unloved.

But, then again, she didn't want to settle for just anyone, either.

Luke didn't quite meet her eyes. "You wound me."

Ach. Not for gut, then. The pencil fell from behind her ear, and she stooped to pick it up, careful not to glance at him as she rose.

"Never without that ever-present pencil, I see."

She winced, hating that he mocked her. It wasn't common to take a pencil to singings, she knew, but what if she wanted to write something down? The name of a book she'd like to read, perhaps, or something she wanted to mention to her students the following week. Maybe even the initials of her number one dream guy, who stood somewhere nearby but didn't pay any attention to her. Who didn't know she was alive. "Sarcasm doesn't suit you."

He sighed. "May I give you a ride home? Looks like things are breaking up."

She took a deep breath. "I'm sorry, but I already have a ride. Maybe another time."

Luke laughed. "Right. I heard how popular you are. Having to beat the buwe off with a stick, ain't so?"

Annie stiffened. "So, you couldn't pay rent on that run-down trailer and ran home to your parents, jah?"

Someone moved up beside her, and she turned her head. Whoever it was didn't register. What she did notice was that others were gathering around her and Luke, watching their exchange.

She was in enough trouble already, having nearly gotten dismissed from her teaching post. The school board had permitted her to continue teaching, provided she was put on probation. All she needed was for one of these eavesdroppers to go home and tell his or her folks. She'd be out of a job so fast, a racing horse and buggy wouldn't be able to keep pace. She searched for something to say, something to defuse the situation.

Luke's glance slid from her to whoever had stepped up to offer wordless support. He sneered, then backed up a space. "Well, since you have a ride, I'll just catch you later, then. Good to see you, Annie."

She forced a smile. "Glad you're back, Luke."

He turned and disappeared into the darkness.

Joshua stood beside Annie for a moment. Silent. Wishing he could say something to salve the hurt she must feel. He sensed the pain radiating from her as she watched the redheaded man walk away.

The whole situation confused him. He'd been attracted to Annie the moment he'd met her, but when he'd fished for more information about her, he'd found out she was taken. Off limits. All but engaged to Luke Schwartz, who had vowed to return for her someday. Apparently, that day was now.

Yet Annie hadn't been waiting with bated breath.

Joshua didn't know exactly what that meant.

He knew only what he wanted it to mean.

The crowd around them thinned as the pairs began to make their ways to their buggies. Joshua became conscious of Rachel standing on the other side of him, twisting her apron in her hand while she waited on him to do something. He wasn't sure what.

He swallowed the lump in this throat and turned to face the brunette schoolteacher. "Um, Annie. I'm going right past your haus. I can give you a ride, if you'd like."

The expression in her dark eyes could have withered a lesser man. "I couldn't possibly impose on a courting couple."

"Ach, you know gut and well Rachel and I aren't courting." He couldn't commit to anyone. Not when his attention had been caught and held by one certain Amish schoolteacher. But he wouldn't approach her—not until he knew for sure what was happening between her and Luke. Or seeing if he could somehow catch her eye. Choosing a future frau was a serious thing. After all, he'd be spending the rest of his life with her.

It wasn't like God would point her out with a bright-neon light, one that he'd be sure to notice in this quiet, rural community. Then again, maybe He had. Joshua had certainly sat up and taken notice of Annie.

"I'm going right past your haus," he repeated, tucking his thumbs into his suspenders to keep from reaching out and touching her arm, grasping her hand, or otherwise physically imploring her to just hush up and come along.

The good Lord certainly hadn't made Annie Beiler into a submissive maidel. Not like Rachel Lapp, who still stood silently on his other side, waiting for him to finish. She'd probably be a docile, obedient frau. Unfortunately for her, he liked a bit of spunk.

Spunk was something that Annie Beiler possessed in abundance, if what he'd overheard during the school board meetings was true.

Ignoring him, Annie turned around and headed for the barn. He watched her go, torn whether to follow or not. Rachel still waited quietly by his side, so he straightened and faced her. "Shall we?"

She met his gaze, her green eyes wide. "Maybe we should wait to see if Annie needs a ride first. Her sister left with a beau, and her brother isn't here." She looked around. "Neither is her best friend."

"Jah." Joshua swallowed, then glanced back at the barn. "I'll ask again."

"Has Luke returned home for gut?" Rachel asked before he'd taken a step.

Joshua shrugged. "He was at the haus when we came back from church this afternoon, and he said he'd kum home."

"Ach, his parents must be so happy."

Joshua nodded, but the truth was, he didn't know. The Schwartzes had both seemed rather skeptical when they'd found Luke on the porch after church. Already, the whole community seemed to know about his homecoming. Who needed a phone when the grapevine was so effective? Annie had looked surprised to see him, however, so perhaps the news hadn't spread as quickly as Joshua thought.

"I'll go see if I can find Annie. Be right back."

Rachel smiled. "I'll wait at your buggy."

Joshua gave a brief nod, then headed back inside the lantern-lit barn, where he breathed in the scents of animals, dust, and hay. He skirted the table, still laden with sandwiches, vegetables, and cookies left over from the singing, and walked toward a far corner where he thought he saw a brown dress in the shadows. Annie always wore brown, as if she wanted to go unnoticed. Hidden from view. Invisible.

Of course, given the recent conflicts with the school board, maybe flying low was the best thing for her.

With a sigh, Joshua paused, backtracked, and grabbed a couple of peanut butter cookies off the table. Taking a bite of one of the crumbly cookies, he retraced his steps toward the corner where he thought Annie was hiding. He swallowed. "Annie?"

No answer.

He rounded a pile of hay bales and saw her, crouched low. "Hey. You'll never find a ride hiding back here."

She jumped up and straightened her shoulders. "I wasn't hiding. I was...." She looked around and picked up a piece of straw, poking it back into the bale. "Cleaning. They missed this corner."

Joshua raised his eyebrows and silently watched her pick up more straw for several moments. Fighting a grin, he leaned against another bale of hay.

Annie balled her fists and planted them on her hips. "Aren't you going to go take Rachel home?"

"It's more fun watching you pick up straw. And I'm sure the Stoltzfuses will appreciate that you took so much time cleaning this part of their barn. By hand, no less. I'll be sure to tell Shanna."

"You're insufferable. Nein wonder your community swapped you out."

Her comment couldn't have been farther from the truth, but he didn't mind. That was just what he wanted everyone to believe—for now, at least. But it didn't matter. The temptation to grin won out. "Jah. I'll just be the thorn in your side, here. Now, quit being so stubborn and admit you need a ride home."

"I'll admit nein such thing."

About the Author

Laura Hilton graduated with a business degree from Ozarka Technical College in Melbourne, Arkansas. A member of the American Christian Fiction Writers, she is a professional book reviewer for the Christian market, with more than a thousand reviews published on the Web.

A Harvest of Hearts follows *Patchwork Dreams* in The Amish of Seymour series.

Laura and her husband, Steve, have five children, whom Laura homeschools. The family makes their home in Arkansas. To learn more about Laura, read her reviews, and find out about her upcoming releases, readers may visit her blog at http://lighthouse-academy.blogspot.com/.